CORDOVA

3º

D1508300

DISCARDED BY
MEMPHIS PUBLIC LIBRARY

Faith of a Vampire

Sophia's Redemption

A Gift From

Friends
of the library

Faith of a Vampire

Sophia's Redemption

Mark A. Sprague

iUniverse, Inc.
Bloomington

Faith of a Vampire
Sophia's Redemption

Copyright © 2012 by Mark A. Sprague

All rights reserved. No part of this book may be used or reproduced by
any means, graphic, electronic, or mechanical, including photocopying,
recording, taping or by any information storage retrieval system
without the written permission of the publisher except in the case
of brief quotations embodied in critical articles and reviews.

This is a work of fiction. All of the characters, names, incidents,
organizations, and dialogue in this novel are either the products
of the author's imagination or are used fictitiously.

iUniverse books may be ordered through booksellers or by contacting:

iUniverse
1663 Liberty Drive
Bloomington, IN 47403
www.iuniverse.com
1-800-Authors (1-800-288-4677)

Because of the dynamic nature of the Internet, any web addresses or links
contained in this book may have changed since publication and may no longer be
valid. The views expressed in this work are solely those of the author and do not
necessarily reflect the views of the publisher, and the publisher hereby disclaims any
responsibility for them.

Any people depicted in stock imagery provided by Thinkstock are
models, and such images are being used for illustrative purposes only.

Certain stock imagery © Thinkstock.

ISBN: 978-1-4759-5670-2 (sc)
ISBN: 978-1-4759-5671-9 (hc)
ISBN: 978-1-4759-5672-6 (e)

Library of Congress Control Number: 2012919386

Printed in the United States of America

iUniverse rev. date: 11/5/2012

PREFACE

My name is Sophia, and I used to be a vampire—a blood-drinking, honest-to-goodness, can't-go-out-in-the-sun vampire, fangs and all. But now, by the grace of God, I am human again.

This is my story. I'm telling it to you because I have grown tired of the lies and ridiculous myths people have come to believe about vampires. So if you're looking for a silly, superstitious story, all about sex, billowy curtains in bedchambers, and (God forbid) sparkly teenagers, then this book is not for you.

Here, I will reveal the truth about vampires—the whole truth. You see, humans aren't the only ones who have misconceptions about vampires. There are certain facts even vampires are forbidden know. The elders have decided that if these truths were to get out, it could cause chaos and civil war within the vampire community. They may be right.

But whatever the consequences, I feel that vampires should know the truth about their history and, more importantly, about the promise of redemption that is available to all vampires if they choose to seek it. Most people, including most vampires, believe this redemption is impossible. The most insidious lie of all is that once you become a vampire, you can never go back to being human again.

The elders of the vampire council have intentionally hidden this lie since the time when the first council was formed. If a vampire so much as mentions a desire to become human again, he or she risks torture and, in some cases, execution. Already, the council's agents dog my steps, seeking to silence me.

But I will not be silenced. The souls of countless vampires are at stake. (Yes, I said souls—the lack of souls is another lie that the council has used to obscure the truth.) For the sake of those vampires who seek to regain their humanity despite the forces arrayed against them, I have decided to come forward with my story.

This is the story of how I found the forbidden path of kohinoor. To vampires, the word *kohinoor* refers to a state of transcendence in which a vampire has purged his or her inner demons and dark desires and found salvation again with God. The elders would have you believe that kohinoor is no more than a myth, that no one has ever achieved it, and that those who have made the attempt have gone mad or died. I am the living proof that they lie.

Who is to say that a vampire cannot follow the commandments of God? It is true that all vampires thirst for blood, but a vampire does not necessarily have to commit a sin to satisfy their thirst.

Although I am in hiding from those who would take my life to silence me, long ago I decided that once I was human again I would dedicate my life to doing whatever it took to bring the truth to as many vampires as possible. They, too, must be allowed the chance to seek out the path of kohinoor so that they can be free from life in the shadows and the terrible thirst.

So here is my story. It begins on a farm outside Weston, Massachusetts, where I lived with my family when I was young and human for the first time ...

I. Végső Öröm:
Ultimate Pleasure

The sun was going down behind the trees at the far end of the wheat field. Through the kitchen window over the sink, I watched as the last rays of light filtered through the tangled branches of the maple trees and bathed the field in a red glow.

Behind me, my mother hummed tunelessly to herself as she bent over the stove. The smell of fried chicken filled the room. Soon, my father and little brother would come in from doing their chores, and we would eat—or at least that's what would have happened any other evening.

All of a sudden, there was a rapid knocking at the front door. Thinking it must be my fiancé, Devin, I wiped my hands on the towel by the sink and hurried to let him in. When I opened the door, I was surprised to see a woman. The sun had now sunk completely below the western horizon, but I could clearly see her in the lights coming from the house. She was very tall and wrapped in a hooded black coat. Her skin was pale—surprisingly so—though her lips were as dark as cherries. She was breathing heavily, as if she had been running, but her eyes were what captured my attention. They were deep black, and I could not look away from them.

Between gasps, she said, "The little one—he is hurt. I think a snake has bitten him. Come quickly!"

I stood as if in a trance and said nothing, but my mother pushed past me and hurried out into the yard, calling for my father.

Still looking into my eyes, the woman said, "Come, my dear. They will need your help too."

I stepped over the threshold. The woman straightened. She no longer appeared out of breath. She threw off her coat, and before I could react, she grabbed me, lifted me over her shoulder as if I weighed nothing, and dashed into the darkness.

My scream sounded weak in my own ears. I pounded madly on the woman's back with my fists, to no effect. I managed to raise my head enough to see my father and brother running after us, but my abductor's speed was astonishing. In moments, she had carried me over the low rise to the east of our house and into a field of tall grass. She let me fall from her shoulder, caught me by the back of my hair, and pulled my head back. Fangs flashed in the dark, and before I could react, I felt them plunge into my neck. Then as quickly as she bit me, she retracted her fangs.

It only hurt for a moment, and then my body went limp. The vampire handled me with surprising tenderness, cradling my head in her hands as I collapsed onto the grass. I tried to fight, but my muscles would not respond. Then a sense of calm washed over me. I felt warm and protected. To my surprise, my fear was gone.

The vampire must have seen my confusion, for she kneeled down beside me and whispered, "Have no fear, my dear. You will live to see your family again." She stroked my cheek gently with the fingers of her right hand, still cradling my head with her left. "Tonight, you and I will have some fun. In exchange for your essence that gives me life, I am giving you a gift of pleasure through my venom. You will experience something few humans will ever experience—ultimate pleasure—what my people call *végs öröm*. So release your fears and relax." She bent over and kissed me on the forehead.

I gasped as a wave of euphoria engulfed me. It was like nothing I had ever experienced—a joy too deep for laughter, and bliss far deeper than I could have imagined. "Who—who are you? What do you want?" I managed to ask.

"Just some of your blood—no more than you can spare. Does that frighten you?" She smiled, showing her fangs.

"A little," I said, although in truth the warm glow of pleasure I was experiencing all but drowned out my fear. "Will it hurt? Will I become like you?"

"No, my dear, it won't hurt at all, and you will not become a vampire. All those stories you hear about us vampires are mere fairy tales to scare little children. Tonight will be an enlightening experience for you, one you will never forget for as long as you live. As I feed on your blood, my venom will allow our minds to share a special bond. We will share one another's thoughts, and you will get a glimpse into the world of a vampire. It is an enlightening experience, my dear, one few humans ever get to experience. It will change your life forever."

I gazed into her eyes as she spoke, hypnotized by their black depths. As the euphoria overwhelmed me, I half-heard what she said. She cradled my face gently in her hands and asked, "Are you ready, my dear?" I simply looked up at her with trusting eyes and nodded. "Then let us begin."

With her right hand, she brushed my hair away from my neck and then turned my head to her left. She slid her left hand under my back and pulled me closer to her. My head fell back, exposing my neck to the vampire.

"That's perfect, my child, just perfect," she said.

I felt her fangs sink deep into my neck. I moaned only slightly, for her venom prevented me from feeling any pain, though I knew in my mind what was happening. I reached over with my left hand and grabbed hold of her right sleeve, instinctively pushing myself away, but her grip on me was too tight. Eventually I gave up and allowed the vampire to feed on me freely.

All of a sudden, I felt a pang of hunger unlike any I had ever known. My body writhed, but the vampire's grip was strong, and I could not escape. It took me a moment, but I realized that I was feeling the vampire's thirst; our thoughts and feelings were beginning to mingle, just as she'd said. Images flashed through my mind: faces of past victims twisted in ecstasy or fear; bodies locked in combat; a still-beating heart clutched in a bloody fist. Our minds were so intertwined that I felt what she felt, smelled what she smelled; I could even taste my own blood in my mouth. To my surprise, it was sweet, and I wanted more.

As darker visions filled my mind, I cried out, "Oh God." I saw a chalice filled with blood and water, glowing red eyes in the dark. I heard a deep, low growl. A moment later, I found myself standing in a graveyard with a red sun behind me, and I heard the dry whispers of the dead who had not passed over begging me for help.

Despite the vampire's venom, fear began to well up inside me. I tried to push her off me, but she held me more tightly and continued to drink. I felt my body becoming weak from the loss of blood, and I panicked, flailing my arms and trying to scream.

Finally, the vampire covered my eyes with her hand and pulled away from my neck. I felt warm blood spill down the front of my dress and then the vampire's tongue licking my neck. She removed her hand from my face and lowered me onto the grass. She sat next to me for a few minutes, trying to catch her breath. Then she reached over and held my hand. I'm not sure if she was trying to reassure me that everything was okay or if she needed comforting. I don't know how long we lay like that, hand in hand, but I no longer felt any desire to escape.

At last, the vampire opened her eyes. "I'm so sorry, my dear," she said. "This was supposed to be a pleasant experience for you. No human has ever seen so far into my mind before—how strange. But now you will need to rest."

She lifted me in her arms like a child, and I was too exhausted to resist. The stars seemed to wheel above me as she ran back over the fields toward the farmhouse. Lights flashed blue and red in my peripheral vision, and then I heard the familiar groan of the barn door, and the smell of horses filled my nostrils. The vampire gently laid me down on a pile of hay, brushed the hair from my face, and asked, "What is your name, dear?"

"Sophia," I whispered. "My name is Sophia."

She bent over me and breathed into my ear, "My name is Sara. Remember it, for I feel certain we will meet again." Then she kissed my forehead once more and disappeared into the night.

2. Awakening

I woke in my own room two days later with a headache and no memory of what had happened. I could recall the woman in the black coat on the doorstep but nothing at all after that. When I asked my parents what had happened, they told me only that I had fallen ill but was recovering. It was not until several weeks later that events forced those memories back up from my subconscious—as you shall see.

Even though I could not consciously remember my encounter with the vampire, it had a profound effect on me. A deep, abiding fear—of what, I didn't know—had lodged itself in my mind. Even in daylight, I was reluctant to leave the farmhouse or wander too far into the fields. At night, the fear was far worse. I lay in bed with my back pressed into the mattress, certain that if I rolled to one side or the other unspeakable presences lurking in the darkened corners of my room would rise up behind me. Needless to say, I didn't get much sleep.

I had a part-time job helping my fiancé, Devin, at his veterinary practice, and I had to call in sick several times because I was too scared to leave the house. He tried to be understanding, but I could hear the frustration in his voice.

On Sunday, I said I had a stomachache and stayed home from church. Usually, Sunday was my favorite day of the week—a chance to wear a nice dress instead of my usual clothes, hear the town gossip, and lose myself in the hymns—but I hadn't slept in days and didn't feel I could face the smiling congregation with the fear still gnawing at me. My mother obviously didn't approve of me staying home but said nothing. My father gave me a pat on the shoulder on his way out the door; I could tell he was concerned for me, but expressing feelings had never been his strong suit.

When they were gone, I soon wondered if staying home had been the right choice. I was now alone in the old house, and every creak of the beams and every tick of the antique clock over the fireplace sent reverberations along my spine. I was twenty years old, a grown woman. Why was I letting these little things bother me so much? I turned the TV on and cranked the volume; it helped some.

About an hour after my family left for church, I heard a car coming down the lane. I looked out the window in time to see Devin's pickup pulling in the driveway. My heart sank. I was engaged to marry Devin, and I guess I loved him, but he could be a bit insensitive sometimes. Anyway, he was probably still mad at me for missing work all week.

As he came up the walkway, I met him at the door. He was dressed in a crisp white shirt, khakis, and a blue tie, and there was way too much gel in his hair, which was another thing that bothered me about him. He never looked completely comfortable out of his work clothes. I gave him a token peck on the cheek.

"Hey," he said. "How you doing? I was hoping to see you at church, but your mom said you weren't feeling well, so I came by to check on you."

"I'm a bit better than I was earlier," I said. He followed me through the living room to the kitchen, and I poured him a cup of coffee.

He took a couple of sips. "Tell me, Sophia. What's going on? Missing work, missing church—this just isn't like you."

I stood there glumly for a moment. If I told him the truth, he'd think I was acting like a scared little girl or, worse, going insane. Still, he was my fiancé. If I couldn't tell him, who could I tell? I took a deep breath.

"I—I think something's wrong with me," I stammered. "I'm scared—terrified—of everything."

The coffee mug halfway to his mouth, he gave me a quizzical look. "That's kind of weird."

Thanks, I thought. "I know it doesn't make sense, but I can't help it. I'm just scared, okay?" I didn't bother to keep the annoyance out of my voice. I poured myself a cup of coffee, more as an excuse to look away from him than because I wanted some, and took a drink. It was bitter from sitting on the hot plate all morning.

"Maybe you just need to do something to get your mind off it," he said. "How about if we go out for ice cream? There's that new place out by the strip mall. If we go now, we can beat the after-church rush."

He flashed me one of his boyish grins. Another time, I might have found it endearing. I knew he was genuinely trying to be helpful, but he clearly wasn't interested in understanding what I was feeling. And I was still terrified at the prospect of leaving the house; even though I knew it was irrational, I felt there could be evil forces in every shadow, around every corner.

"Sorry," I said. "I don't think I'm up for that today."

His face clouded over. Without warning, he slammed his coffee cup down on the counter, sloshing coffee over his hand. "Damn it, Sophia! I'm trying to help here, and you're sure not making it any easier."

If I'm fair, I have to admit he wasn't actually yelling (he raised his voice only slightly), and he had probably burned himself with the coffee. But I was in no mood to be fair. I could feel my fear giving way to anger, and it felt good.

"I think you should leave now," I said with as much venom as I could manage.

"Not until you—"

"I said now!" I took a step toward him, eyes blazing.

He backpedaled and then turned and stomped out of the house. When I heard his truck start, I moved to the living room and flopped down on the couch.

Over the next few days, the fear slowly subsided. It didn't go away completely, but I was able to get back into my old routine and help my mother around the house. I didn't go back to work; I needed to figure out how I felt about the fight with Devin before I saw him again. In a strange way, I think arguing with him helped me to realize that being afraid wasn't my only option—I could be angry too.

It was September, harvest time, so I had plenty to keep me busy. The wheat prices were good that year, and once the harvest was in, Father decided to take the whole family into town for the weekend to do some shopping.

We checked into a hotel just off of Route 20 in Weston. My father made my brother and I share a room.

"So much for my privacy," I mumbled, but deep down I was relieved that I wouldn't be alone while we slept.

As soon as we were all unpacked, my brother ran off looking for a video game store, and my parents planned to look at appliances. Before we split up, my father pressed a roll of bills into my hand—more than I expected. He smiled. "Find yourself something pretty," he said. I kissed him on the cheek and hurried off to find a dress shop.

It took me a while to find a dress I liked, and it was getting dark by the time I left the store. I glanced nervously up and down the street and felt fear clutch at my stomach. Telling myself not to be ridiculous, I squared my shoulders and marched in the direction of the hotel.

When I was almost there, I heard scuffling noises coming from an alley. I turned toward the sound and could just make out two figures struggling together in the dim light. As I watched, the taller man let go of the shorter one, who slumped to the ground. I let out a gasp.

The taller man turned in my direction. In what seemed like the blink of an eye, he was standing right in front of me, and I could see him clearly in the street light. He was a big man, taller and more muscular than Devin or my father. His head was shaved, and he was wearing torn jeans and a leather jacket, but what held my attention was the bright red blood covering his mouth and chin.

I froze. I tried to scream, but my throat felt too tight. Fear gripped my body, and I began to shake uncontrollably. He smiled, exposing two long fangs like a rattlesnake's. Then he grabbed me by the neck with one hand, lifted me off my feet, and swept me into the alley, where he pressed my back against the side of a building. "Well, well," he said. "It must be my lucky day. I get dinner and dessert." He grabbed my hair and twisted my head back to expose my neck.

At that moment, something inside of me snapped. I brought my hand up and slapped him across his face as hard as I could. His dark eyes widened for a moment—clearly, he was not expecting such an act of defiance—but then he growled and pressed me harder into the brick wall behind me. Then our eyes met, and he froze. His eyes were black as coal. A shiver ran down my spine. As terrified as I was, I couldn't look away. I had the strangest sense I had seen eyes like that before.

He turned his head and spat and then, to my astonishment, released his grip. "You have been marked," he growled. He then whirled on his heel and stalked off into the darkness.

I ran back to the hotel room as fast as I could. Fortunately, nobody else was there, and I locked myself in the bathroom. When I looked in the mirror, I saw a smeared, bloody handprint on my neck. I quickly grabbed a washcloth and cleaned myself up as fast as I could. I had just changed into some fresh clothes when my parents knocked on the door and walked into the room. They could tell right away that something was wrong. I guess I still looked pretty shaken up.

"Honey, what's the matter?" my mom said. She hurried forward and put her arms around me.

I knew if I told them about the man's fangs they would think I was crazy and never let me go into town again, so I told them a man had tried to pull me into an alley. My father was furious and lectured me for at least an hour about how dangerous the city could be for a young woman out alone at night alone. Finally, I convinced him I had learned my lesson and would never do it again.

That night I had a horrible nightmare. I saw a face I did not recognize, but the eyes were those of the man who had assaulted me—completely black with no whites at all and filled with malevolence. The face then faded, and I saw a beautiful blonde woman with a pale complexion and dark red lips. It was strange—I felt I had seen her before, yet she still frightened me. I woke up in a cold sweat. The room was dark, and I didn't know where I was. I called out in a panic, but not for my brother or my parents. A name popped into my head, and I cried out, "Sara!"

"You okay, sis? Who's Sara?" My brother's voice brought me back to reality.

In the calmest voice I could muster I said, "Sorry, Josh, it was just a bad dream. Go back to sleep."

I woke early the next morning, my mind in a fog. I wasn't sure what was real and what I had dreamed. Had the man who assaulted me really had fangs, or had I dreamed that? I dressed quickly and headed downstairs to find some coffee.

There was a pot of coffee in the lobby and some tables and chairs set out for hotel guests. Two old men sat at one of the tables reading the paper. As I poured myself a cup, I overheard snippets of their conversation.

"—not unless it was rabid, and I haven't heard any reports of rabies in a while," said one.

"What could it have been, then? You heard what that cop said—completely tore the guy's throat out," said the other.

My ears perked up when I heard that, and as stealthily as I could, I sat down at an empty table nearby.

"Look, I know this sounds crazy," said the first man, "but I think we're dealing with vampires."

"You're right," said the second man sarcastically. "It does sound crazy." He looked at his watch. "I've got to go. Catch you later."

The first man was then alone at the table. A moment later I got up and walked over to him. "Excuse me, sir," I said. "Did I hear you say something about vampires?"

He looked up at me with a grin. "Oh, you overheard that, did you?" He was an older man with uncombed, graying hair and a not-altogether-friendly face. "I wouldn't worry too much about it. The police will figure it all out, I'm sure."

"But is it true that a man was killed in the alley last night?" I asked.

"Yes, ma'am. Throat torn out is what they said. It's the third attack like that this year. They say it's an animal of some sort, but I know better."

He paused to scratch the silver bristles on his chin with a stubby forefinger.

I slid into the seat across from him. "How do you know it was a vampire?" I asked.

He looked at me for a minute and furrowed his brow. I'm sure he was trying to decide if he should tell me more or not, but I could tell he was the type that liked to tell stories, so I waited with an attentive look on my face. Finally he continued.

"Well, missy, one night about a year ago I was heading home after having a drink with a friend, when I saw the damnedest thing. There was this couple in a car in the parking lot. I thought they maybe just wanted a little privacy"—he glanced at me and cleared his throat—"but when I got closer, I realized something wasn't right. The woman was limp, not moving at all. Now, I ain't the hero type, but something made me go and check it out. You're not going to believe what I saw next."

"What? What did you see?" I asked.

"Well, I went over and knocked on the window, and the man looked up at me. His face was all covered with blood, and I swear to God, he had fangs sticking out of his mouth. It was like I was looking at the devil himself. The man looked at me defiantly, as if daring me to do something. I was so scared that I ran as fast as I could back to the bar and called the police."

The room suddenly felt cold. I cupped my hands around my coffee mug for warmth.

"Most people just think I'm crazy when I tell them. The cops wouldn't believe me, and by the time they got there, the car was gone." He shrugged. "I guess I wouldn't believe it myself if I hadn't seen it with my own eyes."

"Thanks for telling me your story, mister. For what it's worth, I don't think you're crazy," I said with a look of understanding.

He smiled a little, raised his mug, and said, "You take care now, missy."

I took my coffee back to the room and waited for the rest of the family to wake up. Even though it was our last day in town, I spent the every minute of it with my family. I wasn't about to go off on my own again after what I had seen the night before. We did some more shopping, had dinner at a local diner, then headed back to the hotel to pack our things.

The sun had set by the time we finished packing the car to go home, but a red glow still lingered in the western sky. As I was about to get into the car a strange feeling came over me. I felt like I was being watched. I looked around the busy street but nothing in particular stood out to me. But then I saw her. The woman from my dream was looking straight at me from the doorway of the dress shop across the street. She smiled as our eyes met.

Without any hesitation, I ran across the street and stopped just in front of her. "Excuse me, but would your name happen to be Sara?"

Her smile widened when I said her name. She cocked her head to one side and said, "Yes, my name is Sara. Do we know each other?"

"Yes—ah, I mean no," I stammered. "Somehow I knew the moment I saw you that your name was Sara, but I don't remember us ever meeting before."

Realizing how foolish I must have sounded, I looked down at the ground out of embarrassment. "I'm sorry. I've not been feeling well lately, and I guess I haven't fully recovered yet. Forgive me for disturbing you."

I was about to turn and go, but she leaned toward me and whispered in my ear, "It's time for you to remember, Sophia." I quickly looked up shocked that she knew my name. As she turned to walk away, she said more loudly, "It was lovely to see you again. Have a safe trip back home."

My father called to me that it was time to go. I turned to answer him, and when I turned back, Sara was gone. I scanned the street, but she was nowhere in sight. My father called my name again, and I hurried to the car.

"Who was that?" Josh asked.

"Just a friend," I answered.

"She looked lovely," said my mother. "That dress must have cost a fortune. You can always tell someone of good breeding from the way she walks and the way she dresses. Where did you two meet?"

I didn't answer. I was still trying to figure out how Sara had disappeared so quickly. And even though I knew her name, I had no idea where I had seen her before.

3. Journey to Nowhere

As the family car pulled away from the curb to head home, I felt my stomach tighten with fear. That was when I realized that while speaking to Sara, I had felt not even a trace of the anxiety that had plagued me during the past weeks—something about her presence had calmed me completely.

At home, I did my best to fall back into my old routine. I mastered my fear sufficiently to start going to church again, and I also went back to work. Neither Devin nor I mentioned our argument; I guess we both figured it was best to pretend it hadn't happened.

One morning a few weeks later, I was helping my mother make lunch for the family. I was slicing an onion when the knife slipped and cut my index finger. I yelped and stuck the injured finger into my mouth. To my surprise, instead of the usual metallic tang, my blood tasted sweet.

I slowly removed my finger from my mouth and stared at the wound. *How strange*, I thought, *to take pleasure in the taste of my own blood.* I hadn't lost much blood, but suddenly I felt lightheaded. I sat down hard on the floor, thinking I was about to faint.

My mother rushed to my side and asked what was wrong, but I barely heard her. My body began to tingle. Then, as if someone had opened a door, a flood of memories poured into my head. The day Sara captured me and drank my blood played out in my mind as vividly as if it had happened yesterday.

Overwhelmed with confusion and fear, I turned to my mother and cried out, "Why didn't you tell me? I had a right to know."

"Tell you what? What on earth are you talking about?" she said.

I stumbled to my feet, pulling away as she attempted to put her arm around me. "The attack! I was bitten by a … a vampire … and you knew and didn't tell me! I had a right to know!" I yelled and ran from the house.

I made it about a hundred yards before I realized it was cold and I hadn't brought a coat. The wind rattled the few dry leaves left on the trees, sending a chill throughout my body. I couldn't stay outside, but I wasn't ready to go back in. I continued down the road until I reached our neighbor's farm. I slipped into their barn, where I sat on a hay bale and began to cry.

I'm not sure how long I sat there, but it must have been several hours. When the tears subsided, I forced myself to think. I was so tired of being afraid. I couldn't spend the rest of my life like this, and none of the people around me—not my parents, and certainly not Devin—seemed to be able to help. Yet in the few moments I had spent with Sara, I had no fear. It was the first time I had felt safe in months. But that didn't make sense; why would I feel safe with the person who attacked me?

As crazy as it sounded, my choice seemed clear. Sara was the key to everything. I thought about looking for her, but where does one go to find a vampire? The only thing I was sure about was that I didn't want to live the rest of my life in fear. Right then and there I made my mind up to go and search for Sara. Somehow, I had to find her. Maybe just by talking to her I would feel safe again. If not, at least I would be doing something to face my fear. I had had enough of cowering at home.

The sun was setting as I left the barn. The cold wind sent shivers across my skin, but as I walked home, a sense of calm came over me. The more I thought about my plan, the more confident I became that it was the right thing to do. There was no reason to wait. Tonight, when everyone was asleep, I would leave to search for Sara.

When I opened the front door of the house, my mother was sitting in her recliner in the living room. She looked up from her magazine with relief on her face. I walked over to her and kissed her on the cheek. "I'm sorry I yelled at you," I said. I could see in her eyes that she wanted to talk, but I told her I was very tired and we could talk about everything in the morning. I hated lying to my mother like that, because I knew I would be long gone by morning. But I was determined to go through with my plan no matter what.

As soon as I closed my bedroom door, I started to pack. I waited a few hours to give everyone time to fall asleep and then quietly made my way downstairs. I left a note on the kitchen table:

Dearest family,

Forgive me for leaving without saying good-bye. I love you all so much that I could never say good-bye to your faces. It would break my heart to say those words out loud. I have to leave while I still have the courage to do so.

I am not the little girl you once knew. I have changed in ways you cannot imagine, and there is something I must do. Regrettably, I must do it alone. Please try to understand.

I promise you that one day I will return, but until then, try not to worry, and know that I take your love with me everywhere I go.

I'm sorry.

Sophia

Next to the note, I left a sealed envelope with Devin's name on the front. It held only the engagement ring. I knew my leaving would hurt him, but I was sure he would find someone else. In time, I would be just a memory to him.

I didn't have a car of my own, so I called for a taxi and gave instructions to pick me up where the lane that led to our house met the main road, to avoid waking anyone.

As I walked out the front door, tears filled my eyes. Somehow I knew that if I went through with this, it would be a long time before I would see my family again. The wind was even colder than it had been during the day so I wrapped my coat tightly around me, picked up my bags, and began my journey.

I almost turned back as I walked down the lane. *How can I leave my family like this?* I thought to myself. But just as I was about to turn around, I noticed the bare, black branches of the trees along the road that stretched out like bony fingers against the dark sky, and I felt that awful fear well up inside me. I was certain that if I turned back, I would never escape it. So I took a deep breath, squared my shoulders, and trudged on.

When I reached the main road, the taxi was already waiting for me. I held my breath, forcing myself to get in, and I let out a long sigh when I closed the door.

"Where to, miss?" the driver asked.

It was only then that I realized I didn't even know where I was going. The only thing that came to mind was the dress shop where I last saw Sara. "Take me to Weston, please."

As the cab pulled away from the shoulder, I said a silent prayer. *God, I know how crazy this journey seems, but you know what compels me to take it. Please give me the strength and courage to see it through and find what I'm looking for. Amen.*

I looked out the window into the darkness. I was tired, and my mind wandered. It's strange how God has a way of lifting your spirits when you're feeling afraid and alone. I thought about how crazy this journey would have seemed to my friends and family if they had known all my reasons for leaving, and for some reason, the whole situation suddenly struck me as hilarious. I even let out a small giggle thinking about it.

"Did you say something, miss?" the driver asked.

I shook my head and just looked out the window.

The sun had risen by the time we arrived in Weston, so I instructed the taxi driver to take me to the local hotel. As I was checking in, the man behind the counter asked me to sign the register. I hesitated for a moment. I knew my family would come looking for me, so of course I could not sign my real name. Then the name Soa popped into my mind. It seemed like a short version of Sophia, but not too obvious. And the last name Dobre was a very common in Weston so I signed the register as Soa Dobre.

After my bags were brought up to my room, I headed out to begin my search. The dress shop wasn't open yet, but I spotted a library down the street and decided to go there. Weston was settled in 1642, so I figured the library would hold a lot of information dating back a long way. I hoped I would find some information about vampires there and hopefully my next clue to finding Sara.

It took a moment for my eyes to adjust to the dim light inside the library, but the smell of dust, binder's glue, and old leather told me it was exactly the kind of place I was hoping for. There was an old woman at the counter with wire-rimmed glasses and gray hair pulled back into a tightly bound bun. I asked her where I could find information about vampires.

She gave me an odd look and said, "You're the third person this week to ask me that. What are you people looking for, anyway?"

I lied and said, "Uh, my brother has to do a book report, and of all things he picked vampires. I told him I'd check to see what information the library had while I was in town."

She got out of her chair and led me between the shelves to a desk in the recesses of the library. On the desk were a stack of books about vampires and a folder full of newspaper clippings. "I was about to put all this stuff away," said the librarian. "I guess it will have to wait. Let me know if you need help finding anything else."

She shuffled back to the front desk, and I sat down to read. I quickly realized my research project was going to take a while, so I went out and found a drug store, where I bought a pen and a legal pad for taking notes. For the next two days, I spent most of my time in the library, except for when I went out to eat. Each time, I made sure to pass by the dress shop, hoping I would get lucky and see Sara there.

After reading everything they had on vampires, and newspaper articles about deaths caused by damage to the throat, my pad was nearly full. Everyone has seen movies or read stories about vampires, but the more I read, the more confused I became. In most stories, vampires were portrayed as vicious, bloodthirsty creatures that kill their prey when they fed. I knew that couldn't be completely true; I felt sure Sara never truly meant me any harm. She even took the time to bring me back to the farm so I could be found. At the same time, I had seen with my own eyes what the vampire in the alley had done to his victim.

As I went over my notes, I noticed there seemed to be a concentration of murder victims with various types of marks on their necks in Boston. I thought that it highly unlikely that these types of murders in a major city would be caused by an animal, as some of the articles claimed. It wasn't much to go on, but it was a possible clue. So having nowhere else to go in Weston, it looked like my next step was a trip to Boston.

It was dark when I left the library, but the hotel was just a couple of blocks away, and there were still plenty of people out on the street, so I felt safe walking.

As soon as I walked into the hotel, the concierge told me I had a message and handed me an envelope. *Who would send me a message?* I wondered. No one here knew who I was, and no one at home knew where I was. Inside the envelope was a letter written in an old-fashioned copperplate script. It read, "Dear Sophia, Go to the dining room and find a table for us. I will meet you there shortly." There was no signature.

I looked around the lobby, as if expecting the letter writer to reveal himself. I thought maybe some man staying at the hotel had seen me and wanted to get to know me better. But how did he know my name was Sophia? Had someone recognized me?

My first impulse was to turn down the offer, but I was burning through my meager savings at an alarming rate. I didn't like taking advantage of anyone, but a free meal sure would help my budget. After all, I was planning to leave for Boston in the morning, so I had the perfect excuse not to see the man again.

The moment I sat down, a waiter appeared to take my order. Not wanting to take too much advantage of a man I hadn't even met, I ordered soup and a salad.

The waiter replied, "Certainly, ma'am. But I have been instructed to bring you anything on the menu at no charge. May I suggest the filet mignon?"

I hesitated.

"It's served with a brandy peppercorn sauce and our roasted asparagus, which, if I may say so, is to die for." He smiled.

"Yes, that sounds lovely. Thank you," I said. I wasn't made of stone, after all.

The food soon arrived, looking and smelling as good as advertised. I waited a few minutes, but the meal began to get cold, so I started without my unknown host. I ate slowly and savored every bite. The filet was a perfect medium-rare and seemed to dissolve in my mouth. I kept expecting my benefactor to reveal himself, but as I finished my meal, I was still alone.

I motioned to the waiter that I was finished and got up to go to my room. I felt strangely happy as I walked away from the table; I had been so intent on enjoying my dinner that I hadn't noticed that my fear was gone.

As I turned to leave, I noticed a woman sitting alone at a table in a dimly lit corner of the restaurant. She wasn't facing me, but something about her posture and blonde hair looked familiar. I took a few hesitant steps in her direction.

I was almost directly behind her when she said in a playful tone, "Would you by any chance be looking for me, Sophia?"

"Sara?" I said.

She twisted in her chair to look up at me. "Of course, silly," she said. "You have been looking for me, haven't you?"

Joy welled up inside me. I wanted to give her a big hug, as if she were a good friend I hadn't seen in ages. I had to remind myself that she was a vampire and that I really didn't know her at all.

"Sit down," she said. "We have a lot to talk about."

I took a seat across from her. A hundred questions popped into my mind. I decided to start with the obvious. "How did you know I was looking for you?"

"Don't you remember yet what we experienced? When we had our ... time together, we created a blood bond. I knew the moment you left home. Now that you've found me, why don't you tell me what was so important that you left your family for it."

I hadn't thought much about what I would say to Sara once I found her, and now that we were face to face, I found that telling her anything other than the truth was impossible. "Since the day we were together, I haven't been the same. I'm afraid all the time. I feel like a stranger in my own home." I paused for a moment to gather my thoughts, and Sara waited patiently for me to continue.

"At the same time," I said slowly, "I feel like I know you, almost like a sister. And for some reason I feel safe when I'm with you. I want to know why I feel this way, but mostly I want to know how to get rid of this fear I have."

Sara nodded. "You feel we're sisters because we are, in a sense. When we were together, a bond was created. Most humans never consciously experience the bond, but there's something different about you. You've begun to awaken."

"Awaken? What do you mean?"

"Look around you, Sophia." I looked around the hotel restaurant. A fat man in a suit chewed a bite of steak with no apparent enjoyment of it while reading something on his smart phone. An elderly couple stared aimlessly at one another over bowls of soup. None of them were looking at us. "You see?" said Sara. "They live their lives as if they're asleep. They do the same thing every day. Isn't that what your life was like back on the farm?"

"Yes," I said reluctantly. "I thought marrying Devin might make a difference, but ..." I trailed off.

Sara's eyes widened. "A farmer's life is not for you, Sophia," she said. "Do you know how beautiful you are? You should be living the life of a noble woman, with men at your beck and call. I've tasted your blood. I know what you're capable of. You could accomplish so much with the right teacher."

I felt my cheeks flush. I wasn't used to hearing someone talk about me that way.

Sara smiled at me and continued. "In spite of your fear, you left your home and family to follow your feelings and seek me out. I have lived hundreds of years and tasted the blood of countless humans, and do you know how many have done what you did?"

I shook my head.

"Not one. You're the first."

I didn't know what to say. I looked down at the table in front of me.

"You're very special, Sophia. In more ways than you know. Therefore, I have a proposition for you. Come live with me, and I'll teach you to realize the potential that lies dormant inside you. I'll also tell you everything you want to know about vampires and show you a world beyond anything you can imagine. You'll live with me in my family's estate and have the most beautiful clothes money can buy, and in time I promise men will do anything just to meet you."

I looked up. Sara was watching me intently, and once I met her gaze I found it impossible to look away. "But why would you do all that for me?" I asked.

She looked down at the table and hesitated before she answered. "I guess you could say I'm lonely. I want a friend, a companion. Someone who I can have fun with and share the knowledge I have learned with. You see, vampires can be arrogant, and they all have their own agendas. I have yet to find a single one I could trust, let alone call a friend, outside my own family. But I think you and I could be friends. So which sounds better: life as a farm girl or life with me?"

As Sara spoke, I felt an excitement growing inside me unlike anything I had ever felt before. However, there was one question I had to ask. I cringed as I spoke, afraid to hear the answer. "This all sounds wonderful, but there's just one thing," I said. "If I went with you, would I have to become a vampire?"

Sara smiled. "No, of course not," she said quickly. "The beauty of this plan is that our differences allow us to complement one another perfectly.

"But there is a catch—a couple of them, actually. We'll have to get permission from my father before you can move in, but I'm sure he'll approve of you. Also, you won't be able to see your family again for a long time—maybe several years. Are you willing to agree to that?"

I thought for a moment. I had already concluded that I might not see my family again for a long time when I left them in the middle of the night. I looked up at Sara and saw that she was grinning.

"You already know what I'm going to say, don't you?" I said with a smirk.

She laughed. "We have a beautiful mansion," she said. "You're going to love it."

I laughed along with her. Part of me was still trying to come to terms with what was happening, but to another part of me, laughing with Sara felt like the most natural thing in the world.

"I know you probably have more questions," she said, "but there will be time for them tomorrow. I have some other business to attend to this evening, but as a treat I've had the hotel move you into a much nicer room for you to sleep in." She then grabbed my hand and placed a room key in it. "Sleep well, my dear," said Sara. She turned and left so quickly I didn't have a chance to thank her.

My new room was a luxury suite, but after my conversation with Sara, enjoying the room was the last thing on my mind. I wondered if the father she had mentioned was her literal father, or was he the one who had turned her into a vampire. Did vampires eat food or just drink blood? How much did they sleep? When did they sleep? What would it be like to live in a vampire mansion? I was both excited and nervous; I barely got any sleep at all.

The next morning I woke at dawn. The beautiful suite confirmed that my conversation with Sara hadn't been a dream. I packed my things quickly and had them taken down to the lobby.

As soon as I stepped off the elevator and the concierge saw me, he handed me another envelope. The note inside said, "Good morning, Sophia. I hope you slept well. Don't worry about your hotel bill; I have taken care of it. Have a nice breakfast. When you are finished, go out the front door of the hotel and look for a black limousine. I'll be waiting inside."

I hurried through breakfast and went outside. Just as the note said, a large, black limousine was in front of the hotel. I hesitated; the windows were darkly tinted, and I wasn't certain Sara was inside.

Then the driver got out and said, "Good morning, Miss Sophia. Miss Sara is waiting for you in the back. Don't worry about your luggage. I'll see that it's taken care of." He then opened the back door of the limousine for me, and I slowly entered. As soon as I was completely inside, the door closed quickly behind me.

It was dark inside the limo; after the morning sunshine, I could barely see anything.

"Good morning, Sophia," said Sara's voice. "Or should I say Soa?"

As my eyes adjusted to the dim light, I made out Sara smiling at me. "Thank you for paying my bill," I said. "How on earth did you know that Soa was me?"

"You'd better get used to it. I know you as well as if we had lived together for years. Are you ready to start your new life with me?"

I felt like a giddy little girl as I looked around the sleek leather interior of the limousine. "It looks like I've already started," I said. "This is beautiful!"

"Wait until you see my house," Sara laughed.

I sat back in my seat and tried to relax. Once my luggage was in the trunk, the driver got back into the limo. Sara leaned forward and said, "Our business is finished here, Randolph. Take us home."

"Where exactly is home?" I asked.

"Boston, my dear. Your new home is in Boston."

4. Meeting a Vampire Clan

Shortly after we left Weston, Sara fell asleep. I thought a little rest after my sleepless night might also do me some good, so I closed my eyes and tried to relax. Before I knew it, Sara was shaking me gently by the shoulder.

"Wake up, sleepyhead. We're almost home."

I sat up and tried to straighten my dress. I could feel my heart pounding in my chest.

Sara must have noticed I was nervous, because she took my hand and said, "You have nothing to fear here. You're safer in my home than any place you can imagine. Trust me."

"I do," I said. "I'm just nervous your family won't like me."

Sara smiled. "They're going to love you."

The limo rolled to a stop. The driver let Sara out first and then came around my side of the limo and opened the door for me. I got out and found myself in an immense enclosed garage. Sara led me up some steps and through a wide wooden door.

Inside, we made our way down a hallway with vaulted ceilings and black-and-white marble floors. Then the hall opened up into the most beautiful place I had ever seen. The floors gleamed. Straight ahead, a wide staircase with curved banisters led up to a landing and then divided to the right and left; I guessed each direction led to a different wing of the mansion. Above us a huge crystal chandelier glittered majestically, reflecting light against the walls.

I followed Sara into what I assumed was a living room. Two men and two women were lined up on the thick red carpet to meet me.

Except for their pale complexions, there was no family resemblance in the usual sense, but they were all impeccably dressed. I knew at once that this was Sara's family.

"Hello, everyone," said Sara. "I'm pleased to present to you the young lady I've been telling you about, Miss Sophia Dobre."

I attempted a curtsy, something I had not done since I was eight years old and pretending to be a princess. I don't think I messed it up too badly.

Then a third man, much older than the others, swept into the room. He had a strong, roman nose and thick, black hair with a touch of gray at the temples. It was immediately clear that the others looked up to him; I assumed that this was Sara's father. He gave Sara a hug, kissed her on the cheek, and said, "It's good to have you home. You have been away much too long."

"Yes, Father," said Sara with a childish grin, "but you know how I love to explore."

"Indeed I do," he said, casting an authoritative glance in my direction, "but it seems this time you have brought home a stray."

"Oh, no, Father," Sara said quickly, "Sophia is no stray. She may be human, but she's my friend."

"So she is the one you've told us about?"

Sara nodded. Her father covered the distance between us in one long stride and took me by the hand. "Your heart, my dear," he said. "It beats like a rabbit. You needn't be afraid; no one in this house will hurt you."

I cleared my throat and replied, "I have to admit I'm a little scared, sir. I've never met a family of vampires before."

He smiled. It was a nice smile, not at all predatory or mocking. "Wonderful," he said. "I'm glad you didn't try to make any excuses for your fear. Such honesty is a rare thing these days." He was still holding my hand, and to my surprise, he bowed and kissed it gently. "My name is Marcus Manori," he said. "Welcome to my home."

I didn't know what to say, so I tried another curtsy and then stood there with my hand in his, trying to look agreeable.

He turned my hand over and looked at my wrist. "May I?" he asked. I wasn't sure what he meant, though in retrospect maybe it should have been obvious. He examined my palm and slid his fingers lightly across my wrist. Then he looked into my eyes and, as if it were a perfectly normal request, said, "Do you mind if I take a little of your blood?"

I glanced over at Sara, who nodded to me, looking surprisingly confident. I looked back at Sara's father and said with a quiver in my voice, "Yes, sir, you may."

Marcus scratched a line across my wrist with his fingernail, and beads of blood welled up along it. To my surprise, it didn't hurt at all. Then Marcus bent down and gently licked the blood from my skin. His tongue and lips were cold and dry. It felt a bit strange, to say the least.

He straightened, eyes closed, still holding my wrist. As he stood up, I looked down at my wrist and could not see blood or any wound where he had cut me. We stood like that in silence for several seconds. Finally, he opened his eyes and smiled again. "Thank you, my dear. That was most enlightening." He then turn to Sara and said. "Come here, daughter." Sara stood next to her father and looked up, waiting for his approval. "Where did you find such a gem?" Sara just stood there and smiled. He turned to me and said, "Miss Dobre, you are welcome to stay here as long as you like. Consider my home your home."

"Thank you, sir," I said. "That is very generous of you."

He then turned to his family. "Since you will be staying with us, Miss Dobre, allow me to introduce you to everyone." Moving to the first of the two women, Marcus said, "This is my daughter Carmilla. She is my oldest."

Carmilla was tall and dressed in a beautiful lavender dress. She was attractive, with very strong features. Her blonde hair was pulled back in a bun.

"She is the scholar of the family, so feel free to come to her with any questions you might have. I'm sure she will be pleased to answer them." Carmilla said nothing but gave me a slight nod of her head.

"And here we have Vanessa," said Marcus.

Vanessa stepped forward and placed her hand gently on my arm.

"Welcome to the family, Sophia," she said with a warm smile.

Vanessa was very attractive. She had full, dark red lips and wore a red dress that hugged her figure without being tacky. Her dark hair gleamed like something out of a shampoo commercial as it lay perfectly across her shoulders and down her back.

"Vanessa has a remarkable talent," said Marcus with a smile. "I'll let Sara fill you in on the details."

"I have one other daughter, but she is away at the moment, visiting the family of her fiancé. Her name is Nora. They have yet to set a wedding date, but I expect it will be soon. You may attend the wedding if you wish. A vampire wedding is something few humans ever have an opportunity to see."

"I would be honored to attend your daughter's wedding. Thank you."

Marcus moved next to the men. The taller of the two men stepped forward. He had short, dark hair and moved with the muscular grace of a dancer. He appeared to be in his late twenties, but since he was a vampire, he was most likely a great deal older.

"This is my oldest son, Nikolai," said Marcus. "He has done this family proud many times. He takes great pride in protecting this family."

Nikolai bowed. "Welcome," he said simply.

The other man, whom Marcus introduced as Dante, appeared to be about my age. He had a broad, freckled face and close-cropped red hair. He flashed me a boyish grin as he took my hand and bowed deeply. I liked him immediately.

"So Miss Dobre, including Sara, you now have six brothers and sisters."

"Please call me Sophia, Mr. Manori."

"Very well, Sophia. Then I must insist that you call me Marcus."

I smiled and said, "Thank you very much, Marcus." I looked around at everyone, smiled, and said, "I'm pleased to meet you all and look forward to getting to know each of you."

Carmilla playfully said, "I wouldn't get too settled in just yet if I were you—if I know Sara, she already has plans to whisk you off to Paris or Rio as soon as possible. But I'm sure eventually she'll bring you back and we'll have a chance to get acquainted."

Sara shot Carmilla a dirty look and put her arm around me. "Come on," she said. "Let's find you a room and get you unpacked. Tonight we'll go out and buy you some new clothes."

As Sara guided me out of the room, I glanced back over my shoulder and saw Marcus saying something to the rest of the family. Nikolai looked up at me sharply with a startled expression on his face. I wondered what Marcus was telling them, but Sara grabbed my arm and hurried me along.

The room Sara led me to contained an antique wardrobe, a dresser, and a beautiful mahogany four-poster bed with a canopy. "I hope you like the colors," she said. "My room is two doors down across the hall. We girls have the whole west wing; the guys have the east wing. We still have a couple of hours until sunset, so make yourself at home. There should be plenty of food downstairs. The rest of us will eat later." She grinned. I grinned back, knowing that their diet probably consisted mostly of blood of some kind.

I was amazed at how quickly I had gotten used to the idea of being around vampires. They all seemed so normal, so unlike those I read about in the library books. Even Sara's subtle reminder of their feeding habits didn't unsettle me.

A wave of happiness washed over me. I took Sara's hands in mine. "Thank you," I said. "You and your family are being so nice to me."

"Oh, but there's a reason for that, and not just because we've bonded," she said. "You'll learn soon enough what makes you so special. All you need to do right now is to get comfortable with your room. You wait here and I'll go see that your things are brought up." She gave me a sly smile and slipped out of the room. I wondered what Sara wasn't telling me. Why had Marcus accepted me into his family so quickly? And what could be so special about me? I still had many questions, but Sara was right. I would find out soon enough.

5. The Grand Tour

A few minutes after Sara left, there was a knock at my door. I opened it, and there stood Sara's youngest brother, Dante, with the luggage.

"Hello," he said. "Where would you like me to put your things?" I told him just to put them on the floor. "Yes, ma'am," he said. "When you get hungry, help yourself to whatever's in the kitchen."

He seemed like such a warm and gentle young man that it was hard to remember he was a vampire. I wondered if he was so pleasant to the people whose blood he drank. I pictured him politely asking to bite someone in the neck. I smiled and shook my head thinking, *What have I gotten myself into?*

After I put away my clothes, I went in search of something to eat. The family seemed to have disappeared, but I guess that was to be expected seeing that it was still light outside. I made a few wrong turns down marble-floored corridors, but eventually I managed to find the kitchen. It was huge by most standards; big enough to cook for a small army with all modern appliances and well stocked with food of all kinds. I loaded a plate with bread, cheese, and some cold cuts and sat at the kitchen table, which was ancient and wooden and could have accommodated twenty people quite comfortably.

I finished eating, and there was still no sign of the family; the house was eerily silent, apart from the ongoing tick of a grandfather clock. I cleaned up after myself as quietly as I could, reluctant to disturb the silence. As I was putting the last of my dishes away, the clock chimed six times. That made me wonder just when the sun would be setting. I moved aside the heavy curtain over the kitchen window and saw that it was stained glass. It was beautiful, but it didn't let enough light in for me to tell whether the sun had set. That was the point, I supposed—not to admit the sun's rays through the windows.

I was almost back to my room when Sara flung open her door, grabbed me by the arm, and pulled me into her room. "Come on," she said. "We have to find you something to go shopping in. No offence, but you simply can't wear what you have on. The first rule of shopping is not to look like you need to go shopping—you'll get much better service that way."

I looked down at the knit dress I was wearing and bit my lip. It was true that my clothes were not as nice as the ones Sara and her family wore.

I began to feel a little self-conscious when Sara grabbed a midnight-blue dress out of her wardrobe and held it up to me. "Yes," she said, "that's perfect." It was a beautiful dress, the sort of thing I would have imagined wearing to a formal outing. This made me wonder just where we were going shopping. I hurriedly slipped on the dress and followed Sara downstairs. The family had reassembled in the living room, or at least the men had. Marcus was sitting on the couch reading a book, and Nikolai and Dante were playing chess with an unusual-looking ornate stone chess set.

"Going shopping, everyone," said Sara. "We'll be back later."

I followed her through the room and out the front door like a puppy trailing behind its master, mumbling an awkward good-bye to those I passed.

Randolph was already out front with the limo waiting for us. Once we got in, Sara directed him to take us first to a place called Strauss's Boutique. It turned out to be the kind of store where they greet you at the door with a glass of champagne and everything is so expensive nothing has a price tag on it. They treated us like royalty, and like everywhere we went that night, everyone seemed to recognize Sara. I tried on what seemed like hundreds of outfits, and Sara bought me so many expensive things I started to feel embarrassed.

I tried to get her to stop, but she just looked and me and said, "Don't be silly. We're going to need all this and more during our travels. I can afford it. Trust me."

It was well after midnight when we got back to the mansion, and I slept in late the next day. When I finally got out of bed and made my way downstairs to find some breakfast, the house was once again silent.

The doorbell rang while I was making myself some coffee. I got to the foyer in time to see Randolph helping a delivery driver unload dozens upon dozens of boxes—no doubt the purchases from last night's shopping spree. I was dying to open them, but I decided it wouldn't be fair to Sara; after all, she was the one who had bought everything. I thought about watching some TV, but the last thing I wanted to do was wake someone. Instead, I decided to go and find a book in the library and read it in my room while I waited for Sara to wake up.

I must have dozed off sometime in the afternoon, because the next thing I knew, Sara was calling my name. I hurried downstairs, where I found her standing next to the pile of packages. "Why didn't you try on your new clothes?" she asked.

"I thought it would be more fun for us to open them together," I said.

"Liar. You've been dying to open them since they arrived."

"I didn't know if you would approve," I said. "I didn't want you to think I was taking you for granted."

"Don't be silly. Anything we buy for you is yours to keep. If they were for me, I certainly would have tried on most of them already."

Still feeling a little uncomfortable, I said, "I'm just not used to being so spoiled like this."

"Well, you'd better get used to it." She grinned. "I didn't ask you to come live here to be your babysitter. I want us to have fun together. Now get your butt down here and help me separate my boxes from yours."

We spent most of the evening trying on our new things and modeling them for one another. I can't remember when I'd had so much fun. After we had tried everything on, Sara said, "I hope you like traveling, because in two days we're going on a six-month trip around Europe."

I knew I was grinning like an idiot, but I couldn't help it.

Sara laughed. "I want you to meet all my friends," she said. "Don't worry about packing. I'll have someone do it for us. All you'll need is a small bag for any personal stuff you might need on the plane. One advantage of being a vampire is not having to deal with those female issues."

"Oh. That must be convenient," I said.

"It is, but on the other hand, we can't have children." She paused to put away a little black dress she'd just tried on. "Oh, and you should probably try to adjust your schedule to sleep during the day. Most of the events we'll be going to during our travels will be at night, and I'd hate for you to miss out on any fun."

"Sure, I can do that." I thought for a moment. "Will all the people we meet be vampires?" I asked.

"Oh, no. I wouldn't expose you to a room full of vampires right away. Not that it would be dangerous—we don't have stupid blood orgies like you see on TV. But many vampires can be quite arrogant. Most spend a lot of time talking about themselves." She shrugged. "Actually, I guess they're not that different from human males."

We both started laughing, and I grabbed a pillow off the bed and threw it at her. She caught it and threw it back at me. The force knocked me off the edge of the bed, and I landed hard on the floor.

"Oh, sorry," she said. "Are you okay?"

"Yeah." I picked myself up, rubbing my backside where it had collided with the floor.

"I'm really sorry. I forgot you were human."

"Don't worry about it. I'm tougher than I look. Just remind me to think twice before starting another pillow fight with you," I said as I got back on the bed. "Are all vampires that strong?"

"No," said Sara. "It depends how old we are. But in most ways we're not that different from humans—we like to dance and laugh and make friends. Some of us run businesses and there are even a few in politics."

I nodded.

"Of course," Sara continued, "there's also a dark side to being a vampire—and I don't just mean having to drink blood. But there will be plenty of time for you to learn about that later. As long as you are with me, you'll be safe."

I wondered what she meant by that; the Manori family had treated me so kindly that it was hard to imagine what kind of dark side they could possibly have. I already felt certain that most of the stories I'd heard about vampires weren't true, so I was eager to learn as much as I could.

The next two days seemed to fly by, and before I knew it, I was sitting next to Sara in a first-class seat on a flight over the Atlantic. Our first stop was Barcelona. The first night we were there, she took me to see Gaudi's Church of the Segrada Familia. I'm not usually one to care a lot about architecture, but I thought it was beautiful. I have to admit that I watched Sara as covertly as I could to see if she flinched when she was near religious symbols, but they didn't seem to bother her. That just reaffirmed to me that all those books I read about vampires was a waste of time.

I bought a postcard with a picture of the cathedral to send to my family. I couldn't tell them exactly what I was doing, of course, but I could at least let them know I was all right.

After Barcelona, Sara took me to Cordoba, Seville, and Madrid. I never had to worry about packing; at every stop, there was someone to pack up our things and see that they were there for us in the next city we visited. Of course, we had to do all our sight-seeing at night, but in a way, it actually made the experience more interesting. In each city, we went to at least one social event—a gallery opening in Seville, a political fundraiser in Madrid—where we rubbed shoulders with the local political and financial elite.

Once the glamour of the fancy clothes and political fundraisers started to wear off, I frankly found those events a bit boring, but Sara explained that it was important for the Manori family to maintain connections with powerful people around the globe. I began to realize that Marcus was a very powerful person.

We spent a couple of weeks in Spain and then caught a flight to Paris. That night, I got my first real taste of the darker side of vampirism Sara had mentioned.

As we were getting into the limo at Charles de Gaulle, Sara said, "I've had enough of monuments and bigwigs for a while. Let's go to a real party." I agreed, and she directed the driver through a maze of dark, narrow streets. Finally, we pulled up in front of an ordinary-looking door.

"Thanks, Jacques," said Sara, tossing the driver a handful of bills. She grabbed me by the hand and pulled me out of the car. I had never seen her in this giddy of mood before, but her exhilaration was contagious. I felt myself grinning as she led me through the door, down a flight of worn stone steps, and into a room with low, vaulted ceilings. From somewhere up ahead, I heard the throbbing beat of dance music.

"Where are we?" I asked.

"A wine cellar," said Sara. Her white teeth gleamed in the dark as she flashed me a smile. Clearly, she wanted this to be a surprise.

At the other end of the cellar was another door. A short, broad-shouldered man in a blue suit stood next to it. He flashed a smile at Sara, obviously recognizing her, and pulled open the door. The music grew suddenly louder. Through the doorway, dim neon lights illuminated a wide-open space. The smells of perfume and alcohol flooded my nose as bodies swayed to the beat in the blue gloom of this hideaway nightclub.

Sara shouted into my ear over the music, "This used to be part of the catacombs, but now it's an exclusive club. Let's go have some fun."

I danced for about an hour and then made my way toward the bar and ordered a glass of wine. While I was waiting on the bartender, a young man sidled up to the bar beside me. He was handsome enough—a head taller than me, slim, with well-groomed dark hair, a chiseled jaw, and a designer jacket—but there was something indefinably sinister about him. He plunked a wine glass down on the bar. With a shock, I realized that the red liquid inside was too thick to be wine.

"You're Sara's new pet, right?" he said. "I can sense her mark on you."

"Excuse me?" I replied.

"I said you're Sara's new toy." He took a sip from his glass and then swept his gaze insolently from my face all the way down to my toes and back up again. I felt my cheeks grow hot. "She does have good taste," he said. He licked a stray drop of crimson from the corner of his mouth with the tip of his tongue and grinned at me, revealing a set of fangs.

I tried to take a step back, but he grabbed my elbow.

"I'm sure she won't mind if we borrow you for a while," he hissed.

Before I even had time to wonder what he meant by *we,* I felt a hand grasp my other elbow. I jerked my head around and found myself looking up into another man's face. This one was blond, broad-shouldered, and even taller than the first, and somehow I knew right away that he was also a vampire.

"*Bon soir, chérie,*" he said in my ear. "No struggling now, yes? Or we tear you in half." His voice deepened to a growl as he finished the sentence.

I swallowed hard and without thinking, I called out as loud as I could, "Sara!"

Still gripping me by the arms, they lifted me off the ground between them and swept me away from the bar at an astonishing pace. I looked around wildly for Sara but didn't see her. They took me under a low arch to the right of the bar, down a dark tunnel, and around a corner. I realized we had left the nightclub and were within the catacombs. We stopped, and the blond one pushed me up against a wall. The rough stones dug into my back.

"We should go farther," said the dark-haired one.

"Why bother? This won't take long"

I felt myself shaking with fear and anger, but I knew fighting back would be suicide. Just about that time, I heard a noise a few feet away.

"You should have listened to your friend." Sara's voice rang out from the darkness.

The vampires froze for an instant and then whirled around. I slumped to the ground, letting out a little sob.

"Not that it would have done you much good," said Sara. "You see, me and my friend have bonded. I would never let anything happen to her. I felt her fear the moment you walked up to her." She stepped from the shadows with her shoulders back and her head held high. A small dagger gleamed in her right hand.

The dark-haired vampire took half a step back, but his accomplice sneered. "You think your little knife can scare us?" he said.

Sara moved so fast my eyes couldn't follow her. There was only a blur, and then she stood back where she had been, licking blood from her blade. I looked at my attackers and saw that each had an ugly, gaping gash across their throat. For a moment, I thought the fight was over, but neither of them fell to the ground.

The blond vampire wiped the back of his hand across his neck and then gave it a shake. My eyes followed his blood as it splattered on the ground. When I looked back up to where there had been a jagged slash across his throat a moment before, I saw smooth skin. I was astonished.

"Nice try, Miss Manori," he said. "But now it's our turn."

Together they charged her, but when they got to where Sara had stood, she was already behind them. They turned around in confusion, and I saw that she had slit both their throats once again. Blood began to soak the front of their shirts. I couldn't be sure, but I thought it took a little longer for their wounds to heal this time.

"Beginning to get the idea, boys?" said Sara.

One of them let out a low growl and rushed at her. Again she whirled out of reach, slashing his throat as she passed. It was almost like she was dancing. This time I was sure it took several seconds longer for the wound to heal. I thought surely they would eventually run away, but for some reason they kept charging at her again and again.

Soon the ground was soaked with their blood. The big blond one was the first to fall. He staggered once and then collapsed face-first onto the stone floor. After one more failed charge, the other man fell to his knees and held up a forearm to shield his neck and face.

"Wait!" he panted. "I'm sorry!" His fangs had retracted, and his eyes looked normal again.

Sara stood in front of him and tilted her head to one side. There wasn't a scratch on her, and, to my amazement, her hair wasn't even out of place. "You're young," she said, "and obviously stupid, so I won't kill you this time."

The man's shoulders sagged with evident relief. Sara took a step toward him, and he flinched. "But I want to make this perfectly clear," she said. "I am the daughter of an elder, a member of an ancient clan, and a master vampire in my own right. You two are no match for me. I have killed insects and felt more remorse than I would feel for killing you after what you tried to do to my friend. If you ever so much as touch one of my friends or family again, you will experience pain beyond your wildest imaginings, and when death finally comes, it will be a relief. Do you understand?"

He nodded, eyes wide. When she turned her back on him and kneeled beside me, he collapsed to the floor beside his fallen comrade, breathing hard.

"Are you all right?" she asked me. I could see the concern in her eyes.

"I think so," I said. She took me by the arm and helped me up. Together, we made our way back through the club and up to the streets of Paris.

Once we were outside, she gave me a hug. "I'm so sorry," she said. "If I'd known they'd started letting in that sort of scum, I never would have brought you here."

"I'll be all right," I said. "I'm just glad you were there."

"I told you that I'd keep you safe. I knew the instance you became frightened. It's part of our bond."

I nodded. I don't know how or why, but I was no longer afraid. Normally I would probably have been hysterical after experiencing an attack like that, but the blood bond Sara kept talking about somehow made me feel safe.

"Come on," she said. "We can't end the night on that note. I know just the thing."

She hailed a taxi and had the driver take us to Montmartre, where we climbed the hill and sat on a stone wall outside the Sacré Coeur. The lights of the city were spread out below us. I spotted the Eiffel Tower and, nearer to us, the glowing red windmill of the Moulin Rouge.

"Wow!" I said.

"Now you know why they call it the city of lights," said Sara. We sat in silence for a moment, taking in the view.

"Sara?" I said at length.

"Yes?"

"How come your family's so different from other vampires?"

"What do you mean?"

"The ones who attacked me tonight—they were no better than animals. You're nothing like that."

Sara looked uncomfortable. "I'm afraid there's not a simple answer for that," she said after a pause. "The thing is, there's a part of me that's exactly like them. All vampires have an insatiable thirst for blood. We sometimes call it 'the beast.' We can learn to control it, but it's always there."

"Is that why those two vampires kept trying to attack you?"

"Not exactly. The beast is the thirst for blood, but when vampires lose too much blood, they go into a state we call a bloodlust. When this happens, vampires lose control of their conscious minds, and their basic instincts take over. Those two vampires were in a fight when they went into a bloodlust, and because of their loss of blood, their instincts told them to keep fighting. They could not stop themselves until they killed me or were too weak to go on.

"Don't worry—I had no intention of killing them. They just pissed me off, and I wanted to teach them a lesson. Now the word will get out, and no one will try to harm a hair on your head again. I promise ..."

The night air suddenly felt colder than it had a moment before. I shivered. It was hard to believe there was a part of Sara that could be like those men.

"Do you remember the Picasso painting we saw in Madrid? The one called *Guernica*?" Sara asked.

I nodded.

"Do you know what inspired it?"

"Kind of," I said. "It was a town that got bombed in World War II, right?"

"The Spanish Civil War," she said, "but yes. Just about everyone in the town—men, women, and children—were killed in less than two hours. And the town wasn't even important—strategically, I mean. The Germans just wanted to see how well their bombs worked."

"I don't understand," I said. "What does that have to do with vampires?"

"Nothing," she said. "Humans did that." She looked away from me out over the city.

"I don't get it," I said.

"Well, Sophia, what makes you different from the people who bombed Guernica?"

I thought for a moment before finally I understood what she was getting at. "Oh, I see what you're trying to say. Whatever it is that made the Germans different from me is kind of the same thing that makes you different from those vampires. It's all about the choices we make, right?"

Sara simply nodded. I reached out and took her hand, and she squeezed back gently. We spent the rest of the night sitting there together and talking. It was a night I will definitely never forget.

6. The Accident

T he rest of our time in Europe flew by. We visited Germany and Italy, and Sara even showed me one of the castles she used to live in during the Middle Ages, which was quite a revelation. I had known she was old, but I'd had no idea she was that old. However, her age certainly didn't prevent her from having fun. We always stayed in the finest hotels, and I tasted food and wine more delicious than anything I could have imagined. It was easy to see why Sara liked traveling so much.

We returned from Europe three months later, but being home did nothing to slow the pace of Sara's social life. It seemed like every time I turned around we were shopping or attending one event or another. I must admit that I enjoyed every minute of it. My whole life I had wanted to see the world beyond the city of Weston, but I had no idea just how much world there was to see.

We had been home for a few weeks when one night Sara told me we needed to make a special trip to an up-and-coming senator's house. "It's not a social call," she said. "We have an ... unusual ... relationship with this particular politician. I think you'll find it educational."

Randolph drove us to the senator's house in the middle of the night. The grounds took up most of a suburban block and were surrounded by an intricate, wrought-iron fence. A few months earlier, I would have found it fascinating, but now I barely noticed.

The senator himself met us at the door. He looked more haggard in person than in his campaign photographs. "Miss Manori!" he exclaimed, taking her hand. "It's absolutely wonderful to see you. Please do come in."

"Senator," she said. "The pleasure is all mine." She introduced me as her friend, and then the senator led us into a sort of den where there were a couple of couches and a television. A man in a trench coat sat on one of the couches. He sprang to his feet as we entered, and I saw that he was carrying a leather bag, the kind doctors use to use to make house calls. He opened the bag and produced a little brown bottle sealed with rubber at the mouth. "Ready when you are, Miss Manori," he said.

Sara nodded and stepped forward. She opened her mouth and extended her fangs. For a second I thought she was going to bite him, but then she took the bottle and bit down on it so that one fang punctured the seal. She stood completely still like that for almost a full minute, and it suddenly dawned on me what she was doing. Sara was filling the bottle with her venom. When the bottle was full, she retracted her fangs and handed it back to the man in the trench coat. "Here you are, doctor," she said.

We didn't stay long after that—as she had said, it wasn't a social call. The senator showed us to the door. "Thank you again," he said. "I really can't tell you how grateful I am."

She smiled at him. "Of course, Senator. I'm sure you'll have an opportunity to show your gratitude one of these days."

The senator briefly looked as if he had swallowed something unpleasant, but he quickly regained his composure. "Of course," he said. "Of course." He stood at the threshold, watching us and rubbing his hands together nervously as we walked back to the limo.

As soon as Randolph closed the limousine door behind us, Sara grinned at me. "What did you think of that?" she asked.

"It was weird," I said. "What did he want your venom for?"

"He has a son who came back from Iraq with post-traumatic stress disorder. It calms him down enough for his treatment to work."

I remembered the sense of calm and joy I had felt the first time Sara bit me. I nodded slowly. "So I guess in exchange for your help, he'll use his political influence to help Marcus one day when he needs it, right?" I said.

"Exactly," she said with a smile. "See? I told you it would be educational." Sara then leaned forward and said, "Take us home, Randolph. Our business is finished here."

"Yes, ma'am," said Randolph. It amazed me the way he always responded calmly and obediently to commands from the Manori clan, no matter how they were delivered. I had asked Sara about it, and she explained that Randolph served the family out of loyalty. I don't know all the details, but apparently at some point Nikolai and Marcus saved his family from a rogue vampire, and he vowed to pay back his debt to the Manori family by working for them. The job must take a toll on him, but I never once heard him complain.

We were about halfway home when all of a sudden we heard a loud bang. The limo swerved sharply. We weren't wearing seatbelts, and I slid across the leather seat into Sara. We couldn't see what was happening through the tinted windows, so Sara slammed her hand down on the button to drop the glass separating us from the driver's compartment. There was another bang, and a crack appeared in the window beside me.

"What's going on?" I asked.

"I think we're being shot at!" yelled Sara.

Randolph swerved again. This time Sara slid into me, and I slammed into the door.

"Hold on, you two!" Randolph yelled. "There are a couple of guys on motorcycles shooting at us. I'll do my best to lose them."

With some difficulty, Sara and I managed to get our seatbelts on. More shots rang out from both sides of the limousine. Surely by then the attackers had to realize the windows were bulletproof, but they kept shooting. A spider-web pattern of cracks had appeared in the front windshield, and Randolph was having trouble seeing.

"Randolph, what the hell are you doing?" Sara shouted. "Just run the bastards over!"

"Yes, ma'am." Randolph swerved at the assailants, but their bikes were far more maneuverable than the limo.

We were just a few miles from home. If we could make it there, they wouldn't dare follow us into the Manori compound; the whole family would attack them. Unfortunately, there was an underground tunnel between us and home. I saw its dark mouth looming out of the night ahead, and as the walls closed around us, I began to panic.

A series of concrete pillars divided the lanes inside the tunnel, and the space between them and the limousine seemed impossibly narrow. I clenched my teeth as they whizzed by at a terrifying speed.

I heard the motorcycles shift into high gear as they weaved around the pillars to overtake us on the left. A staccato rhythm of gunshots echoed down the tunnel. Then I heard Randolph swear, and the back end of the vehicle fishtailed out of control. They had shot out the tires.

Randolph tried to keep the limo straight, but eventually the back end of the limo slid out of the lane, and we crashed into one of the concrete pillars. My body jerked, and I clearly heard the loud sounds of metal bending, then something hit me in the face.

After hitting the pillar, the limo continued down the road, sliding on its side. Then there was a crunching sound, and something pushed up against my side. I noticed something warm and wet in my mouth. It tasted sweet, and just before I lost consciousness I realized it was my own blood.

*   *   *

The next thing I knew, I was lying on soft grass. The sun warmed my limbs, and it smelled of summer. I opened my eyes and saw a worn path leading into a grove of trees. Without thinking, I got up and followed it.

I soon reached a clearing where a dozen or so people were talking and laughing together beside a pool of water. I wasn't sure why, but some of them seemed familiar to me.

At first, none of them paid any attention to me, but then a man in overalls with weather-worn cheeks and a kind smile looked straight at me and said, "Hello, Sophia, welcome." He walked over to me, smiling like he hadn't a care in the world. "Do you know who I am?"

I shook my head.

"I'm your grandfather."

"I'm sorry, sir, but I never met my grandfather. You must have me confused with someone else," I said in a polite manner.

"That's true, Sophia. I'd already passed on before you came along, so it's no surprise you don't know me."

"Where are we?" I asked. "I don't think I've ever been here before, but it seems familiar somehow."

"Everything's going to be all right," he said. "There's a special place here for people like you."

I didn't understand what he meant, but I didn't respond. He looked thoughtfully into the pool of water for a moment. I followed his gaze, but all I saw was my own reflection.

"Your friend Sara loves you very much," he said. "She's trying so hard to save your life." He turned from the pool and looked me in the eyes. "Whatever happens, Sophia, don't ever lose your faith in God, you hear me! No matter what happens."

This time I said aloud, "I don't understand," but not understanding didn't seem to matter much. The clearing was such a lovely place; I thought how nice it would be to spend some time here.

Then the man calling himself my grandfather cocked his head to one side, as if listening to something. "I'm sorry, my dear," he said. "It seems it's not your time. You have so many things left to do. But don't worry. We'll see each other again soon."

The clearing faded, and I found myself alone in the dark. I cried out, "Grandfather! Where did you go? Please! Where are you? I want to stay."

There was no answer. Then, in the dark, I began to see images—the same images I had seen when Sara first bit me all those months ago. There was the bloody fist, and the chalice of blood and water. Eyes glowing in the darkness. As the images flashed before my mind's eye, excruciating pain began to shoot through my body. It was unlike any pain I had ever experienced. I screamed, and tears flowed down my face. "Oh God," I sobbed. "Help me, please."

As suddenly as it had come, the pain left me. Once more I was alone in the dark. Then, as if over a great distance, I heard Sara's voice calling my name.

"Sophia, please don't leave me," she called. "Come back!"

I followed the sound of her voice in the inky nothingness. I opened my eyes, and there was Sara's face. It was caked with blood, and I could tell she had been crying from the tracks where her tears had washed the blood away.

"What happened?" I said. "Are you okay? You're covered in blood."

She hugged me and kissed me repeatedly. "You're back," she said. "You're really back. I didn't lose you."

I no longer felt any pain, but I was covered in blood, so I did a quick inventory of myself just to be sure. I couldn't find any injuries on me, so I said, "Yes, I think I'm fine. In fact, I feel better than I have in a long time. Is Randolph okay?"

She finally stopped kissing me long enough to speak. "He'll have a headache for a few days, but it's nothing serious. Right now, we need to get you home as soon as possible." She looked around for Randolph. I followed her gaze and saw him standing nearby with a bloody bandage around his head. "Randolph, get us a taxi," said Sara.

"Yes, ma'am," he said. He gave me the strangest look before he hurried off.

"What's all the fuss about?" I asked Sara. "I'm fine, aren't I?"

She shushed me, and I lay contentedly in her arms listening to the sirens wail in the distance until Randolph reappeared with a cab.

7. Changed Forever

The taxi driver gaped at us. "Are you ladies okay?" he asked as we slid into the cab. "Do you need me to take you to the hospital?"

I looked at Sara and then down at myself. We were both covered in blood, and my clothes were torn to shreds.

"We're fine," said Sara. "The blood is from one of the other passengers. We just need to get home."

During the drive, I tried to remember the accident. It seemed impossible that I could have come through without as much as a scratch. I remembered something hitting me in the face and side, but there were no wounds. I turned to ask Sara what was going on, but she put her finger to my lips. "I'll explain when we get home," she said.

When we got back to the mansion, we immediately headed upstairs to shower and change into fresh clothes. When I came back down, Sara and the family were gathered in the living room. They had obviously been talking about something, but silence fell as I stepped through the doorway.

Marcus got up as I entered and gave me a hug. "You two were very lucky tonight," he said. "Once you've had a chance to speak with Sara, I would like a word, if you're up to it, Sophia. I will be in the library." With that, he left the room.

As I sat down on the couch next to Sara, Nikolai, Dante, and Carmilla got up to leave. Nikolai paused in front of me. "We're glad you made it home safely," he said. He bowed to me ever so slightly and then swept out of the room, but he glanced back at us from the hall.

"Okay," I said to Sara as soon as he was gone, "what the hell is going on?"

Sara pursed her lips for a moment before answering. "I'll explain everything, but I need a moment to gather my thoughts. Would you like a glass of wine to calm your nerves?" She got up and poured me a glass from the bar.

I was already feeling fairly calm, but I accepted the glass, thinking it would help me sleep. I noticed vaguely that it wasn't a wine I'd had before; it was sweet and rich. However, I was too focused on Sara to pay much attention to it.

When we were seated again with our wine, she said, "Prepare yourself, because what I'm about to tell you may be difficult to hear."

"Ok," I said, waiting patiently to hear what happen.

"You were hurt very badly in the accident, and if I hadn't saved your life, you would have died tonight."

I was a little confused, but I took her by the hand and said, "Well, whatever you did, Sara, worked, because I feel fine. Thank you. How can I ever repay you?"

Sara put down her wine and looked me in the eye. "Well," she said, "you can start repaying me by not getting mad when I tell you *how* I saved you."

"What do you mean?"

"When I finally reached you after the limo came to a stop, I realized you were dying. You had already lost a lot of blood, and I couldn't feel a pulse. I knew that the only way I could save you was to give you some of my blood."

"You gave me some of your blood," I said. "How is that even possible?"

"You know that vampires heal quickly, right?"

I nodded, remembering how quickly the vampires' throats healed in Paris.

"Well, we vampires can also help humans to heal by giving them a small amount of our blood. In a controlled situation like a hospital, an IV is used. When that is not possible, the person has to literally drink our blood."

From the look on Sara's face, I was beginning to get concerned. "Just how were you able to get me to drink some of your blood?" I asked.

"You were so close to death, Sophia. I got scared. I was frantic but determined to keep you alive, so I had only one option left. I first bit my wrist and held it against your mouth, but you were not responding. That's when I realized that your heart was not beating. I had to bite you and inject some of my venom into your system to get your heart beating again. The venom acted like a shot of adrenalin to your heart. After that, you started to drink my blood on your own." She gulped down the last of her wine and got up to refill her glass.

I could tell she was worried about how I was taking this. It did sound a little gross, but if it had saved my life, I wasn't going to complain. "So now I'm completely healed?" I asked.

Sara avoided my gaze. "Yes, but there's more I need to tell you. You see Sophia, you had lost almost all of your human blood, and I had to give you a lot of mine to save you."

Finally, I began to realize what she was trying to tell me. Trying to fight the anxiety growing in my chest, I said quietly, "Sara, just what are you trying to say?"

"Well, because you needed so much of my blood, your body now has more vampire blood in it than human blood."

Almost in a panic, I stood up and screeched, "Sara, what did you do to me?"

Sara's shoulders slumped, and she finally looked me in the eye. "Because you have more vampire blood in you than human blood ... well, you are now one of us."

I stood up and exclaimed, "One of you? Just what do you mean when you say 'I'm now one of you'?"

Sara walked over to me, took my hands, and said, "Sophia, you must understand that if I didn't act right away you would have died. The truth is ..." she took a deep breath and said, "the truth is you are now a vampire."

My body suddenly went numb, and I slowly sat back down. I gulped down the rest of my wine without even tasting it, and Sara immediately refilled my glass.

"I'm sorry," she said. "I wanted this to be your choice—one you wouldn't even have to think about, until many years from now."

"I don't understand," I said. "How can I be a vampire?"

"Under normal circumstances, when a human decides to become a vampire, the vampire drains the human of most of their blood. Then, at a precise moment, the vampire cuts their wrist and feeds their blood to the human. Eventually the human has more vampire blood in them than human blood. When I tried to heal you, in a sense the same thing happened. Your human blood was replaced with my vampire blood."

Sara sighed and sat down next to me. She turned toward me and clasped my hands tightly in hers.

"But I don't feel any different," I said.

"That's because you haven't completely changed yet," Sara explained. "The transformation usually takes about three days, but with my venom also in your system, it's probably going to happen a lot quicker than that."

My mouth felt dry. I felt my hands shake, in spite of Sara's firm grip. "If I'm a vampire, is my body—I mean, am I dead?" I asked.

Sara let out a long sigh. "To be honest, I don't know. It is true that some vampires believe our bodies are dead." I swallowed hard when she said that, but she continued. "Personally, I don't think that makes sense. Think about it. Our bodies heal more quickly, and we're a lot stronger than humans. We also have many abilities humans don't have. Frankly, I think we're actually *more* alive than humans. We just need fresh blood to maintain our health. Who knows, maybe we're the next step in human evolution."

As Sara was speaking, I felt anger building up inside me. *How dare she turn me into a vampire without my permission*, I thought to myself. *Even though I was dying, it wasn't her decision to make.*

Eventually, I couldn't contain my anger anymore, and I leaped to my feet and hurled my wine glass at the fireplace. My aim was off, and I hit the stained-glass window instead. The wine glass shattered, and a piece of stained glass fell out of the window, letting in the rays of early-morning sunlight. The light fell on my face.

At first, all I noticed was the warmth of the sun, but then I felt pain as the sun actually burned my skin. I gasped and quickly jumped back into the shadows. The smell of burning flesh filled the air. When I brought my hand up to my cheek, the blisters were already healing. I turned to Sara in stunned silence. My own flesh burned simply from sunlight. In that moment, I realized that everything Sara said was true. I was becoming a vampire.

Sara looked down at the floor and in a quiet voice said, "There's something else I need to tell you. When I bit you to inject my venom, we shared each other's thoughts, just like we did back at your farm. I saw what you saw and felt what you felt. I heard that man say he was your grandfather. I believe you were passing from this life into the next. Vampires live so long that we never really think about the afterlife."

As Sara lifted her head, I saw tears running down her face. "I've never felt so much love," she said. "I feel like I deprived you of your chance for peace. I'm so sorry, Sophia. Can you ever forgive me?"

"You saw that too?" I said. "I thought it was only a dream."

Now I was more confused than ever. I didn't know what to think. All I knew was that I had to get away from Sara for a while. Without a word, I ran upstairs to my room. I sat on my bed for a long time, just thinking. Once I calmed down, I decided I wasn't mad at Sara—not really. She had acted out of compassion for me and had saved my life. At the same time, I was terrified. I had always heard that vampires have no souls. Did that mean I no longer had a soul?

I remembered my conversation with Sara in Paris. She had shown me that there were good and bad vampires, just like there are good and bad humans. However, was it fair to compare the two? I felt sure that even evil humans have souls. The Bible tells us that. Maybe vampires do too.

As I sat there on my bed, I remembered Marcus saying that Carmilla was the scholar of the family; maybe she would have the answers I needed. I went out into the hallway and tapped on her door.

"Come in."

I had never been in Carmilla's room before. On a long table against one wall, an assortment of glass containers was lined up, filled with what looked liked different types of herbs and other stuff I didn't recognize. Every other wall was lined with bookshelves. On her desk were neatly organized stacks of notes and a laptop computer, and in the corner were two overstuffed chairs. She was sitting in one of them with a book, but she closed it when I entered, leaving a finger between the pages to mark her place. "Hello, Sophia," she said. "Please come in."

I was a little intimidated by Carmilla, who I hadn't gotten to know very well. I walked into her room, and I smoothed my dress over my knees self-consciously as I sat in the chair across from her.

"With everything that's happened, no doubt you have questions," she said. "What's on your mind?"

I took a deep breath, paused for a moment, and then blurted out, "Carmilla, do vampires have souls?" Immediately after the words left my mouth I felt like I was back in school and had just asked a stupid question. I felt my body sink into the overstuffed chair in embarrassment.

She looked at me, clearly a bit surprised by my question. However, without hesitation she said, "Honestly, Sophia, I don't know. Most of my studies have to do with things that are more ... empirical." She waved her hand at the table that held her collection of herbs and whatnot. "I'm not sure I believe in souls at all. Why do you want to know? Are you afraid you had a soul but now you've lost it?"

I nodded.

"I see. Do you feel any different?"

"Well, no," I admitted.

"Then I don't see any reason to think you've lost anything," she said.

"But how would I know?" I said in despair. I had really hoped she would be more helpful than this.

Carmilla sighed. "We older vampires don't tend to think too much about religion," she said. "We've accepted what we are. We're creatures of the night—of darkness. If souls are of the light, then having a soul might kill us. Maybe that's why people think we don't have them."

She paused for a moment. Maybe she realized I wasn't feeling very reassured, because then she said, "If you're really concerned about this, you should ask Father. If anyone can answer your question, he can."

"Father? You mean Marcus? I always feel like I'm bothering him when I ask him questions. I know he has more important things to do."

"Well, it's up to you," she said. "But if you want my advice, I'd just forget the whole thing. It's not like you can do anything about it, and that kind of question can get you into trouble." She turned back to her book, and I knew that was my cue to leave.

Her last words didn't really sink in until I was closing the door behind me. *Get me into trouble?* I thought. *What on earth could she mean by that?* In spite of her advice, I knew I wouldn't be able to let the question drop. I might be a creature of darkness, but I still believed in God. What was the point of living, even for centuries, if I didn't have a soul? I needed to know for sure, so I finally decided to talk to Marcus.

8. Revelations

I stopped just outside the door to the library. I needed to have my emotions under control before speaking to him, so I took a few deep breaths. I was about to knock when he said, "Come in, Sophia."

I pushed open the large wooden door. Marcus was sitting in his favorite chair by the fireplace with a pile of books and a glass of wine. "Come and sit with me, my dear," he said. "From the noise I heard earlier, I take it Sara explained what happened."

I nodded and slid into the chair next to his.

"I realize the idea takes some getting used to, but I truly think you will like being a vampire," he said. "For one thing, I can now embrace you as a full member of the family. If you feel comfortable calling me Father instead of Marcus, please do. I have already come to think of you as one of my daughters."

Pleasantly surprised by Marcus comment, I replied, "I must admit that I have come to look up to you as a father, but I was not sure if it was appropriate because I was human. I will enjoy calling you Father. Thank you."

"Wonderful," he said. "But I sense there is something troubling you. Tell me what it is, my dear. I'll understand."

I felt myself tremble, afraid of the answer he might give. "It's just—I was raised to believe in God, and I always felt I would go to heaven when I died. Now that I'm a vampire—well, I've heard other vampires refer to themselves as the damned." My voice quavered, and I felt tears begin to well up in my eyes. "Is that what I am? Do I no longer have a soul?"

"I see," he said quietly. "So that's what is bothering you." He got up from his chair and poured me a glass of wine from his decanter. "Wipe your tears, my dear, and I will tell you what I know." I did as he asked and took a sip of wine.

He clasped his hands behind his back and paced back and forth in front of the fireplace for a moment or two. Then he turned to me and said, "Many myths have become associated with vampires. I'm sure you've heard that we can turn into bats and that our reflection can't be seen in mirrors."

I nodded.

"Of course, those are silly superstitions. The only reason I mention them is to remind you that many of the things people say about vampires should be taken with a grain of salt—and that includes the idea that we don't have souls."

"But how can I know for sure?" I asked.

"You can't," he said simply. "But that is also true for humans; no one has ever provided proof that souls of any kind exist. But what I can tell you is that in all my life—and I have lived a very, very long time—I have seen no evidence that vampires *don't* have souls. Is that any help?"

"I think so," I said. It wasn't the definitive answer I wanted, but it was better than nothing.

"Let me ask you a question," he said. "How do you think someone without a soul would act?"

I thought for a minute. "I don't know," I said slowly. "I suppose that person wouldn't have any emotions at all. He would act only on instinct and would kill or steal without any remorse."

"Well," Father said, "there was a time when vampires behaved exactly like that—we hunted whenever we felt the urge, and we killed everyone we fed upon. We had no idea how to control our thirst for blood. If you think about it, primitive man acted in much the same way. The only difference is humans died, but we lived on and learned to control our thirst. We older vampires still carry those memories with us to this day.

He looked down for a moment, and when he looked up again, there was a strange intensity in his eyes. "That was a terrible time," he said, "and if I do have a soul, I will surely have to pay for the sins I committed back then."

I didn't know what to say, so I just sat there in the uncomfortable silence, waiting for him to continue.

Then a warm smile crept across his face. "However, things change. Today we vampires love and care for our families. We recognize that it is wrong to kill for food, and most of us want our children to have a better life than we did, just like humans do. Tell me, Sophia. You have lived with us for several months now; do you think we act as if we don't have souls?"

"No, Father," I said without hesitation.

"I'm glad to hear you say that. I'm sorry I can't give you a simpler answer, but perhaps you have already answered your own question."

He looked at me; eyebrows raised waiting for me to grasp what he just said. It took me a moment but then it hit me. I had just told Father that I believed vampires had souls. A smile slipped across my face that almost turned into a laugh.

"Very clever, Father," I said.

He reached over and held my hand. "Sophia, I have no proof to give you, but personally I feel confident that your soul is fine and exactly where it ought to be."

I stood and gave him a kiss on the cheek. "Thank you," I said.

"You're welcome, my dear."

I turned to go, but then he said, "There was something else I wanted to say before you brought up this soul business. Have you ever heard the word *dhampir*, my dear?"

I mouthed the word after him: *dhampir*. I shook my head.

"Do you remember the first day you came to this house?"

"Of course, Father. You drank some of my blood."

"That's right. And have you ever wondered why I accepted you into the family so quickly?"

I shrugged my shoulders. "I'm not completely sure, though Sara did say there was something special about me—but she never told me what it was."

He clasped his fingers together, resting them on his chest. "When vampires drink fresh blood from another person, they can see into the mind of the person. More experienced vampires can see into a person's past—their genetic past, I mean. When I drank your blood, I saw that in your bloodline long ago was a human woman who became pregnant by a vampire and gave birth to a male child."

"I thought vampires couldn't have children," I said.

"Female vampires can't," Father explained, "but human women can give birth to children fathered by male vampires. Such a child is called a *dhampir*. A dhampir is born human, but after it has tasted vampire blood, it can possess some of the abilities of a vampire. However, if the child never tastes the blood of a vampire, those abilities will remain dormant, and the child will grow up human. That is what happened with one of your ancestor."

"Uh, okay," I said. Compared to finding out I was about to become a vampire, none of this seemed very important.

Father continued. "The reason I'm telling you this, Sophia, is because those dormant abilities are genetic traits passed down from generation to generation. Therefore, that makes you a dhampir. I believe that is the reason you had such a strong desire to search for Sara after she bit you and you two bonded. Her venom must have awoken some part of your dhampir abilities."

"When I accepted you into this family, I hoped that over time we would be able to awaken your dormant abilities. As a dhampir, you would not thirst for blood as we do, and you could walk in the sun without harm. You would be unique among humans and vampires. Now, of course, that won't happen, since you will soon be a vampire."

"Are there many other dhampirs like me?"

"No, there are not. There are many reasons why, but we can talk about that later. It's important for you to know about your past because it may make your transition into a vampire a bit easier. It may also intensify your vampire abilities, which could prove useful."

"Useful?" I questioned.

"Sophia, I must be truthful with you. The attack on you and Sara was not random. I fear we stand at the brink of a war, and I will use every advantage to ensure this family's survival." A hint of a growl crept into his voice.

I had been so preoccupied with becoming a vampire that I hadn't even thought about our attackers since the accident. "Who were they?" I asked. "The guys on the motorcycles, I mean."

"I don't know," said Father. "Sara was too busy tending to you to chase them down, and they were long gone by the time I heard what had happened. I have my suspicions, but I will keep them to myself until I've had a chance to gather more information."

He shook his head, and his expression softened again. "But you have more pressing matters to deal with. Don't be angry with Sara. She saved your life. If you were the vampire and Sara the human, would you not have done everything in your power to save her life?"

My eyes widened. "Of course, Father. I love Sara. I'm no longer mad. I think I was still in shock from the accident when Sara told me that I will soon become a vampire. And on top of that, thinking that I might not have a soul, really scared me. That's a lot for a person to take in all at the same time."

"Yes, I'm sure it was. Now go and find Sara. She's worried about you."

"Yes, Father," I replied.

"Listen to what she tells you, Sophia. She will help you prepare for your transformation."

I kissed him on the cheek once more and left. When I looked back from the doorway, he was still standing in front of the fireplace, deep in thought.

9. Training Day

I found Sara in the parlor and gave her a big hug. "I'm sorry I yelled at you," I said.

"It's okay. I've lost my temper once or twice myself."

I took a step back from her and looked her in the eyes. "I'm going to need your help to get through this. I have to admit, I'm a little scared. You'll be there for me, won't you?"

"Of course. I'm the one who sired you, so I'm responsible for you. And anyway, I could never turn my back on you. Especially now"

She then walked over to the bar and pulled out a bottle. "It's time for a little education. This is what we call Bloodwine. It is part blood and part red wine. You've been drinking it all morning."

"That was Bloodwine? I actually like it."

"Good, because you need to drink as much of it as you can. Don't worry about getting drunk—the closer you get to being a vampire, the less the alcohol will affect you. The Bloodwine will help you control your first cravings for blood. If you start to feel like you have a knot in your stomach, let me know right away."

"All right," I said. "What else do I need to know?"

"Your senses will probably start to become heightened sometime in the next day or two. It can be overwhelming at first, but in time you'll figure out how to control it. Tomorrow, we'll worry about the next step."

"What's the next step?"

"I said we'd worry about it tomorrow. Right now, I need some blood, and rest. You should eat something before you go to bed to keep your strength up. It may be the last human meal you ever have, so enjoy it." She kissed me on the cheek, grabbed a full bottle from under the bar, and headed upstairs.

I headed to the kitchen to follow her advice. I was famished. If this was going to be my last meal with real food, I was going to go all out. It was still morning, so I decided on breakfast food. I opened the refrigerator door to get bacon and eggs and was immediately overwhelmed by the smell. It was so strong that for a moment I thought something had spoiled, but it didn't smell quite like that. I quickly realized that everything just had a stronger scent than normal. I knew vampires had a strong sense of smell, but this was far beyond anything I had imagined.

I heated a skillet and dropped a couple of strips of bacon into it. The smoky smell of cooking bacon fat was more than I could handle. I gagged, switched off the stove, and stumbled out of the kitchen. The smell seemed to follow me. I rushed to the front door and flung it open, hoping to get some fresh air, but I had forgotten about the sunlight. The skin on my face blistered almost instantly. I slammed the door shut and staggered backward.

I had thought the smell of bacon was bad, but the scent of my own skin burning was a thousand times worse. I rushed up the steps to my room and doubled over the sink in the adjoining bathroom. When I had finished vomiting, I soaked a wash cloth in cold water and pressed it over my nose and mouth. It dampened the smell a little, but not much.

A few moments later, there was a knock at the door, and I answered it with the cloth still over my face.

Carmilla stood in the hallway. "I heard you being sick," she said. "Is your sense of smell changing already?"

I nodded.

She looked concerned and grabbed my wrist as if to check my pulse. After a moment, she relaxed. "Don't worry," she said. "This is normal. Your body hasn't turned yet, but your sense of smell is changing first. That means it will probably be more sensitive than your other abilities. Once you turn completely, you'll be able to control it. For now, drinking some more Bloodwine would probably help. Or, if you like, I can make you up a potion that will dull your sense of smell for a while."

I mumbled through the washcloth, "If you don't mind, I think I'll try the potion."

She grinned. "I thought you might say that. I'll go mix it up."

When she came back, I must have been a sorry sight. I was sprawled on the bathroom floor next to the toilet, soaked in sweat, and I was sure my face was a lovely shade of green. Carmilla held out a small vial of purple liquid. "Just inhale the scent," she said. "It's a very powerful potion, so don't use any more than you need, and whatever you do, don't ingest any of it."

I held the vial under my nose and took a deep breath. I felt better instantly. "Thanks so much, Carmilla," I tried to give her a hug, but she backed away. Maybe it was just her usual reserve—or maybe I looked even worse than I thought.

Being sick all morning had wiped me out, so I collapsed into bed as soon as Carmilla went back to her room. I fell asleep the moment my head hit the pillow.

*　　*　　*

When I woke up, Sara was standing over me with a glass of Bloodwine. I grabbed it and downed it in one gulp.

"Good evening," she said. Before I could reply, she took my hand, pulled my arm toward her with my palm up, and bent to sniff my wrist. Then she made me open my mouth and prodded at my gums and teeth with her fingers.

I pulled my head away. "Hey," I said, "I don't know where those fingers have been!"

"Very funny," she said. "You're progressing nicely. Shower and then meet me downstairs. And wear something comfortable that you don't mind getting dirty."

The smell of my shampoo was enough to make me vomit again, but fortunately I remembered Carmilla's potion just in time. As before, it worked right away.

Sara, Nikolai, Vanessa, and Dante were waiting for me at the bottom of the stairs. I stopped a few steps above them. "What's going on?" I asked.

"It's training day," said Nikolai with a devilish grin.

"What do you mean? What kind of training?"

"Normally, a vampire's abilities develop naturally during the transition," Nikolai explained. "But Father thinks we can make your abilities stronger by putting you in situations that will force you to concentrate on one or more of your senses before your transformation is complete. It will be like awaking what you already have within your genetic bloodline."

"Okay," I said. "What do you guys have planned for me?"

None of them answered. I turned to Sara.

"Don't look at me," she said. "This is all Father's idea. He told us not to tell you what was going to happen because it might make the training less effective. But don't worry—he knows what he's doing."

Randolph was waiting outside with a brand new limousine. Once we all got inside, I noticed a bandage on Randolph's head.

"Are you okay, Randolph?"

"Yes, Miss Sophia, I'm fine, but thank you for asking."

No one else said a word. Father's instructions, I was sure.

We drove for about an hour to an industrial district and parked in front of a warehouse. As we got out, I noticed that Carmilla's potion was starting to wear off; the smells of oil and asphalt and industrial chemicals flooded my nostrils.

As we walked up to the door, Nikolai said, "There's only one way in or out of this warehouse. Inside, it will be completely dark. Your job will be to get to the far end of the warehouse past all the obstacles. There you will find a bell. Ring it, and we'll come get you. "Now, don't think this is just a test for your sight—there's something in there to test all your abilities. Do you understand?"

I was starting to feel nervous, but I nodded. Sara placed a black hood over my head. "Don't worry Sophia," she said, but I could hear the concern in her voice. "The hood is just so you won't know where the door is. You can take it off once you are inside. The key is to trust your instincts. You can do this."

"Okay," I said. "I just hope nothing stinks in there."

Nobody answered, which struck me as a little ominous. I heard a loud bang followed by metal sliding against metal. Then someone took my hand—from the size of the hand, I guessed it was Nikolai—and led me a dozen paces forward. "Okay," said

Nikolai's voice, "as soon as you hear the door close, you can take off the hood and begin the test."

I nodded. A moment later, I heard the door bang shut behind me. I took off the hood, but it didn't make much difference. I was standing in total darkness. I strained to see, but everything was black.

I stood completely still for a moment, trying to get some sense of which way to go. I could smell a whole jumble of scents—concrete, plywood, steel, and was that rotten meat? All the scents together made me slightly queasy, but none of them told me anything useful. I couldn't hear anything except the shuffle of my own feet as I turned in a circle with my arms stretched out. *Well, so much for my supposed vampire abilities*, I thought. I was beginning to think this was a waste of time, but I knew that if this test was really Father's idea, there was no way they would let me out until they heard that bell.

I tried to stay calm and think about the situation logically. If I found a wall, I would be able to follow it all the way around to the other end of the building. I tried to shuffle to my right, but after just a few steps, I ran into something solid—it seemed to be a big wooden crate of some kind. I felt along it as high as I could but couldn't reach the top. I tried to go around it, but there was another crate in the way. My idea wasn't working.

I gave up on my plan in frustration and stumbled into the dark at random with my arms stretched out in front of me.

As I shuffled along the floor, my right foot hit something. There was a soft popping noise, and something smacked into my leg. It didn't hurt much, but when I reached down, my shin felt wet. At the same moment, the smell of blood reached my nose. Something had cut me.

"Hey, you guys! I'm bleeding in here!" I yelled. "Nobody said anything about this being dangerous!" Anger began to surge through me, and I thought for an instant that I could dimly make out the shapes of the crates stacked here and there around the warehouse. Then everything went black again. I tried to focus, but it was no use. "What the hell?" I muttered. My leg healed quickly, and I started to walk forward again, more cautiously this time.

By now Carmilla's potion had completely worn off, and as I shuffled through the darkness, my sense of smell continued to sharpen. The smell of rotten meat I had noticed a moment before remained, but now I realized it was made up of several distinct scents; there were actually dead animals in some of the crates. One of the crates to my left held rotting fish. Somewhere to my right was a dead rabbit. I wasn't sure how I even knew what a dead rabbit smelled like, but I was certain that was what it was. I clenched my teeth and willed myself not to be sick. Throwing up wouldn't do anything to get me out of here.

Then something growled in the darkness. I froze. My nausea vanished, chased away by a surge of adrenalin. Suddenly, I could see again. This time it lasted for several seconds. There was a path through the crates just ahead; on top of one of them was a cage. Behind the bars, I could barely make out a huge, canine shape, the hair on his back raised when he noticed me. *Well,* I thought, *at least it's caged and can't get to me.*

As I calmed down, everything faded to black again. I sniffed the air and could now make out the smell of wet dog. I had been so overwhelmed by the rotting meat that I hadn't noticed it before.

I took another step forward, and out of nowhere, someone shoved me from behind. I fell forward, and my head collided with one of the crates. A hollow boom echoed through the warehouse. I rolled into a sitting position, rubbing the lump on my skull. "Son of a bitch!" I shouted. "Just what kind of training is this?"

I tried to stand up, but someone pushed me down again, and this time whoever it was used a blade of some kind and sliced the skin along my upper arm. I hit the floor with a grunt. This time, I heard a faint rustling as my attacker made his retreat.

I rolled into a crouch with my back to a crate and grabbed my wounded left arm with my right hand. The cut was already healing, but my shirt sleeve was soaked in blood. As the pain left me, I began to get angry. I could feel it well up inside of me, and I felt all my muscles tense. I tried to stay calm, but it was no use. I was really starting to get pissed off. Then my vision suddenly returned. It was much sharper than before, and every sound and smell in the room was now crisp and distinct.

There was a figure standing perfectly still a few feet ahead of me. He was dressed all in black, and a mask covered his face. A scalpel glinted in his right hand. Instinctively, I knew not to let the figure know I could now see. I deliberately looked wildly around the warehouse, pretending to peer into the darkness. He charged again, and this time I clearly heard his feet padding softly along the concrete floor.

When he was close enough, I balled my right hand into a fist and punched upward with all my might. At the same time, I pushed off from the floor with my legs. My fist collided with the figure's chin with a loud crack. His head snapped back, and he crumpled like a rag doll.

A feeling of pride overcame me as I took down my attacker. Still able to see in the dark, I looked down at my assailant. With anger in my voice I said, "I may be a girl, but I'm no weakling. If any of you thought I would sit down and start crying at the first sign of trouble, well, you have grossly underestimated me. I will get through this damn test one way or another."

The masked figure recovered. As he sprinted away, I was gripped by a ferocious joy and almost went after him, but then I remembered that I had to find the bell at the other end of the warehouse. I forced myself to relax and took a few deep breaths. As I regained my composure, my vision faded again. "Damn," I said aloud.

With newfound confidence, I trotted off toward the path I had seen between the crates. Then the sound of a chain sliding across metal followed by a loud bang stopped me in my tracks.

I sighed. "What more do I have to do?" Then I heard a dog panting somewhere to my left and realized the metallic sound had been the cage opening. This time, my fear did nothing for me; I couldn't see a thing. I stood perfectly still, my heart lodged in my throat, trying to concentrate on my other senses. Something about the dog didn't smell right, and its movements seemed erratic. *Was it rabid?* I wondered. *Had they really put me in here with a rabid animal?*

There were some scuffling noises and then the sound of splintering wood. It sounded like the dog was trying to get at the dead animals in the crates. Thinking maybe I could find my way to the bell while the animal was distracted, I took a cautious step forward. Immediately, the warehouse fell silent. Then I heard a low growl, followed by padded paws falling on concrete.

Crap, I thought. It was coming for me. I began to panic, and fortunately, my night vision kicked in again. I sprinted toward the opposite end of the warehouse, but I wasn't nearly fast enough. I had gone only a couple of steps when I felt the beast's jaws close on my calf. I lost my balance and fell face-first onto the floor.

The dog dug his teeth into the flesh of my leg, and I screamed in pain. I twisted around in time to see it leaping for my throat. I flung my hand up to defend myself and felt the creature's teeth sink deep into my forearm. It tugged, trying to tear the flesh from my bone. I beat on his head with my other hand, but it didn't let go.

As we thrashed around on the floor of the warehouse, I was dimly aware that it was slick with my own blood. My calf wasn't healing the way my arm did, and I could feel myself getting weaker. Through my panic, I knew with absolute clarity that if I didn't do something soon, I was going to die. Sara's words from earlier then popped into my head: "Trust your instincts."

As soon as that thought entered my mind, my fear disappeared, and I was overcome with pure rage. I heard a growl and realized with a shock that it was coming from my own throat. Then something snapped inside my head, and I completely lost control.

I didn't black out or lose consciousness. It was as if the part of me that normally felt emotions and made decisions faded into the background. I was still there, watching everything that happened, but something else was happening to me.

I no longer cared about getting away from the dog. In fact, all I wanted to do was rip it apart. Its jaws were still clamped around my arm, but I no longer felt any pain. I grabbed the dog's back legs in my other hand and twisted it onto its side. I threw back my head, let out a loud growl, and then bit down on the creature's neck as hard as I could. The taste of wet dog hair filled my mouth, and then there came the warm, tinny taste of fresh canine blood. That sent me into some kind of frenzy. I bit down again and felt my teeth close on the dog's windpipe. I jerked my head back with all my strength and felt flesh rip away from the dog's throat.

Warm liquid poured into my mouth and over my chin. The dog's body went limp, and I flung it against the wall. I stood up, chest heaving, completely oblivious to the pain, and looked around for something else to kill. Apart from my heavy breathing, the warehouse was silent.

Once I no longer felt threatened, I began to regain control. I fell onto my hands and knees and spat out blood and clumps of hair.

The bites on my arm and leg burned fiercely, but I could tell they were already beginning to heal. After a moment, I realized I could still see in the dark. I stumbled around another row of crates and spotted the bell. I straightened, walked slowly over to it, rang that damn bell, and shouted, "Get me the hell out of here—now!"

10. The Dhampir's Past

A minute later, the main warehouse door opened, and I could clearly see my way out of the warehouse. I stalked out into the parking lot. The others were leaning against the limo, waiting for me.

"What the hell was that?" I said. "I could've died in there!"

Dante and Vanessa looked concerned but said nothing. Nikolai wore his usual blank expression. Sara hesitated for a moment and then took a step toward me. "I know it seemed that way," she said quietly, "but it had to. Nothing else would have sent you into a bloodlust. You may not believe me, but you were completely safe."

"Completely safe?" I yelled. "That's your idea of completely safe?"

Dante backed her up. "She's telling the truth, Sophia. We didn't let the dog out until we were sure your abilities would kick in. That's why we sent Nikolai after you first."

"Nikolai?"

Dante mimed an uppercut and grinned. Vanessa looked like she was about to giggle, and Sara actually did. "You broke his jaw," she said. Nikolai grunted and suddenly became very interested in his fingernails.

That satisfied me a little, but I still didn't see the humor in the situation. Every muscle in my body ached, and my hair was caked with congealed blood. I glared at them all, and, to my surprise, I let out a low growl. "I don't see how that justifies letting a rabid dog come after me," I muttered.

Sara put her arm around me, apparently oblivious to what a mess I was. "You knocked down a five hundred-year-old vampire with one punch. None of us expected that," she said.

"Especially not Nikolai," said Dante with a smirk.

"After we saw that, we knew there was no way a dog was going to get the better of you." Sara smoothed a bloody clump of hair out of my face. "I know it was horrible," she said, "but you did excellent, Sophia."

The anger drained out of me, and suddenly I felt completely exhausted. I had to lean against Sara for support. "Can we go home now?" I asked in a small voice.

"Yes, sister," she said. "Let's go home."

*   *   *

I fell asleep on Sara's shoulder as soon as we were in the limo. When I woke up, I was in my own bed, and the clock on my night stand told me it was seven o'clock in the evening; I had slept straight through the rest of the night and the following day. I was ravenously hungry.

I was still covered in dried blood, but my hunger pangs were so urgent that I didn't even shower before I trotted downstairs barefoot to find something to eat. The smell of the food in the kitchen turned my stomach, so I went and got a bottle of Bloodwine from the bar in the parlor, popped the cork, and took a swig straight from the bottle.

I heard a noise behind me and whirled around, wiping my mouth with the back of my hand. Nikolai was standing in the doorway. "I see you've gotten used to the taste of Bloodwine," he said.

"Sorry," I said, suddenly painfully aware of my disheveled, bloody appearance. "I was starving, and nothing in the kitchen appealed to me."

He smiled. "It's okay," he said. "This was bound to happen eventually. How about something a little stronger?" He went behind the bar, pulled out a different bottle, and poured me a glass.

It was much darker and thicker than what I had been drinking. I took a sip. It was the most wonderful thing I had tasted in my life. I gulped the rest down greedily and held out my glass for more. "What is this stuff?" I asked. "It's delicious."

"Blood," he said calmly. He refilled my glass and poured one for himself. He swirled his glass around and sniffed the bouquet. He raised his glass as if in a toast.

I sniffed my own glass and shrugged. The idea of drinking pure blood still sounded a little gross to me. But it smelled delicious. My stomach grumbled as I mirrored Nikolai's gesture and then sucked the red liquid down. I drank two more glasses before I was satisfied.

"If you're feeling better, I think Father wants to speak to you," said Nikolai. He glanced down at my ragged, blood-stained clothes. "But you might want to get cleaned up first."

I thanked him and headed up to my room. After a hot shower, I felt almost human again, and I went to look for Father.

As usual, I found him in the library. He was sitting in his favorite chair when I entered, but he got up to greet me. "Good evening, Sophia," he said, giving me a kiss on the cheek. "How did you find your training?"

"I found it ... difficult, Father."

"I know it's been hard, Sophia, but you've done very well. Astonishingly well, in fact." He gestured to the two chairs in front of the fire, and we sat.

"I suppose I should tell you why I put you through such a difficult situation."

Remembering how difficult yesterday was, I was not in the best mood, so I just sat there, patiently waiting for an explanation.

"Sophia, you are unique. If I were to let you transition into a vampire naturally, you would probably have the same abilities as any other vampire, but I decided to put you through this training because of your dhampir bloodline."

"What does my bloodline have to do with me turning into a vampire?"

Father got up and pulled an ancient, leather-bound book from one of the library shelves. He flipped through the book until he found what he was looking for and then held it open in front of me. "This," he said, "is the vampire whose bloodline you inherited."

On the page was an image of a very thin man. He had a long, narrow face and a deeply sinister expression. Underneath the picture were the words *Vadim Preda, Fifth Elder of the High Council of Lamia.*

"Council of Lamia," I said. "What's that?"

"Twelve vampires whose daunting job it was to oversee the entire vampire community. At the time this image was made, the council's primary duty was to keep the balance between humans and vampires. There was concern that there might not be enough food to go around, which could have led to an all-out war between the clans." He snapped the book shut and returned it to the shelf. When he turned back to me, there was a look of sadness on his face. "You have to understand, my dear, that a vampire war is a terrible thing, both for the clans involved and the humans who are inevitably swept up in it. To avoid that, the council decided to limit the number of vampires in any particular area."

"Okay," I said slowly. I assumed he would get around to explaining what all this had to do with me eventually.

Father began to pace in front of the fireplace, his hands behind his back. "At first," he said, "they tried to get some clans to move away from the cities where there were too many vampires to less populated areas, but many refused to relocate." He sighed. "So they resorted to more drastic measures."

I listened, fascinated, as he told me how the council had created a secret society of vampire assassins to kill clan leaders in cities that were overpopulated. Once a clan leader died, he explained, the rest of the clan usually scattered, and the problem was resolved.

"Of course," he went on, "once the vampire community began to realize what was happening, they wanted the council members killed. Fortunately, no one at that time knew who the council members were. Even the names of the assassins were a closely guarded secret.

"Vadim Preda died a long time ago, and it is now common knowledge that he was a member of the council. Many of the ancestors of the vampires he ordered killed are alive today. If word were to get out you are even remotely related to him, they would hunt you down and kill you without a second thought. They would see it simply as a matter of family honor."

A chill ran down my spine, and I felt the color drain from my face. Father must have seen how unsettled I was, because he kneeled beside my chair and squeezed my hand in his.

"I did not tell you this to frighten you, my dear," he said. "Only Sara and I know your true lineage and only because we have tasted your blood." He stood and resumed pacing in front of the fire. "But it does have bearing on your training. Vadim Preda was an ancient and immensely powerful vampire. His strengths lie dormant within your blood. I want to awaken those dormant abilities so that if your secret ever does get out, you will be able to protect yourself.

"If you continue with your training, in the coming days you will surpass even Sara, and she is a master vampire."

I felt a knot forming in the pit of my stomach. "There's going to be more training?" I said weakly.

"Oh, you needn't worry," said Father. "It won't be anything like last night. But you can learn a great deal from your siblings. Nikolai is an accomplished fighter, and Vanessa is an expert in the art of seduction. I believe you have already benefited from Carmilla's skill as a chemist."

I nodded, relieved.

"I know this is a lot to take in, but there's something else I wanted to talk to you about," said Father.

He stopped pacing for a moment and looked at me. "Even if your secret remains safe, the family may have need of your abilities soon. I haven't been able to track down the men who attacked you and Sara, and I have to believe they will try again. I need you to do your best to awaken your abilities to their full potential.

"Sophia, you are now a part of this family, not as a human but as a vampire. As a family, we protect our own. As my daughter, I will help you in any way I can. But there may come a time when the family needs you."

"I understand, Father," I said.

"Good. Now run along and find yourself something to drink. Transformation is a thirsty business—and so is humoring an old man who has grown too fond of his own voice."

I jumped to my feet and kissed him on the cheek. "Don't be silly, Father," I said. "I love the sound of your voice."

He smiled at me affectionately and ushered me from the room with a wave of his hand. I closed the heavy wooden door behind me as I left.

On my way back to the parlor, I bumped into Sara in the hall.

"Hey," she said, "want to go to a party?"

After the past few days, it was a bit of a shock to find that things as frivolous as parties were still part of Sara's agenda. "Uh, sure," I said.

"What's the matter?" asked Sara.

"It does sound nice to do something fun after the past couple of days," I said. "It's just that I'm still kind of freaked out by the way my bloodlust took over in the warehouse last night. What if that happens when there are people around?"

"It won't," she said. "Bloodlust only kicks in when your life is in danger and your rational self can't find a way out. Then the beast takes over and saves your butt. If you hurt anyone at that point, they'll probably deserve it. The only other time it might happen is when you get really low on blood. Speaking of which ..." She led me down the hall to the parlor and poured me a glass of blood.

"Thanks," I said.

"No problem. You won't need this much once you've fully changed, but right now it's important to keep drinking."

I took a sip. "All right, let's go to this party of yours."

"Excellent. Tonight we'll celebrate your transformation. But I should warn you that it will be a little different from when you were human. Your abilities are strong enough that some other vampires will be able to sense them. And your intuition will tell you things it didn't used to—like whether someone is lying to you or even if they like you. It takes some getting used to, but I'm sure you'll catch on quickly."

"Okay," I said, but my heart sank.

"What is it?" she said, seeing my expression.

"I was just hoping this might be a chance to have some fun, not another training exercise."

"Who says it can't be both?" she asked. "I certainly intend to enjoy myself. But you have to remember that you're an ambassador for the family now. The friends we make at parties like this one could someday make the difference in one of Father's business deals. Making a good impression now will help him behind closed doors later."

I nodded dismally. This was sounding like less and less fun by the moment.

"Oh, don't look so depressed," she said. "We're going to have a great time. Now go put on something nice and meet me back down here."

I hurried off to my room, where I put on my favorite little black dress, put up my hair, and put on a little makeup. I decided I looked nice enough not to embarrass the family. When I met Sara back in the parlor, she was wearing a deep blue dress, and a string of sapphires glittered blue against her pale throat. "You look stunning," I said. "I hope what I'm wearing is okay."

Sara waved her hand dismissively. "You could dress up in rags and the men would flock to you."

I smiled at the compliment. I felt a rush of affection for this woman who had become like a sister to me. "I'm sorry I've been such a bother these past few days," I said. "I know I can't have been easy to live with."

She took my hands and looked into my eyes with a serious expression on her face. "Don't be ridiculous," she said. "What you're going through is normal. I'm just glad I didn't lose you. For a moment after the accident, I thought I was going to, and it terrified me. You and I have a special bond, and that makes me so happy. I hope you feel the same way."

I gave her a hug and said, "You know I do. I would be lost without you."

We separated, but she held onto my hand. "All right, Sophia," she said, "are you ready?"

I smiled at her nervously and nodded. By the time we got into the limousine, I was actually looking forward to the party.

II. Finding Sara

The limo pulled up in front of a trendy nightclub in downtown Boston. The attendants immediately opened the limo doors, and I followed Sara directly to the VIP entrance. A man who recognized Sara motioned for us to follow him. He unlocked a door and led us upstairs to a private part of the club that catered to a select clientele.

Polished glass glowed in the dim light behind the bar, and the room was full of swaying bodies. My nostrils flared as I took in the odors of alcohol, pheromones, and expensive cologne. I quickly realized I could pick out even more precise scents. I found that I could tell which people were humans and which vampires just from the way they smelled.

Sara grabbed my elbow and pulled me aside before I could join the crowd. "Try to do a little mingling," she said into my ear so I could hear her over the music. "I know your sense of smell is the strongest, but don't let it be a crutch. This is the perfect situation for you to learn how to read people."

Almost yelling over the music I asked, "How do I do that?"

"We vampires have the ability to sense the energy people give off. Tonight, just pay attention to what your intuition tells you about each person you meet, especially through your sense of touch. I don't mean how they physically feel; I'm talking about the energy they give off. Everyone has a different energy, and you will immediately notice the difference the more people you touch. Just relax and notice how they make you feel. Once you master this you will be able to know a lot about a person simply by being in the same room.

"Oh, and Sophia?"

I looked at her and saw that she was grinning. "What?"

"Try and have a little fun." Still smiling, Sara walked off to join some friends she had spotted in a corner, leaving me alone.

I walked off in the opposite direction, skirting the edge of the dance floor as I made my way to the bar. As I opened up and stretched out my feelings, I found I knew every time Sara looked over at me. I was amazed how clear the sensation was, but now was not the time to think about Sara. It was time for me to get to work.

The crowd around the bar was striving for the bartender's attention. This seemed like a good opportunity to touch some people without anyone noticing. I first brushed up against a young red-headed man in a navy blazer at the back of the group and nearly gasped. He was a riot of conflicting emotions—I felt lust, envy, arrogance, and below it all an obsessive need for another drink. I could tell by his smell that he was a vampire, but I also had the sense that he wasn't very old. Maybe that was why I sensed so many emotions from him.

When I reached the front of the pack and raised my hand to get the bartender's attention, I allowed my wrist to brush the hand of a short, solidly built female vampire in a white dress. This time I was ready for a wave of emotions, but I felt only a steely reserve and perhaps just a hint of amusement. I knew immediately that she was old—far, far older than the other vampires around her—and that she was quite powerful. I glanced at her, and she gave me a quizzical look before turning away into the crowd, protecting her drink as if it was a precious gem.

After that, I decided to be more careful—I was supposed to be the one observing them, not the other way around—so I got my glass of Bloodwine and found a seat where I could observe the other guests without drawing attention to myself.

Before long, I had memorized the scent of every person in the room, and once I had a person's scent, it wasn't any trouble at all to remember the face that went with it.

After an about an hour, I got bored memorizing smells and decided to go find Sara. Once I thought about it, I realized I hadn't felt her looking at me for some time. I walked around the perimeter of the room but didn't see her anywhere. I stepped outside to see if she had left without me, but there was Randolph, leaning against the limo, a cigarette hanging out of his mouth as usual.

I ran back inside and started to get worried. We had never found out who the motorcyclists were; what if they were here? My mind raced. For a second I wondered if this was some new part of my training, but then I realized it didn't matter. Either way, I had to find Sara.

I took a deep breath and tried to concentrate on her energy and scent. I could smell her all over the club, but the scent was stronger near the kitchen door, so I pushed through the crowd and into the kitchen, nearly knocking over a man with a tray of hors d'oeuvres. I sniffed the air, ignoring the man's outrage, and followed Sara's smell straight through the kitchen to another door.

She hadn't come this way alone. I recognized two other scents from the club and mentally matched them to the faces of two young male vampires I had seen earlier. Why would she have come this way with them? They weren't nearly strong enough to have overpowered her. Where the hell was she?

I followed the scent down a dark hallway and found myself at a freight elevator. We were on the top floor, so the only place to go was down. As I walked onto the elevator I was overwhelmed with a strong chemical smell. I stopped the elevator on the ground floor and got out. After a few seconds of fresh air, my head cleared. I couldn't detect Sara's scent here, so I was pretty sure she was still in the building.

I plunged back into the elevator and made my way back up floor by floor, trying to detect Sara's scent, all the while trying not to inhale the chemical fumes in the elevator. When I stuck my head out on the third floor, I caught a whiff of Sara's scent. I stepped off into the darkness, and the elevator doors slid shut behind me.

As my eyes adjusted to the dark, I saw that I was in a large open space full of pallets stacked with pipes and boards and other construction materials. On the far side of the room were a couple of offices with large windows. Behind one of them, a light glowed behind closed blinds.

I crouched and ran lightly between the pallets toward the light. The scents of Sara and the two men grew stronger as I approached.

When I was about a dozen paces away from the office door, I heard a man's voice ahead and froze.

"—only member of the clan who goes to clubs. It has to be her," said the voice.

There was a muffled moan, and I knew instantly it was Sara. They must have found some way to overpower her.

"We're going to bleed you dry, missy. Once we're done with you, there won't be anything left but ashes," said one of the men. I then heard a dull thud and another moan.

I knew I had to do something, and fast. I looked around for something I could use as a weapon and saw a pile of rebar on a pallet to my right. I lifted one from the pile, careful not to let it clank against the others. It felt surprisingly light and flimsy in my hands, but I decided it would work reasonably well as a spear. My idea was that if I could incapacitate one of them with my homemade spear, I felt confident that I could take the other one.

Standing there outside the door with my homemade spear, I began to feel some anxiety. I knew the danger, but I couldn't stop myself even if I wanted to. I had to try to save Sara, even if it meant my own life.

Standing there, ready to make my attack, I felt a burning sensation deep inside me as my anxiety grew. With every second, it grew to the point I could not stand it anymore. I could wait no longer. I took a deep breath, and then with all my strength I kicked open the door.

One of the two men was standing right in the doorway. I had my target. He whirled around toward the door, and I charged forward, my spear leveled at his chest. But my aim was a little off, and the rebar struck him on the shoulder. The rebar pierced his skin, and I didn't stop until he slammed into the far wall, the metal punched through his flesh. I continued pushing and felt the tip of my makeshift spear crunch into the drywall behind him and through to the outside wall. For the moment, he was pinned.

I spun around and scanned the room. Sara was gagged and bound to a chair with leather straps. A pool of blood lay on the ground under her. There were cuts and bruises on her face and arms, but she seemed alert. I then focused my attention on the other vampire.

He looked surprised for a minute, but then he grinned and extended an old-fashioned straight razor in his right hand. I could tell he had been using it to cut Sara, and that turned my anger into rage. I stood there, muscles tense, waiting for him to make a move.

"You just made a big mistake, girl," growled the vampire.

I said nothing. I knew he would try to slit my throat with his first attack. If he was successful, I knew I would lose a lot of blood since I had not yet completed my transition into a vampire. My healing would be too slow for me to recover quick enough to fight back. But if he missed, I had him.

He lunged toward me, but it was a clumsy attack. I stepped into him, grabbing his right wrist as I slipped under his arm. His momentum carried him forward, and I grabbed the razor and twisted it out of his hand. Before he could catch his balance, I plunged it into his side with all my strength and sliced upward and across his abdomen until I felt the blade grind against his ribcage. I yanked it free. He gasped and clutched at his wound, falling to his knees.

I quickly turned to Sara and cut the leather straps that held her to the chair. As soon as she was free, she leaped out of the chair and tore the gag from her mouth. Her jaw was set, and her nostrils flared. I had never seen her like this—not even when she fought the two vampires in Paris had she looked so angry. She yanked the rebar out of the vampire I had pinned to the wall, and he slumped to the floor, clutching his shoulder. Then she picked him up by his belt as if he weighed nothing and threw him through the window. The glass shattered, and moments later there was a crunch as he landed three stories down, followed by the insistent wail of a car alarm.

Sara turned to the other man, who was now curled on the floor in a fetal position, cradling his stomach with bloody hands. Staring at him, Sara said, "Wait outside, Sophia. I don't want you to see this."

I was about to protest, but then I caught sight of the rage smoldering in Sara's eyes. I stepped outside the office, closing the door behind me.

A moment later there was a blood-curdling scream that rattled the blinds against the window beside me and sent a shiver up my spine. Then there was silence. The door swung open and there was Sara, covered in blood from her face to her feet. Without looking at me, she stalked toward the elevator. I followed closely behind.

A crowd was beginning to gather outside when we left the building; it seemed the vampire Sara had thrown out the window had landed on someone's Ferrari. A few people stared at us, but none of them dared to say anything as we made our way to the limo.

Randolph hurriedly stubbed out his cigarette and opened the door for us. "Home, ma'am?" he said to Sara. She nodded and slid across the seat to let me in after her.

During the ride home, I bit back the many questions I wanted to ask. Who were the two men who had attacked her? Were they the motorcyclists? Sara's jaw was still set, and she stared rigidly ahead. I knew better than to speak to her.

When we pulled in at the mansion, Randolph came around and opened her door first. To my surprise, she leaned over and kissed me on the cheek. Then she got out and went straight to her room.

I met Randolph's impassive gaze and shrugged. I hoped she would tell me what had happened tomorrow, but mostly I was just glad she was safe.

12. The Beast Escapes

When I got back to my room, I showered and went straight to bed. A few hours later, I woke up with a terrible headache.

I thought that maybe a glass of blood would help, but when I flipped on the light on my nightstand, it was like someone was sticking daggers in my eyes. *What the hell is going on?* I wondered. I was pretty sure vampires didn't get migraines, but then again, I hadn't fully transformed yet. Maybe this was part of the transformation. I turned away to give my eyes a moment to adjust and noticed a few drops of blood on my pillow.

My first thought was that when I showered earlier I must have missed some blood from the fight, but then another red spot appeared on the pillow, and I realized I had a nosebleed. I tilted my head back and hurried to the bathroom, doing my best to ignore the throbbing ache in my head.

I sat on the toilet with a wad of tissue pressed against my nose, hoping the bleeding would stop. My headache was getting worse; even the nightlight in the bathroom sent jabs of pain into my eyes.

I noticed a drop of blood on the white tile floor, and as I bent down to mop it up with another tissue, blood gushed out of my mouth. There was so much I almost choked on it. I stood up unsteadily and pressed a towel to my face. In a few seconds, it was soaked. I glanced into the mirror over the sink and saw blood coming from the corners of my eyes. I started to panic.

Another burst of pain exploded in my head, and I swayed. I had to drop to my knees to avoid falling. I doubled over, spat a mouthful of thick blood onto the floor, and managed to let out a scream.

A moment later Carmilla appeared in the bathroom doorway in a nightgown. She took one look at me and turned and ran, calling for help.

The pain continued to build, and I rolled onto my side and lay there shaking on the bathroom floor, sobbing and gasping for breath.

I was only dimly aware of Father and Nikolai standing over me, the rest of the family hovering behind them. "Damn," said Father. "She's going into the final phase. Nikolai, run and get as many bags of fresh blood as you can carry." Nikolai dashed off.

This was it, then. My body was about to undergo its final change, and after tonight, I would be a vampire. Would I be the same person as before? Would I still have a soul?

Father crouched beside me and said over his shoulder to the others, "No matter what happens, don't let her out of this room. In her current state, she could go into bloodlust and kill someone. And remember that she isn't a typical vampire, so be ready for anything."

Every muscle in my body was on fire. The pain was so bad I couldn't think straight. I was losing control. I tried to fight it, but it was no use. The part of me that was still me fled to an out-of-the-way corner of my consciousness and curled into a whimpering ball. After that, my instincts took over, and all I could do was watch.

Father reached out to grab my shoulder. I knew he only wanted to help, but my body interpreted the action as a threat. Fangs sprouted from my gums where there had been none before, and I struck like a snake, burying them in the flesh of his forearm.

He swore in his native tongue and jumped back into the bathroom doorway. "Looks like we're going to have to do this the hard way," he said. "I need to examine her to see if there's anything unusual about her transformation. Guard the door in case she gets away from me."

He distracted me with his right hand and then grabbed my hair with his left and pulled my head back as far as it would go. He forced my jaws open with his right hand and peered into my mouth, ignoring my growls and attempts to squirm away. "Soft spots behind her fangs," he said. "She'll have some type of venom, like you, Sara, but it's too early to tell what kind." He pulled a vial out of his coat pocket and scooped up some of the blood that was still pouring out of my mouth. Then he let me go and jumped back into the bedroom.

I dropped into a defensive crouch, growling and hissing. Pain shot down my spine, and I fell to the floor again, writhing in agony. After a moment, it subsided to a more bearable level, and I jumped to my feet and charged toward Carmilla and Dante, who were standing in the door. I almost broke through, but Dante managed to get his shoulder under my ribs and fling me back into the bathroom.

Carmilla closed the door, and I lashed out like a caged animal. I tore down the shower curtain, kicked and shattered the toilet tank, and then smashed the sink. The door caught my attention next. I put my fist through the wood, trying to break through. After two more hits, it split down the middle and fell out of the frame.

Nikolai showed up with the blood just as I destroyed the door. He tore the top from a one-liter bag and tossed it past me into the bathroom. Crimson blood gushed out and spread over the floor. The smell of fresh human blood drew me instantly. I seized the bag in both hands and hunched over it like a wild animal, growling to keep the others away. I sucked huge gulps of the delicious liquid down my throat. Drinking the blood eased the pain a little, but it was far from enough. When the bag was empty, I looked around for more. Nikolai carefully placed another bag of blood just outside the bathroom door and took a few steps back into my room. I pounced on it immediately and tore into it with my fangs.

While I was preoccupied with the fresh bag of blood, Sara and Dante—who had positioned themselves out of sight on either side of the door—lunged forward and grabbed my arms. The blood fell to the floor, and I struggled wildly with all my strength. I managed to yank one blood-slicked arm from Dante's grip, but Sara held on long enough for Father and Nikolai to jump forward with thick leather straps, which they used to bind my arms and legs together.

Once I was restrained, Father lifted me gently onto my bed, and they held me down. Vanessa picked up the bag of blood I had dropped on the floor and held it up to my mouth, allowing me to drink. When it was empty, Sara appeared at my side with another.

With each bag of blood, I felt a little better, and eventually I calmed down and stopped pulling against the restraints. I must have downed half a dozen liters before Father and Nikolai decided to ease their grip. I didn't try to escape. As long as I was getting blood, I was content.

Father stepped back and wiped his forehead with the back of his hand. "This should never have happened," he said. "Her training was designed to avoid exactly this situation. What happened last night must have triggered her transformation prematurely."

Sara looked down at me sadly as I guzzled blood out of the bag she was holding. "I should have seen it coming," she said. "She only switched to pure blood yesterday. She didn't have nearly enough in her system for something like that."

Father stepped forward and put his arm around her. "We all should have thought of it. We were too preoccupied with the attack to give her the attention she deserved." He sighed. "Well, at least it's over now. The transformation will be finished before sundown. From this day forward, she is a Manori; there will be no doubt about that."

The others nodded.

"Sara, keep giving her blood as long as she wants to drink. Your presence might help calm her. The rest of us should try to get some sleep."

"Yes, Father." Sara opened another bag of blood and caressed my forehead with her left hand as she guided the torn corner of the plastic to my mouth with her right. The rest of the family filed out of the room.

Halfway through the next bag of blood, I closed my eyes out of exhaustion and fell sound asleep.

13. The Evening After

When I woke up that evening, my hands and feet were still bound in leather straps. I sat up in bed and looked around. Sara was sound asleep at the foot of my bed. Then I noticed the bathroom. It looked as if someone had set off a bomb in there. A few splinters of the door still hung on the hinges, and fragments of glass and porcelain spilled out onto the bedroom carpet. Blood was smeared and splattered everywhere.

I gazed at the destruction in confusion for a moment, and then memories of the night before began to swim up out of the murk of my subconscious. "Oh," I said.

Sara stirred and stretched. She opened one eye and asked, "Feeling better today?"

"Um, I think so," I said.

Sara got up and removed my restraints. Then she poured me a glass of blood. I held it with both hands, worried that I might drop it; I was still a bit shaky. I stared at the shattered bathroom. "Is everyone okay?" I asked.

"Everyone's fine," she said in the middle of a yawn. "A little tired, but fine."

"What happened to me? I woke up with a headache, and then—"

"Your body was starving for blood. Your heroics at the club—for which I'm very grateful, by the way—used up what little blood you had in your system. You eventually went into a bloodlust and your survival instincts took over.

"To make matters worse, the lack of blood in your systems also triggered your final transformation into a vampire. That is why you were in so much pain. What should have been a gradual process was accelerated by your bloodlust."

I looked down at the rumpled bed covers. "Is Father mad at me?" I asked.

"Why would he be? If anything, he's grateful you were there to save me."

"I remember biting him."

"Well, you'll have to talk to him about it, but I wouldn't worry too much." She yawned again, covering her mouth with her hand. "He wants to have a family meeting at ten to talk about what happened, and I think I'm going to try to get some more sleep before then. You can use my bathroom until yours is fixed up. I'll probably be dead to the world by the time you get there." She grinned, no doubt thinking her choice of words was funny.

I stared at her blankly.

"That was what's called a joke, Sophia," she said. Still smiling, she got up off the bed and walked down the hall to her room.

I finished the glass of blood and poured myself another. I peeked into the bathroom. It was completely unusable. Fortunately, my wardrobe was intact; all the nice clothes Sara had bought for me had escaped my rampage.

I grabbed a pair of jeans and a T-shirt and went to Sara's room to take a shower. Sara was fast asleep on top of her covers, and I realized she must have stayed awake with me for most of the day. I thought how lucky I was to have such a close friend and sister.

When I had showered and dressed, I left Sara sleeping and made my way downstairs to the parlor. Father was sitting on the sofa, but he got up to embrace me as I entered the room. Then he poured two glasses of blood from the decanter. He handed one to me and held up the other in a toast.

"To the completion of your transformation," he said. Our glasses clinked, and we both drank. He sat down and gestured for me to join him on the sofa. "Of course, it didn't go exactly as planned, but you are now one of us, Sophia, a Manori vampire. I'm very proud of you."

I looked at my feet. "How can you be proud of me?" I asked. "All I did was mess up the bathroom. And—and I bit you."

He laughed and waved my concern away. "I've been bitten hundreds of times in my lifetime. What's a little puncture wound compared to saving Sara's life? No, my dear, don't worry yourself about that."

"Thank you, Father."

He leaned forward and squeezed my hand. "It is I who should be thanking you. You have brought honor to this family, and I wish to honor you in return. If there is any favor I can do for you, please do not hesitate to ask."

My thoughts went immediately to my family—my human family—and I felt a pang of guilt. What were my parents and my brother doing at that moment? Were they worried about me? Ever since starting my life with Sara and her family, I had pushed thoughts of them away, knowing I could not see them, but I missed them so very much. "I do have something in mind," I said, "but now is not the time to ask. Once I finish my training, I will ask for the favor I want, if that's okay."

"Very well," he said. "I will not forget."

The grandfather clock tolled ten times, interrupting the conversation. Father stood up. A moment later, the rest of the family began shuffling into the room. Sara, still bleary-eyed, took a seat beside me on the sofa and held my hand.

When everyone was assembled, Father adopted his usual speaking position, his hands clasped behind his back, and said, "It has been clear for some time that someone is attempting to destroy or discredit the family. The attacks on Sara and Sophia—first on the highway and then in the club last night—were the most brazen acts of aggression against this family in decades. Perhaps even more disturbing, is that my usual sources have been unable to find out who is behind these attacks." He paused and let that sink in. The rest of us waited in solemn silence for him to continue.

"Until we know more, there is little we can do except to remain vigilant," he said. "But we do have one asset that our enemies, whoever they are, do not. As you all know, Sophia, having the bloodline of a dhampir, is already far stronger than anyone would expect for a vampire her age. As she continues to develop her abilities, she could become stronger than any of us."

The rest of the family looked at me. I felt my cheeks flush, and I stared at my feet. Sara squeezed my hand.

"In the days and months ahead, that strength may mean the difference between life and death for this family," Father went on. "For Sara, it already has. So I call on all of you to help Sophia as much as you can. Each of you has something to teach her."

"Father," said Nikolai, "may I make a suggestion?"

"Of course, Nikolai. What is it?"

"We should recall Nora from the Németh clan. It's too dangerous for her to be away from the family right now."

I hadn't thought of Nora since the first day Father introduced me to the family. She was Father's youngest daughter—or had been, until I came along. She was currently staying with her fiancé's family in New York.

Father stroked his chin in thought for a moment before answering. "I understand your concern," he said, "but I don't want to insult Vladimir by implying that the Németh clan is unable to protect her. We need all the allies we can get. I'll make sure he knows what happened so he can be on his guard. Does anyone else have anything to add?"

The room was silent.

"Very well," said Father. He looked around at each of us once more, nodded, and left the room.

Vanessa was the first to rise from her chair after he was gone. She turned to me. "Perhaps it would be best to put off any more ... strenuous ... training until you've fully recovered from this morning," she said. "If you feel up to it, you can come to my room. I can show you a little of what I know about the art of seduction."

I would have liked to have rested a bit more, but the last thing I wanted to do was to sit around replaying the events of last night in my head. I thought going with Vanessa would be a good distraction.

"Okay," I said. "That sounds like a good idea."

I wasn't sure what to expect as I followed Vanessa's swaying form up the stairs, but I was determined to live up to Father's expectations of me. When we got to Vanessa's room, she closed the door behind us and turned to face me. I looked around the room. It was much like mine except larger, and I counted three mahogany wardrobes, in addition to the closet. Along one wall was a vanity that held a staggering array of makeup and other cosmetic products.

My first lesson with Vanessa was all about clothes. She expounded at length on color, texture, and fit, pulling out garment after garment to illustrate her points. "You must never reveal too much," she said. "Show just enough skin to stimulate a man's interest. His imagination will do the rest."

"Now let us talk about true seduction. The first thing to understand," she said, "is that seduction is not about sex. I like to think of it like a song. If you play all the right notes on a person's desires, any man—or woman, for that matter—will dance for you. The key is to use your senses to find out what stimulates a person. I'm not talking about the obvious things like sex, power, or someone's need for attention. What you need to look for are the subtle things that are lacking in a person's life. You see it's easy to get someone's attention, but you have to determine what it is that simulates and inspires them to keep their attention. Learn this, and soon you will have them eating out of your hand."

"Another thing to remember is never give too much. Always leave them wanting more. Here is where you must be strong. You must always be the one in control. If not they will lose respect for you, and then you are just another face in the crowd. However, when you gain a man's respect and can fulfill hidden needs or desires, he will pamper you to no end—buy gifts for you, take you places, and do just about anything just to get a smile or a word of approval from you. He will crave your attention like a drug. Once you show him even a little attention, you have him, and he will do just about anything for you."

When Vanessa felt she had crammed as much information into my head as she could for one day, she sent me to find Carmilla, who began at once to instruct me how to concoct various tinctures, potions, and salves that she thought I might find useful. I soon learned that she had been honing her craft since around AD 330, when she was part of the Roman Empire and many had regarded her as a great sorceress and alchemist.

When I finally left her room, I had a notepad filled with herbal formulas and a list of ingredients. It was four o'clock in the morning, and I was exhausted. To my surprise, Sara was waiting for me in the hall with a pint glass full of fresh blood. "Here," she said.

I drained the glass and wiped my mouth with the back of my hand. I hadn't realized how thirsty I was.

"When your body tells you to feed, don't ignore it," she said. "We don't need a repeat performance of yesterday morning. And it will be even more important to get plenty of blood once you start your combat training."

Over the next few nights, I settled into a routine. I spent the first two hours after dusk in Vanessa's room learning about seduction and the next two hours studying potions with Carmilla. Once or twice a week Sara took me out to work on my social skills and to practice what Vanessa had taught me, and three nights a week I spent several hours practicing combat training with Nikolai.

I quickly found that I had an uncanny aptitude for fighting. After the first month, I could usually beat Dante and sometimes even Sara when we sparred together. A month later, I surpassed Sara, and I even beat Nikolai in an unarmed match for the first time.

He shook his head as I helped him up off the training mat. "I've never seen anything like it," he said. "I've been doing this for centuries, and you just kicked my butt."

Weapons training I enjoyed the most. My favorite weapons were throwing stars—what the Japanese call *shuriken*. The first time I threw one, it took the practice dummy's head off. Nikolai stared at me, eyes wide. I grinned. "So that was good, right?" I asked. He just shook his head in disbelief and trotted off to collect the shuriken from the wall behind the target.

My biggest problem turned out to be mastering the art of seduction. Vanessa was patient with me, but she had her work cut out for her; I hadn't had many opportunities to interact with men growing up on the farm. Devin had developed feelings for me without the need for any encouragement from me, and that was the extent of my romantic experience. Under Vanessa's guidance, I slowly learned that even the way I walked could make the difference between whether a man ignored me or fell instantly under my spell.

When Vanessa felt I was ready, Sara showed me how to use my newly acquired seduction techniques to acquire fresh blood. Most men, it turned out, were surprisingly eager to be lured into the dark corners of nightclubs or the more secluded parts of public parks for a little time alone. Sara taught me how to pierce a victim's skin with my needle-sharp fangs so precisely that they didn't even feel it. Once I had finished my snack, I quickly licked the wound, which congealed the blood and stopped the bleeding—another benefit of being a vampire. Then I'd either ask for another drink or make up some excuse for why I had to go home.

I would usually pull away from my victims with a laugh and a playful glance, and they usually let me go with no more than a wistful look in their eyes. If they pressed for more than that brief kiss on the neck—well, I was more than strong enough now to repel any unwanted advances.

As the months passed, I became more and more proficient at the skills my new siblings were teaching me. The more I learned, the more confident I became; I had to remind myself not to be arrogant. Becoming a vampire had not changed the essence of my personality, but there was no denying there was something different about me. I felt powerful. I feared nothing, and my chief desire was to bring honor to my vampire family and to make my father proud.

14. SECRETS

One evening while I was relaxing in the living room with everyone, Father walked into the room carrying a rolled up parchment of all things. He cleared his throat to get our attention.

"I just received a letter from Cadmus. Lord Illyrius has called a meeting of the elders, and I'm supposed to be in Hlohovec at the next new moon."

I exchanged a blank look with the others.

"When is that?" asked Dante.

"Three days from now," said Father. "Why that man can't use a normal calendar like everyone else is beyond me. Better yet, why can't he learn to use e-mail? This damn letter took two weeks to get here."

"Lord Illyrius isn't the only one who could stand to move with the times, Father," said Vanessa, smiling. "If you're not careful, you'll end up just like him—all wrinkled and covered in dust. You spend far too much time in that library of yours. I know some charming young women who are just dying—"

"That's quite enough, Vanessa," said Father. "My personal life is doing very well, thank you."

"Of course, Father," said Vanessa, still grinning. "You know best, I'm sure."

Father rolled his eyes and continued. "The point is I'll have to leave tomorrow. I want you all to be extra careful while I'm gone. We still don't know who attacked Sara and Sophia, but we have to assume we haven't seen the last of them. No one is to leave the house alone until I return. Is that understood?"

We all nodded in agreement.

"Very good. Now, if you'll excuse me, I should go pack."

When he was gone, I turned to the others and asked, "Who are Cadmus and Lord What's-his-name?"

"Illyrius," said Sara. "He's the head of the vampire council. He lives in a damp old castle in Slovakia, which is in Central Europe. When you're ready, you'll go there for your initiation."

"My what?"

"Lord Illyrius has to approve new members of the family, since Father is an elder," said Dante.

"It's just a formality, really," said Nikolai. "Nothing to worry about."

"As long as you don't mess with his books," said Sara. "He treats them like they're made of gold. If you're very, very polite, he might let you read one, but don't let him catch you near the library without permission."

"Okay," I said, "I think I'm beginning to get the picture. What about Cadmus?"

"He's the council's bookworm," said Dante. "He takes notes at all the meetings—by hand, mind you—and manages the library."

Sara rolled her eyes at Dante. "He's the council's official scribe," she explained, "and he's almost as old as Lord Illyrius. Legend has it he was a Phoenician prince when he was human. I've even heard that he was the first to adapt the Phoenician alphabet for writing in Greek. I don't know if that's true, though."

"See?" said Dante. "A bookworm."

"So Father is an elder on the vampire council?" I asked.

"That's right," said Sara.

"Wow."

*   *   *

Early the next evening as Randolph was driving Marcus to the airport, the head of the Manori clan got out his cell phone and made a call. "I'm leaving Boston now," he said. "I should be there by tomorrow at the latest. Is everything in place? Good. I'll see you when I get there."

As he returned his phone to his inside jacket pocket, the limo hit a pothole. Marcus's briefcase slid off the seat and snapped open, scattering papers over the floor. "Damn it, Randolph, watch where you're going!" he barked.

"Sorry, sir," said Randolph blandly. "I'll be more careful."

Still grumbling, Marcus gathered up his things. Among the papers was a vial of red liquid labeled *Sophia*. He checked to make sure the vial was intact and then carefully placed it back inside the briefcase and secured the lock.

The next evening Marcus's plane landed in Budapest, where a private jet was waiting to carry him to Hlohovec. From there, a limousine drove him three hours into the countryside to Lord Illyrius's castle.

It was an ancient tradition for each member of the council to wear a gold and crimson robe embroidered with the insignia of his or her house. As soon as Marcus entered the castle and the massive oak doors boomed shut behind him, a servant helped him on with his robe and placed a glass of warm blood in his hand.

Once he was properly attired, Marcus proceeded to what had once been the great hall. The other council members were already whispering in groups of two or three around the room. Covering one whole wall was a massive tapestry displaying the insignia of Lord Illyrius's house. Under it, the ancient, emaciated form of Lord Illyrius himself stood waiting.

Marcus's footsteps echoed as he strode across the ancient room. "Greetings, Lord Illyrius. As always, your hospitality is unparalleled." He smiled and raised his glass as he rose from his bow. "The blood is excellent. It has been a long time since the council last met. I hope we can find time to catch up."

"Welcome, Marcus, welcome," Lord Illyrius replied. "You have always had a way with words—I've always liked that about you. And you still show honest respect for your elders and have not completely discarded the old traditions, which cannot be said of everyone these days." His voice was like wind rustling dead leaves. He licked his thin lips with the tip of a pale tongue. "May I ask if you brought the item you wrote to me about?"

"I did, my lord. I think you will be pleased with the results."

"Excellent. Once we are done with council business, you must come to my library for a private talk."

"As you wish, my lord."

Marcus bowed again and retreated to a convenient nook from which to observe the other council members. There were eleven of them, not counting Lord Illyrius. Each elder represented a particular region of the world. The council had not met in years, and the room buzzed with speculation about the purpose for this meeting.

Marcus was the last of the elders to arrive, and as soon as he had finished his drink, Lord Illyrius called for the council meeting to begin. The elders raised their gold and crimson hoods and filed silently out of the great hall down a long corridor, where they reached a heavy wooden door that look as if it was centuries old, yet solid as stone. Lord Illyrius unlocked it with an ornate iron key that hung on a chain around his neck, and the hinges groaned as the door swung outward. A narrow flight of stone steps, worn by the shuffling feet of vampire elders over countless centuries, led down into darkness.

Deep below the ground, they came to the council chamber. Its walls were of dry-laid stone carefully cut to fit together perfectly, without any gaps. Cadmus sat at a desk in the corner, ready to take down the events of the meeting. A candle flickering at his elbow provided the room's only light. In the center of the chamber was a round wooden table with twelve seats—eleven for the council members and one for Lord Illyrius. At each elder's place, there was a small ceremonial dagger with a jeweled hilt, and as Lord Illyrius took his chair, a robed servant scurried out of the darkness and placed a golden chalice on the table in front of him.

Without hesitation, Lord Illyrius picked up the dagger in front of him and drew it across his wrist, over the mouth of the chalice. Dark blood trickled over the vampire's pale, leathery skin and into the cup. After a moment, he bent over to lick the wound clean, and the servant stepped forward again to carry the chalice to the elder from Africa, who sat to Lord Illyrius's left. The cup made its way around the table, and when it returned to Lord Illyrius, it held a little of each council member's blood.

The ancient vampire stood, threw back his hood, and raised the chalice in both hands. "I drink now this blood willingly, given that I may know without doubt that each of us is true to the sacred calling bestowed unto him and unto all of us, from the first night till this night and for all nights to come," he intoned. "Woe to any who has strayed from his sacred vow, for retribution will be swift."

He brought the cup's brim to his lips and drained it in one long, slow swallow. The servant took the chalice away, and for a moment Lord Illyrius stood perfectly still with his eyes closed. Finally, he leaned forward to place both of his hands on the table and fixed his gaze on the representative from East Asia. "Master Woo Pinyin Shi. I see your thoughts in my mind. Must I speak them aloud, or will you speak on your own behalf and explain yourself?"

Master Shi stood and lowered his hood to address the council. "Members of the council, as you know, more than one-and-a-half billion humans live within the borders of the People's Republic of China. Most live in poverty. I respectfully request that, in order to reduce overpopulation, the council grant the vampires in China special permission to kill the humans on whom we feed."

There was some murmuring from the elders. Master Shi's request was in direct contradiction to the council's first and most sacred rule: vampires must not kill their human victims except in defense of their own lives.

Master Shi hurriedly continued. "We would feed only on those in poverty-stricken areas and would dispose of the bodies properly. In the long term, we believe such a policy would improve the conditions in these areas. Thank you for listening to my request." He raised his hood over his head and sat down.

Lord Illyrius stared implacably at the Chinese elder. It was difficult to be sure in the flickering candlelight, but Marcus did not think the head of the council had blinked since first fixing Master Shi with his gaze.

There was a long moment in which nobody spoke. Then Lord Illyrius said, "Master Shi, it seems some vampires in your region have already adopted the practice of which you speak. Is this not true?"

"Regrettably, it is true, Lord Illyrius."

"Regrettably, you say. And what measures have you taken to put a stop to these killings?"

A barely perceptible quaver crept into the East Asian representative's voice as he responded. "My lord, the human population in my home country is large, and so is the vampire community. As soon as I heard about this situation, I sent emissaries to speak to the clan leaders responsible, but they would not listen."

"And once news of this rebellion reached you?"

"We have few assassins in my country, and many have spoken out in support of the practice. It seemed prudent—"

"Master Shi," Lord Illyrius cut in sharply, "every member of this council knows the laws set down by the original elders. They are there for a reason. When one of these laws is broken, it is your responsibility as an elder to take action. By your own admission, you failed to do so."

Lord Illyrius nodded slightly, and a masked figure slipped silently from the darkness behind Master Shi's chair. Marcus caught the gleam of a piano wire in the candlelight, and an instant later Master Shi's body slumped headless in its chair. A fine mist of blood sprayed across the table. The dead man's head hit the floor with a sickening thud, and the assassin was gone.

The council sat in silence as the servant reappeared and spread a white sheet over the corpse. A red stain blossomed on the shimmering satin cloth before the body of Master Shi began to turn to dust. The blood-stained sheet fell to the floor, where a servant quickly picked it up.

"A shame," said Lord Illyrius, as if to himself. "I expected better from Master Shi, and now I will have to find a replacement." He turned to the rest of the council. "As you all know, it is your duty to take swift and decisive action whenever one of our laws is broken. Now let's move on to other business."

Each member then gave a brief report on his or her region, and when they were done, Lord Illyrius folded his hands on the table and looked in the eyes of each member of the council. A dead silence filled the room. Finally Lord Illyrius spoke. "The reports from each of you show that throughout the world the vampire population is growing faster that it should. If this keeps up, the delicate balance between humans and vampires will become disproportionate. It is our duty to make sure this does not happen. If the growth of the vampire population cannot be stopped, decisive action will have to be taken. Therefore, I am ordering the immediate halt of the turning of any more humans until balance is restored. It is your duty to inform the vampire community of this order and, if necessary, enforce it. That is all."

Everyone knew what Lord Illyrius meant by decisive action. He would send out his assassins to kill the clan leaders who did not comply with his order. Then, if necessary, other vampires would have to be killed to thin out the population. It was imperative that the human population never know of the existence of vampires. More importantly, these actions would send a message to the vampire population that the council's power extended throughout the world.

After the meeting adjourned, most of the council members hurried off to bed. Marcus stayed behind and waited in the great hall. He did not have to wait long before Lord Illyrius appeared with a bottle of blood and asked Marcus to join him in the library.

Lord Illyrius's library was immense. Shelves towered more than thirty feet high along every wall and in the center of the room there stood row after row of bookshelves with rolling ladders attached to each one. Lord Illyrius led Marcus to a niche along one wall where two wingback chairs faced one another over a low table. When they were seated, Lord Illyrius poured two glasses of blood.

"So," he said, handing Marcus his glass, "tell me more about this dhampir you have adopted."

Marcus nodded. "Her name is Sophia, and I think you will be surprised when I tell you the name of the vampire who fathered the first dhampir in Sophia's bloodline. I thought it best not to commit it to writing, or I would have informed you sooner."

"Who was the ancient vampire?" asked Lord Illyrius.

"Vadim Preda, fifth elder of the Council of Lamia."

"Very interesting," said Lord Illyrius. He took a sip of blood. "Tell me more about this Sophia."

Marcus gave a brief account of Sophia's friendship with Sara, the accident in the limousine, and Sophia's transformation. "I had never heard of a dhampir becoming a vampire before," he concluded, "so during her transformation I put her through some training to try to awaken the vampire traits within her DNA. The results have been nothing short of astonishing."

"Really now. In what ways?"

"She has only been training for a few months, my lord, and her abilities already match those of a master vampire." Marcus set down his wine glass and placed his briefcase on the table. He opened it and took out the vial of Sophia's blood, which he handed to Lord Illyrius.

The old vampire read the label and then removed the cap and brought the vial to his lips. He closed his eyes for a moment. When he opened them, he said, "I admit I'm intrigued. She may prove useful to the council. Of course, now that she's a vampire, she will need to undergo the usual test."

"Of course, my lord," said Marcus. "When would you like to test her?"

Lord Illyrius waved his hand dismissively. "There is no need to hurry. Let her train for a few more months and then bring her to me." He paused and gazed intently at Marcus across the table. "Do not let your affection for this girl blind you to your duties. We stand at the precipice, Marcus, as you know all too well. The balance is in need of adjustment. If all goes well, your Sophia will be a great asset to the vampire community—and she will reap the rewards that go with her service. But nothing can be certain until she is tested. Let us not speak of this again until you bring her to me."

"As you wish, my lord," said Marcus. "If there's nothing else, I would like to go to my room and rest. It's been a long night."

The old vampire nodded. "I plan to do the same shortly. Sleep well, Marcus."

"And you, my lord."

Marcus rose and left the library. When he looked over his shoulder, Lord Illyrius was still in his chair. His shoulders were hunched and his brow furrowed, as if in deep thought.

As soon as Marcus woke the next evening, he said his good-byes to Lord Illyrius and the other elders and began the long journey home to Boston.

15. THE STREETS OF BOSTON

E arly one evening a few days after his return from Hlohovec, Father knocked gently at my bedroom door. I was surprised to see him; usually he summoned me to the library when he wanted to talk. I invited him in, and he took a seat in the overstuffed chair. I perched on the edge of my bed and waited for him to speak.

"How do you feel your training is progressing, my dear?" he asked.

"Pretty well, I think—well, I'm not so great at seduction, but Nikolai seems impressed with how well I can fight," I said. "I've been working hard, Father."

"I'm sure you have," Father said with a grin. "The others have told me of your progress. I'm very pleased with what you have accomplished. But now it's time to take what you've learned out into the real world."

"What do you mean?"

"One of my sources has finally unearthed some information about the vampires who abducted Sara at the nightclub," said Father. "It seems one of them has connections to a clan in one of the less savory parts of the city. I want you to go there tonight with Sara and Nikolai and see if you can gather any information about the attacks."

Apprehension welled in my chest, but at the same time, I felt a thrill of excitement.

Father looked at me seriously. "I want to make it clear that the neighborhood where you will be tonight is very dangerous. The vampires of the lower classes are not always as … civilized as we are, Sophia. They feed on the drug addicts and prostitutes that live on the streets. I don't expect them to give the three of you any trouble, but if something goes wrong, you are to listen to Nikolai and do exactly what he says."

"I understand, Father."

"Good. I'll leave you to prepare. Meet Nikolai and Sara downstairs in an hour." Father got up, kissed me on the cheek, and left the room.

Once he was gone, I changed into some comfortable clothes. My apprehension kept gnawing at me for some reason. Perhaps it was because I had never fought against another vampire as a full vampire before. To ease my mind, I decided to arm myself, just in case we did run into trouble. I slipped a dagger into one boot and a wooden stake into the other. My shuriken, which I had now become very proficient with, were thin and light enough for me to conceal a good supply of them in a leather pouch strapped to the small of my back. They were tipped with silver, so if I managed to lodge one in a vampire's body, the wound would stay open and continue to bleed until it was removed.

When I was fully dressed, I took a deep breath and looked at myself in the mirror. My reflection stared back, grim and confident—maybe even arrogant. I saw no sign of the innocent farm girl who had set out from home in search of answers more than a year before. That girl was long gone.

I found Sara and Nikolai waiting for me in the parlor. I nodded to them, and the three of us marched out to the waiting limo without a word. Randolph pulled out of the garage without waiting for instructions; apparently, he already knew where we were going.

Nikolai turned to Sara and me. "Here's the plan," he said. "I know a guy who runs a bar on Dudley Street. He may be able to point us in the right direction. If we stick together and don't draw too much attention to ourselves, we should be able to avoid any trouble."

Sara squeezed my arm. "You've been kicking ass in training," she said, "but this is the real thing. Stay sharp, and don't try anything heroic."

"Don't worry," I said. "I'm not that stupid. Is there anything else I should know?"

"Yeah," said Nikolai. "If things go wrong and we end up in a fight, leave the close-up stuff to me and Sara. You run and find some high ground so you can cover us with those fancy ninja stars of yours."

"They're called shuriken," I said teasing Nikolai. "How did you know I brought them?"

"I couldn't help but notice the slight bulge at you back. I know that's where you like to keep them," said Nikolai.

A little annoyed, I folded my arms and said, "All right, Nic, you're the boss."

The limo rolled up to a stoplight on Dudley Street, and Nikolai motioned for us to get out. When we were all standing on the corner, Randolph rolled down his window. "I'll meet you back here in two hours," he said. "If you need me sooner, call the limo number."

Nikolai responded with a curt nod. The light changed, and Randolph pulled away from the curb, leaving us stranded in one of the worst neighborhoods in Boston.

As I looked around, I saw a hodgepodge of buildings lining the street: a low-rise apartment with cracks in the concrete blocks; single-family homes whose wooden siding was badly in need of repair; a Laundromat with a flickering neon sign. The air was thick with the stink of decomposing trash and a sea of plastic bags and fast-food wrappers littered street.

The few people out on the sidewalk stared at us openly. Even our casual clothes were far nicer than anything anyone else on the street was wearing—and of course, we had just hopped out of a limousine. So much for being inconspicuous.

"This way," said Nikolai quietly, and we followed him down the sidewalk. We had only gone half a block when six men poured out of the front entrance of an apartment building right in front of us. I knew instantly that they were vampires.

As soon as they saw us, they stopped and formed a semicircle, blocking the sidewalk. One of them stepped forward. His black hair was slicked back, and there was fresh blood on his face. "What can I do for you three?" he asked.

"No need to worry about us, friend," said Nikolai. "We're just here to take a quick look around. Then we'll be on our way."

The vampire took another step forward and made a show of looking Nikolai up and down. "I think you should leave now, *friend*. You obviously don't belong here. It would be a real shame if anything happened to those pretty clothes of yours." One of the other vampires snickered.

They began to spread out, trying to flank us. Sara caught my eye and jerked her head toward an alley we had just passed on our left. I nodded, spun on my heel, and made a dash for it. Jeers filled the air behind me. I turned the corner into the alley and stopped to listen. There was no sound of following footsteps. The apartment complex towered above me. My initial leap carried me past the first-story windows, and my fingers found a crack in the concrete. That was all I needed. Seconds later, I was crouched on the roof.

The scene in the street below hadn't changed. Nikolai and the other vampire stood inches apart, staring one another down.

Nikolai blatantly sniffed the air between them. "Junkie blood," he said, his mouth twisting in disgust. "I have to say I've never understood the appeal. Do you get high from it, or are you just too lazy to catch a healthy human?"

The other vampire's eyes narrowed to thin slits, and he let out a low hiss. Quick as a snake, he drew a switchblade from his pocket and flicked it open. Before he could strike, Nikolai grabbed his wrist, spun him around, and twisted his elbow upward, immobilizing him. "Drop it," he ordered. The knife clattered on the pavement. The other vampires edged forward. I reached into my pouch and slid a shuriken into each hand.

"Stay where you are," said Nikolai calmly, "or I'll tear his arm off."

The vampire in Nikolai's hold grunted in pain. The rest stayed where they were.

"Good," said Nikolai. "Now listen up. We don't want any trouble. If you leave us alone, we'll leave you alone."

There were a couple of hesitant nods from the group, and Nikolai shoved the slick-haired vampire back toward his companions. They caught him and began to back away. I let out a breath I didn't realize I'd been holding.

My relief was premature. One of the six who had been hanging back behind the others stepped forward. As he stepped under the streetlight, I got a good look at him, and I gasped. The last time I'd seen him, I'd jabbed a steel bar through his shoulder.

"This is the bitch that killed Damon," he said, his gaze fixed on Sara. "Her and the other girl. We can't let them go."

Without any hesitation, Sara slid a wooden stake from her boot, stepped forward, and plunged it through the vampire's heart. Clearly, she still had some pent-up feelings about being captured. He crumpled onto the sidewalk, already turning into ash.

Everyone on the street stood completely still. All eyes turned to the vampire who had first confronted Nikolai. He took one look at his friend's ashes and turned and ran into the apartment building. The others scattered. I looked around and saw that all the humans had already fled the street. It was like a scene in an old Western, I thought ominously—the scene just before the gunfight.

Nikolai jumped forward and stood back to back with Sara, who yelled out, "That was personal, between me and him. Now either you can let us leave in peace, or we can give this place a new name, Via Sanguinis. For all you uneducated filth, that means—"

"Blood road." A rich, deep voice from the darkness interrupted her. "I rather like that. Gives the place a bit of class, don't you think?"

The owner of the voice stepped from the shadows. He had broad shoulders and salt-and-pepper hair and was well dressed in dark jeans and a sport coat. I wasn't sure why I hadn't been able to sense him before, but I certainly could now. He was older than the other vampires and much stronger by far. I realized that Sara and Nikolai might not be able to take him. As the vampire walked into the light, I tightened my grip on my shuriken.

He walked across the street toward Sara and Nikolai, who were still standing back to back under the streetlight. "My name is Vaine," he said, "and this is my domain. Do you think you can come here, kill one of my children, and then just walk away?" He shook his head. "Foolish child. Death must always pay for death."

As he spoke, vampires rushed from the apartment complex below me and from several other buildings along the street. There were close to a dozen of them, and they closed in on Sara and Nikolai from all directions.

Vaine turned to one of the approaching vampires. "Take as many as you need and go find the other female. I can still smell her nearby. Go!"

I eased back from the edge of the roof and pulled a small bottle from my pocket. It held a potion Carmilla had taught me to make to hide my scent. I poured the oily liquid on my hands and rubbed it on my face, hair, and clothes.

I crept forward and risked a peek down into the street. The circle of vampires had tightened around Nikolai and Sara, but they weren't attacking yet.

"Where are you from, boy?" Vaine said to Nikolai.

Nikolai said nothing. I could tell the vampires in the street below were starting to get restless. If they charged, there was a good chance they would be able to overpower my adopted siblings. There were just too many of them. And to make matters worse, I couldn't spot the ones Vaine had sent after me. Sooner or later, they would surely think to look up. I had to act, and quickly.

Vaine took another step forward and growled, "I asked where you—" He stopped midsentence and took half a step back, a puzzled expression on his face, one of my shuriken protruding from his forehead. He reached up and pulled it out. Blood oozed from the wound for a moment, but it healed quickly. "What the hell is this?" said Vaine. "Does your friend honestly think she can hurt me with a child's toy?" He tossed my weapon contemptuously away and focused again on Nikolai.

As soon as the shuriken left my hand, I sprinted across the rooftop and leaped over the alley. I somersaulted to a stop on the roof of the Laundromat next door. As soon as I came to a stop, I threw another shuriken at Vaine. This time, it buried itself in his neck, and a bright arc of blood spurted from the wound as the silver tip severed his carotid artery.

Vaine yanked the shuriken from his neck and let out a gurgling noise that resolved itself into a stream of profanity as his vocal cords stitched themselves back together. "Find her, damn it!" he shouted, and several of the vampires around Nikolai and Sara dashed toward the Laundromat.

Fortunately, I was no longer there, having leaped into a narrow space between two houses across the street while all eyes were on Vaine. I threw two shuriken in quick succession. The first struck

Vaine in the thigh, followed by another gratifying spurt of blood. The second shattered the window of a beauty salon two buildings down. That was all the distraction I needed to sprint around the house to my left and climb swiftly to a new position on the roof of a brownstone directly behind Vaine. Despite the danger, I felt a thrill of exhilaration as I slipped two more throwing stars into my hands.

As Vaine bent to pull the shuriken from his leg, Sara and Nikolai finally sprang into action. There were only a few vampires clustered around them now—most were stumbling through nearby alleys looking for me. Sara lunged and staked one through the chest, and Nikolai swept another off her feet with one hand and crushed her throat with the other.

Vaine turned toward them, but I jumped from the rooftop and landed in a crouch in the street about twenty feet behind him. "I must be the belle of the ball," I said. "It seems everyone wants to dance with me tonight."

At the sound of my voice, Vaine spun around.

"How about you, handsome?" I taunted. "Wanna dance?" I threw another shuriken, but he caught it in his hand. I turned and ran up the street away from the others, and he took off after me. He was fast for his size—faster than I expected—but I was a little faster. When I had gained a couple of yards, I whirled and hit him in the chest with two more shuriken. He lowered his head and accelerated, not even bothering to pull them out.

I ran on, groped for more shuriken, and realized I only had one left. I knew then that I was going to have to stop and fight. Just ahead of me, an uneven slab of concrete jutted an inch above the rest of the street. I pretended to trip over it. I heard his feet pounding the street behind me. Just before he reached me, I hopped to one side and spun my leg around in a low arc, sweeping his feet from under him.

He went down hard and skidded for several feet along the street, but he rolled to his feet before I could press my advantage. We faced one another, circling slowly. His clothes were in blood-stained tatters, but his movements were sure. "There's something different about you," he said. "What is it?"

"I'm the one who's going to kick your ass," I said arrogantly.

He charged. I tried to slip away, but his long fingernails raked across my face. It threw me off balance for a moment, but I didn't feel any pain. We danced around one another, exchanging attempts to hit each other, dodging and blocking one another's attacks. We growled and hissed as we fought, and I realized that I was in a fight to the death: only one of us would walk away from this.

Somehow I knew that Vaine was an old European vampire, and he fought like one—he barely thought of his legs as weapons at all. He charged again, and this time I leaped into the air and did a flip over his head. I landed in a somersault, and as I rolled to my fleet, I shoved my last shuriken into the toe of my boot, turning it into a weapon.

But I had taken a fraction of a second too long. Before I could regain my balance, Vaine landed a solid punch to the back of my head. I fell forward but managed to twist around and land on my back. Vaine picked me up by the front of my shirt with his left hand. His right hand moved in a blur, and he tore deep gashes across my face and throat with his fingernails, first one way, and then the other. I blocked with my arms as well as I could, but many of his attacks landed on me hard. My feet scrabbled on the pavement, but I was unable to get enough footing to get to my feet. I could feel myself weakening as blood gushed from my wounds.

Then with all my strength, I kicked Vaine in the thigh with the shuriken in the toe of my boot. Out of anger, Vaine flung me down the street. The back of my head struck the asphalt, and my teeth came together with a snap. I lay there, lungs heaving, as he strode toward me. "I'll teach you to make a fool out of me, bitch," he growled.

He stood over me gloating, thinking I was defeated, but I still had some strength left. I felt the cuts on my face begin to heal, which gave me a boost of confidence. He picked me up again and threw me farther down the street, but this time I was ready. I landed in a controlled roll and was already sprinting away before he realized his mistake.

I turned at the first corner and doubled back down a dark alley behind a cheap pizza shop. I pressed my back to the brick wall next to a Dumpster and tried to hide in the shadows. I was too weak to run or find another hiding place. I only hoped that my body would have enough time to heal before Vaine found me.

Then the unexpected happened. I felt a rage build from deep within my body, and my exhausted muscles throbbed with a deep burning pain. This time I knew what was happing. I was going into a bloodlust.

I heard the crunch of Vaine's boots at the mouth of the alley, and my anxiety put me over the edge. I screamed from the pain and then lost control. Just as before, my instincts took over, but this time things were different. I was now in a full vampire bloodlust.

As Vaine came into view, I flung my body forward and leaped at him, fangs fully extended and my jaw open wide.

He was unprepared for such a ferocious onslaught, and he stumbled back, eyes wide. Before he could bring his arms up to defend himself, my fangs sank deep into his neck. I hadn't learned to use my venom yet—I didn't even know what kind of venom I had—but instinctively my body knew exactly what to do and injected a massive dose of my venom into his body.

Vaine gasped. His hands clutched weakly at me once or twice, and as soon as I released my bite, he collapsed onto the broken asphalt. I stepped back and stared down at him. His eyes rolled wildly in their sockets. Other than that, he was completely paralyzed.

I smiled and dropped to one knee on his stomach. I jerked out one of the shuriken that was still lodged in his chest and straddled him. Slowly, I used the blade to slice a deep gash down his cheek, from the corner of his eye down to his jaw. It healed, so I did it again, and again. The more blood he lost the slower he healed. Vaine let out a muffled whimper.

I grabbed his chin with my left hand and forced him to look me in the eyes. Without looking away, I balled up my fist and thrust my right hand deep into his chest with a tremendous force. There was a popping sound as his ribs gave way. My fingers closed around his heart, and I yanked it out and held it in front of his face. A look of horror filled his eyes for an instant, and then he was gone.

As I stood up, Vaine's body began to crumble into ash. I stood there trembling, still deep in a bloodlust. Now that Vaine was gone, my thirst for blood became more powerful than lust for revenge. I sniffed the air and scanned the alley for a source of food.

Just then, the back door of the pizza parlor swung open. A shaft of light from inside pierced the shadows, and the aroma of baking pizzas filled the air. A young man in a red visor and a white polo shirt stepped into the ally carrying a garbage bag, and the door swung shut behind him.

I pounced, snarling. I slammed his body up against the wall, and my fangs found the jugular vein in his throat. Somewhere deep inside, the part of me that could still think, the part that still had a conscience, cried out for me to stop, but it was no use. I drank until I had sucked the last remains of blood from his veins. As his blood made its way through my system, my bloodlust began to subside. I stumbled away from his corpse in confusion and staggered out into the street.

"Sophia! Sophia, are you okay?" I looked up and saw Sara running toward me. Nikolai was a few paces behind her. They guided me back to the sidewalk, and my head began to clear. "Are you okay?" Sara asked again.

I looked down. My clothes were in shreds, and I was completely soaked with blood. I felt exhausted. "I think I've been better," I said. I swayed, and Sara put her arm around me for support.

"Where's Vaine?" asked Nikolai.

"Dead," I said. In spite of the horror I had just experienced, I felt a thrill of triumph. A grin spread over my face. "I killed him."

Nikolai's eyes widened. "Holy shit, sis. You took him out by yourself? I wasn't sure that Sara and I together could've taken him out."

"We should get you home," said Sara. "We're not going to find out anything useful tonight, not after all this."

Nikolai called Randolph, and together we made our way back to the rendezvous point, Nikolai and Sara supporting me between them. Randolph, noticing my condition and blood-soaked clothes, opened the trunk, pulled out a blanket, and placed it over my shoulders. Sara then wrapped it around me as we got into the car.

As we made our way back home, Sara noticed the shuriken in my boot. "Good idea, sis," she said. "We should get some built in to your next pair."

I nodded, but I wasn't really listening. As soon as we were safely out of the area, I passed out from exhaustion.

*   *   *

The next evening, I woke in my own bed. Sara and Nikolai must have carried me up to my room. Before I even sat up, the events of the night before came crawling into my head. I felt numb. I didn't know whether I ought to feel bad about killing Vaine—he had been trying to kill me, after all—but I was shocked by the brutality of what I had done to him before he died.

And then there was the pizza boy. I stared at the ceiling for several minutes, trying to come to terms with what I had done. I expected to feel devastated, but there was only a mild sense of guilt, the same sort of thing I might have felt for telling Devin a white lie back when we were engaged. Surely that was wrong. I imagined the boy's mother crying when she learned of his death and searched my feelings again. Still nothing. Well, maybe the crushing guilt would come later.

As I sat up, I realized I was covered in dried blood and still wearing my clothes from the night before. I got into the shower with my clothes and peeled them off once the caked blood began to soften. The water ran red down the drain. When I was finally clean and dressed in fresh clothes, I went in search of something to drink.

I found Sara and Nikolai sharing a bottle of blood in the parlor. "Any left for me?" I asked.

Nikolai jumped up. "Let me get you a glass," he said.

I took a seat on the sofa next to Sara, a little shocked that Nikolai was waiting on me. He handed me a fresh glass and then topped off Sara's and his own. We clinked them together and drank.

"That was quick thinking, distracting Vaine the way you did last night," said Sara.

"It was," said Nikolai. He flopped back into his chair and put his feet up on the ottoman. "When he first showed up, I honestly thought we were dead."

"I was scared too." She smiled at me. "That's the second time now you've saved my butt."

"You both would have done the same for me," I said.

"Wouldn't have had to," said Nikolai. "It seems you can take care of yourself."

I rolled my eyes at him, but I had to take a drink to hide my smile.

"Oh, I almost forgot to tell you," said Nikolai. "Father wants to see you in the library for a debriefing, but I'm sure he won't mind if you finish your drink first."

When I got to the library, Father was seated in his usual chair by the fireplace. "Come in, my dear. Come in," he said, waving me into the room. As I slipped into the other chair, he said, "How are you feeling this evening?"

"Surprisingly, I feel good, considering what happened last night."

"Excellent," said Father. "Since this was your first fight with a vampire, I want you to tell me everything you can remember about last night. Even the smallest detail could be the clue that leads us to whoever is conspiring against the family."

I started haltingly, but once I got going, it all poured out in a rush: Vaine chasing me up the street, the fight, his claws ripping across my face. As I spoke, Father listened silently with his head cocked to one side. When I got to the part about going into bloodlust, my telling of the story slowed again.

"—I then bit him, and it was like he couldn't move," I said. "I think my venom paralyzed him."

"Paralyzed him? Well, now, that's very interesting," said Father, looking up at me sharply. "What happened then?"

I remembered the look of terror in Vaine's eyes as I slowly drew my shuriken down his cheek and the blood welling from the cut. Somehow, telling Father about the events of the night made them feel real again. "I tortured him, Father," I stammered, lowering my head in shame. "And then I—I—tore out his heart."

Father's eyes widened. He was no doubt surprised that I was able to accomplish such a deed, even while in a bloodlust.

"Oh, Sophia," said Father. "It's all right. You have to remember that you've only been a vampire for a very short time. In many ways, you're still a child. You can't be held responsible for something you did while in a bloodlust. The beast is a terrible thing. It takes most vampires centuries to learn to control it."

I nodded, but I didn't look up from the floor.

"Truly, my dear, you did nothing wrong," said Father gently. "I'm sure this Vaine meant to kill you—and he would have, if your bloodlust hadn't saved you."

Emotion finally overwhelmed me, and tears began to flow down my face. I looked up at Father and saw the kindness in his eyes. Somehow, I found the courage to tell him the rest of the story. "It wasn't just Vaine," I said. "There was a human, a boy. He came into the alley after Vaine was dead, and I bit him, and—and I couldn't stop." I covered my face with my hands, and deep sobs wracked my body.

Father was at my side in an instant. He kneeled beside my chair, and I felt his strong arms around me. "Oh, my dear Sophia," he said. "I know you're upset, but it will be all right—truly, it will. You are not responsible for what happened. I was the one who sent you into such a dangerous place, and it was Vaine who started the fight. In a way, we're the ones who killed that boy, not you. Look at me, Sophia."

I looked up into his face, wiping the tears from my eyes.

"You are not to blame," he said in a clear, deliberate voice. "What happened last night was not your fault. Do you understand? You were only acting on instinct. With your strength I doubt if five vampires could have stopped you."

I nodded, still sniffling.

"You acted bravely to defend your family," said Father. "Sara and Nikolai told me how you saved them. You acted nobly, Sophia. What happened during your bloodlust—well, that's on Vaine's shoulders, and maybe a little on mine."

I buried my face in Father's shoulder and cried quietly for a while. When I regained my composure, I looked up at him. "But won't I get in trouble?" I asked. "I mean, isn't ... what I did ... against vampire law?"

"Let me worry about that," said Father. "You aren't the first young vampire to lose control. There are ways to deal with these situations."

I wrapped my arms around his neck and gave him a kiss on the cheek. "Thank you, Father."

He held me for a moment longer and then patted me gently on the shoulder and rose to his feet. He turned to face the fireplace, clasping his hands together behind his back. "If it makes you feel any better," he said, "I intend to find the boy's family. They'll never want for money again. It won't bring him back, of course, but I thought you might like to know."

I nodded, even though Father was still facing away from me. It did make me feel better—not much, but a little. I scrubbed the last tears from my eyes, rose quietly, and left the room, leaving Father alone with his thoughts.

16. Πora

Over the next few nights, I settled back into my old routine, and my sense of guilt gradually faded. After the first week, I stopped thinking about it altogether.

Early one evening while the whole family was gathered in the parlor for a drink, Father's phone rang. He stood in silence for several minutes, listening. His expression turned cold. We could tell something was wrong, but all we could do was wait.

"How long ago did this happen?" he asked. There was a pause. "And you're just calling me now?" Anger crept into his voice. "Vladimir, that's impossible!" Another pause. "We'll be there as soon as we can." He ended the call, and his phone slipped from his fingers and clattered across the marble floor. He stared straight ahead with a blank expression for a moment.

Then his face hardened. When he spoke, his voice was almost a snarl. "Your sister Nora is dead. We leave for New York in half an hour." He turned abruptly and strode out of the room.

The rest of us sat in shocked silence as what he said sank in. I looked around at my brothers and sisters and saw grief and anger etched into their faces. After a moment, Nikolai stood and marched toward the stairs. The rest of us got up to follow.

In the hallway upstairs, I grabbed Sara by the arm. "What do I do?" I asked. "I've never seen Father like this."

She looked at me and said coldly, "You do your duty to the family. We're going to find out exactly what happened to Nora, and when we do, we're going to hunt down and kill everyone involved."

I stared at her, stunned. She had never spoken to me that way before.

"Pack your things," she said. "We don't have much time. Now go!" She whirled and disappeared into her room. The door slammed shut behind her.

I went to my room and packed a gym bag with a few changes of clothes and my favorite weapons. Then I hurried downstairs to the living room and waited for the rest of the family to assemble. It didn't take long. Father was the last to appear. "Is everything ready?" he barked at Nikolai.

"Yes, Father."

"Then let us go avenge your sister and restore honor to the Manori clan."

We filed into the garage, where Randolph was waiting with the limousine. No one spoke during the four-hour drive. From what I had heard, the Németh clan were almost as ancient and powerful as we were with respect to their bloodlines. The union of our two families would have made us the most powerful clan east of the Mississippi. Now, with Nora gone, that could never happen.

The Németh mansion turned out to be a massive Victorian, built of brick and situated on a lushly forested estate just outside New York City. As we stopped in front of the mansion entrance, Father told us to wait in the limousine while he went in first. As soon as Father reached the front steps, an old vampire came to the door. I guessed it was Vladimir Németh, the clan leader. They spoke for a few minutes and then disappeared inside.

Hours seemed to pass before Father finally reappeared and beckoned us to join him on the steps. "I have spoken at length with Vladimir," he said. "He told me that Nora and Michael were walking home from a friend's house in a suburb near here when they were attacked by a vampire hunter. It seems Michael was badly hurt in the attack as well. For the moment, I believe Lord Németh's story. Come now and look upon your sister."

We entered the mansion behind Father. Vladimir Németh met us with a solemn bow and motioned for us to follow him. He led us into a massive room with inlaid wooden floors and a vaulted ceiling. In the center of the room was a casket made of clear glass, bouquets of white and pink flowers arranged around it.

I expected Nora's remains to be ash—she was, after all, a vampire—but her pristine body in a clean white dress lay serenely inside the casket. She was quite beautiful, with dark red lips and red-gold hair that neatly framed her pale face. The way she looked, I half expected her to sit up and greet us. I shot Sara a puzzled look and saw that her brow was furrowed in confusion.

Dante took a step toward the casket. "There are no signs of decay," he said. "Could this be a mistake?" He rolled up his sleeve. "Father, let me feed her. Perhaps all she needs is the blood of our clan."

Father took Dante by the arm. "Wait a moment, my son," he said. He turned to Vladimir. "Can you explain this, old friend?" he asked.

"It's just as much of a mystery to me," said Vladimir, "but more than a week has passed since the attack, and she shows no sign of life. We tried to feed her, but she didn't respond. No vampire her age can go so long without blood. Judge for yourself, Marcus, but I sense no life in her. Only an empty shell remains. I'm sorry."

Father walked slowly to the side of the casket and looked down at his daughter. "May my family and I have some time alone with her?" he asked.

"Of course," said Vladimir. "Take as long as you need to say your good-byes." He bowed deeply once more and left the room.

As soon as he was gone, Father began inspecting the casket. "Something isn't right here," he said. "Can any of you sense any life from Nora?"

We all shook our heads.

"Sophia," he said, turning to me, "your senses have surpassed those of the rest of the family. I need you to concentrate and tell me whatever you can about your sister."

I slowly approached the casket and walked around it. Nora lay perfectly still. I could smell nothing from the casket at all; there was not even a hint of death or decay. I placed my hands on the glass, but still I felt nothing.

"That's odd," said Sara. "It's completely sealed. Look—there's a lock on the lid."

"Can I break the lock?" I asked Father. "I might at least be able to smell something then."

He nodded. "Nikolai," he said quietly, "keep a watch on the doorway. If Vladimir is hiding something, I don't want him to know we suspect."

Nikolai trotted silently back to the entryway, looked back, and shook his head, indicating that we were unobserved. I reached down and snapped the brass lock with my hand. The sound echoed disconcertingly in the cavernous room. Slowly, I opened the lid.

Nora's scent filled my nostrils at once. There was still no smell of decay, but there was a hint of something else—a vaguely familiar chemical scent. I placed a hand gently on her chest and closed my eyes. After a moment, I sensed a faint pulse of energy like a miniscule electric spark. "She's alive," I said. "Just barely, but she is alive."

Without a word, Father lifted Nora in his arms and hurried outside. The rest of us followed. He laid her gently across the backseat of the limo, and Sara cradled Nora's head in her arms while Nikolai retrieved a large metal briefcase from the trunk. When he opened it, I saw that it was full of surgical tubing, syringes, needles, and medical equipment of all kinds. Working quickly, he inserted an IV into Nora's arm and attached it to a bag of blood.

Vladimir Németh ran down the front steps of the mansion. "What foolishness is this?" he cried. "You are giving false hope to your family. I promise you, Marcus, I checked many times. Nora is dead!"

Marcus rounded on him angrily. "My daughter, who is just over a year old, was able to tell Nora was alive as soon as we opened the casket. What does that say about your abilities? When was the last time you went on a hunt? When did you last visit the old country or pay your respects to Lord Illyrius?"

Vladimir backed away, but Father followed him step for step.

"You have grown weak," Father spat, "and my daughter may still die because of your weakness. If you weren't my friend, I'd rip your heart out here and now."

The two vampires stood face to face, their fangs extended and eyes black as coal.

"Would you two stop it?" shouted Carmilla. "You should both be trying to help Nora. She's not responding to the blood."

As all eyes turned to Nora, I finally realized where I had smelled the blend of chemicals from the casket before. "Father!" I said.

He tore his gaze away from Nora's limp form. "What?" he barked.

I quickly explained about the chemical scent. "It's the same odor I smelled the night Sara was abducted," I said. "Just inhaling it knocked Sara unconscious, but if it was somehow injected …"

Marcus turned to Carmilla. "Could Sophia be right? Is there some poison that could make Nora appear to be dead?"

She nodded slowly. "Yes, several. But it would take someone extremely skilled to make such a drug subtle enough to fool a vampire."

Marcus turned to Vladimir. "How were Nora and Michael attacked?"

"They were struck by arrows. We assumed they were poisoned, because Michael has been in a coma since the attack—we've given him blood, but it doesn't seem to help. But I've never heard of a poison that could make someone seem so lifeless. Clearly, Nora absorbed more of the poison than Michael. I'm sorry, Marcus. If I'd had any idea she was alive, I would have done everything possible to help her."

"Carmilla, this is your area of expertise," said Marcus, ignoring Vladimir's apology. "What can we do?"

She thought for a moment. "The poison must still be in her body. It's somehow preventing her from absorbing human blood," she said slowly. "We could try a transfusion of vampire blood. It should be easier for her to absorb, and it might let her heal enough to start taking in human blood again. It's the only thing I can think of."

"We need a room with two beds," said Nikolai.

"Of course," said Vladimir. "Follow me."

Nikolai removed Nora's IV and picked her up, and we all followed Vladimir back inside. He led us up a flight of stairs and down a hall to a simply furnished room with two twin beds. Nikolai placed Nora gently in one of them.

"We should start by getting some of the poison out of her system," said Carmilla. "I know it's primitive, but we'll have to bleed her."

Vladimir hurried from the room and came back a moment later with two porcelain basins. Carmilla positioned Nora's left wrist over one of them and made a neat cut across her vein. As bright red blood began to trickle into the milky bowl, I could clearly smell the astringent scent of the poison.

When the basin was almost full, Carmilla said, "All right, we need to start the transfusion before we take any more. Who's first?"

Nikolai hopped onto the bed next to his sister with an IV line and rolled up his sleeve. He quickly found a vein, and a moment later his blood was flowing through the transparent tube into Nora's right arm. At the same time, Carmilla switched out the full basin for the empty one and continued to take blood from Nora's wrist.

When Nikolai had given as much blood as he could spare, Vanessa took his place. Sara went after her, then Dante, and finally me. By taking turns, we were able to keep a steady supply of blood flowing into Nora's veins as we emptied basin after basin of her blood into the bathroom sink. Vladimir brought us human blood to replenish what we had lost.

Hours passed without any sign that the process was working. Every so often Father asked if I could sense anything, but all I could tell him was that Nora was still alive.

Finally, after almost four hours, Nora's fingers twitched. A moment later, she let out a moan. It was working. Father sat on the edge of the bed and took Nora's hand. "Your father is here, my dear," he said into her ear. "We're going to make you well again. Everything will be all right."

When Vladimir saw that Nora was really alive, he hurried off at once, calling for the rest of his family to come perform the same transfusion process on Michael.

Not long after Nora began to move, I noticed that I could no longer detect the chemical smell in her discarded blood. As soon as I was sure, I told Carmilla, who stopped the transfusion and started Nora on an IV of human blood.

"It's working," she said almost at once. "Her body is accepting it."

I breathed out a long sigh of relief. Nora was going to be all right. As I watched my adopted family crowd around her, it reminded me of the way my human mother and father used to care for me when I was sick. Even though I knew those days were gone forever, I still missed my human family. A few tears welled up in my eyes, and I stepped into the hall for a moment to regain my composure. A minute later, Father joined me. He put his arm around me, and I leaned up against his chest.

"Once again you have saved one of my children's lives," he said. "This family owes you a great deal, my dear. What more than my love can I give to you, my daughter?"

"I didn't do anything, Father. Carmilla came up with the transfusion idea."

"But you were the only one who could sense that she was still alive."

I said nothing and just let Father hold me as I leaned into his shoulder. After a few minutes, Dante stuck his head into the hallway and said, "Hey, sis, there's someone in here who wants to meet you."

I wiped my face and tried to make myself somewhat presentable before going back into the room. Nora was sitting up in bed with a glass of blood in her hand. As soon as she saw me, she smiled and stretched out her arms for a hug.

I stayed with Nora for more than an hour, long after the rest of the family had gone to get some rest. She welcomed me to the family and told me all about her fiancé, Michael, who sounded much more pleasant than his father. Finally, we both fell asleep.

Father woke us as the sun was setting. "If you feel up for it," he said to Nora, "I'd like to take you home tonight."

Nora nodded. "How's Michael?" she asked.

"Recovering even more quickly than you," said Marcus. "He had much less poison in his system. I expect he'll be able to come say good-bye before we leave."

There was still a little light in the western sky as we carried Nora to the limousine. Michael was already well enough to join the rest of the Németh clan in seeing us off. As a token of thanks for curing his son—and also, I suspected, as an apology for not taking better care of Nora—Vladimir gave us a full chest of fresh blood bags for the long drive home. As for me, I just wanted to get home as soon as possible. I longed for a full day's sleep in my own bed.

17. The Ties That Bind

A week after we brought Nora home from New York, Sara woke me with news that Father wanted to see me in the library.

He met me at the door and guided me to the chair by the fireplace. A fire crackled in the grate, filling the room with red, flickering light and the smell of wood smoke. In Father's hand was a letter marked with a wax seal that had been broken.

"Well, my dear," he said once we were seated, "the time for your test has come. A week from tomorrow, I will take you to the old country to meet Lord Illyrius."

I felt a nervous flutter in my stomach. "What kind of test will this be?" I asked.

He gazed into the fire for a few moments. When he turned to me again, there was a look of concern on his face. "In most cases the test is a mere formality. Lord Illyrius usually tastes some blood, asks a few questions, and if the person shows respect, then they are allowed to stay with their clan. But in your case, I'm afraid he may ask for a more tangible demonstration of your skills. I can't give you specifics, because I don't have any. I just wanted you to be prepared. The only thing I can tell you is that Lord Illyrius already knows of your dhampir bloodline."

I swallowed hard. What would Lord Illyrius ask of me? I wondered. Father's concern made me think I wouldn't like it, whatever it was.

A log shifted in the fire, and a crackling fountain of sparks leaped up.

"Father," I said, "do you remember when you asked if there was anything you could do for me?"

"Yes, of course," he said. "I do not make such promises lightly. Tell me what you wish, and if it's in my power to give, it's yours." He looked at me expectantly.

"It's been quite some time since I left my family—my human family, I mean. If it's all right, I'd like to go and see them again before you take me to meet Lord Illyrius."

"Is that all?" He smiled and rose from his chair. "Of course you should go visit your family. Take Randolph and leave whenever you wish. Just be back here by Friday, packed and ready to leave."

I jumped to my feet and gave him a hug. "Thank you, Father."

"Of course, my dear. All I ask is that you don't tell them where you're living now or what name you're using. Is that understood?"

I nodded.

"Good. Now get out of my library," he said, shooing me away with a playful wave of his hand. "I have important brooding to do before the fire burns out."

*   *   *

Randolph and I left the mansion at about four o'clock the next afternoon. I wanted to arrive at the farmhouse right at sunset. That would avoid any awkward questions about why I needed to stay out of the sun but would give me plenty of time before my parents went to bed. The trip went faster than I expected, so I asked Randolph to park out by the main road until it was safe for me to get out of the limo.

While we were waiting Randolph asked, "Miss Sophia, are you okay? You look a little nervous."

"To be honest, I'm scared to death, Randolph. The only communication they have had from me since I left were postcards. I at least wanted them to know I was alive and okay."

"Of course, Miss Sophia. That's perfectly natural," said Randolph.

"I've come up with a story that explains why I have been gone for so long. I think I am going to tell them that I have been a personal assistant to a wealthy entrepreneur. I'll say that the condition of my employment was that under no circumstances could I tell anyone who he was or when we planned to travel. I'll say he is a bit eccentric and one of the conditions of the job was that I had to cut all ties with my friends or family for at least the first year. How does that sound?" I asked.

"Actually, it sounds pretty good, Miss Sophia. It would explain a lot without going into many details. I think they will believe it, especially since you will be showing up in a limousine."

I gave Randolph a smile and then looked out the window, waiting for the sun to set. Finally, the sun disappeared over the horizon, and Randolph drove slowly down the gravel lane to the house. It was exactly as I remembered: the peeling yellow paint on the wooden siding and the purple lilacs blooming in the front yard. Even the old swing was still there on the front porch. Randolph got out and opened my door. I took a deep breath, stepped out of the limo, and started walking toward the front door.

Before I had a chance to ring the bell, I saw someone look out the window. The door opened, and there stood my dad. He looked at me blankly for a moment.

"Hello, Daddy," I said.

"Sophia? Is that you?"

"It's me." My voice cracked a little as I replied.

He wrapped me in a hug that lifted me off the ground. Then he set me down, looked me over from head to toe, and hugged me again. "Lauren, Josh," he called over his shoulder, "it's Sophia."

My mother and brother appeared behind him. Josh was a whole head taller than the last time I'd seen him. I grinned at him, "Hey stranger," I said. I gave him a bear hug, and my mom wrapped her arms around both of us. After a few minutes, my mom got everyone to come into the living room. It seemed smaller than I remembered, and the furniture shabbier.

"You've sure been traveling a lot," my mom said as I settled onto the couch. "We got your postcards."

"Oh, good. I'm glad.

Josh sat down beside me, and I ruffled his blond hair with my hand. "Is that your limousine?" he asked.

"No, it belongs to my employer," I said. My dad raised an eyebrow at me, so I trotted out my story about finding a job with an eccentric entrepreneur. "I'm sorry for making you all worry," I said. "I thought the postcards would at least let you know I was okay, but I wasn't allowed to say any more about where I was or what I was doing. I'm one of the few people my employer trusts. That's about it. Again, I am so sorry for leaving the way I did. I'm sure you were worried sick."

"We're just glad to see you again, honey," said my mom.

Over the next hour, my parents filled me in on all the town gossip. After they could think of nothing more to tell me, the room fell silent for a moment, and a significant look passed between my parents.

My dad walked over to my mom and whispered something in her ear. She turned to him and shook her head. With my enhanced vampire hearing, I heard her whisper, "She doesn't have to know."

"Lauren, she needs to know," said my dad. "What if she got sick and needed her family's medical records?"

My mom's shoulders slumped. "All right, if you think it's necessary."

"Sophia, there's something we need to tell you," my dad said. He paused for a moment and passed his hand through his hair. Then he said, "You know those anxiety attacks you had just before you left?"

I nodded.

"Well, your mother had them too."

I looked at my mom. "You had anxiety attacks too?" I asked.

She said nothing, but I knew from the look on her face that she was upset.

"No, not your mom," said my father quietly. "Your biological mother."

It took a moment for his words to sink in. I stared at him in disbelief. "Are you saying—are you trying to tell me I'm adopted?"

"For a long time, the doctors thought your mother and I wouldn't be able to have children of our own, so we decided to adopt. We fell in love with you as soon as we saw you." He smiled at the memory. "They told us your parents had been killed in a car accident. We don't know their names, but the agency gave us their medical histories. Your mother's says she suffered from anxiety and panic attacks. That sounds like what you experienced after you were attacked."

I looked from my father to my mother and back again. "How come you didn't tell me this sooner?" I asked.

"We didn't want you to think we loved you any less because of it," said my mother. She was on the verge of tears.

"And we don't," said my father firmly. "We love you every bit as much as Josh. But I thought it might help to know there was a family history of panic attacks. Anyway, you should probably have these medical records now that you're out on your own."

My father got up and went into the next room. When he returned he was carrying a dark brown folder. He slid it across the table to me. I just stared at it.

"Sophia, are you okay?" he asked.

"Yes," I said, focusing my eyes on him again. "I'm fine. Thank you for telling me."

To vampires, bloodline is the bond that ties them together as a family, and I just learned that I had none with my human family. I immediately lost my desire to stay any longer. I rose, gave my parents a hug, and said. "This doesn't change anything. You'll always be my mom and dad—and you my little brother," I said as I looked over at Josh.

My mom nodded and wiped the tears from her eyes.

"Well," I said, stepping back from her. "This has been quite a night. I hate to say it, but I have to be back in Boston before it gets too late."

"You mean you can't stay?" my mother asked.

"No, Mom, I have a flight to catch in the morning. I'm sorry I can't stay. But I have some vacation coming up, so maybe I'll be able to stay a few days with you then."

I hugged them all again and gave them an e-mail address where they could write to me. I also promised to do my best to visit more often, but I knew even as I said the words I was lying. In fact, almost everything I'd said that night had been a lie. I just hoped my visit made them feel better and that my story would help then not to worry about me. As for the medical records, I left them sitting on the table.

When Randolph saw me coming out of the house, he stomped out his cigarette and held the limousine door open for me without saying a word. I turned to wave to my family one last time, and then the door slammed shut behind me.

"Let's go, Randolph," I said as he slid into the driver's seat. "I have some packing to do."

"Yes, ma'am."

On the way home, I wondered if I really would ever see my human family again. The news that I was adopted actually came as a relief to me. I loved my human family, and I knew I always would. But I had always felt guilty about leaving them the way I did. Learning that I had no blood ties to them gave me permission to let go of that guilt. But at the same time I felt a little sad. I would have liked to have known my biological parents, especially my mother after learning that she suffered from anxiety attacks. I can only assume that she was the dampier in my bloodline. I guess I'd never know for sure.

We had only been gone a few hours before we returned to the mansion. I walked into the living room, and Sara was there. She asked me what happened.

"I just found out that I was adopted," I said in a soft voice. "Once I found out, I had no desire to stay with them overnight. It was strange, Sara. Finding out I am not blood-related to my human family has put everything into perspective for me. I can now put my human life behind me without any quilt and embrace the fact that I am a vampire and that this is my true family."

Sara gave me a smile of encouragement and simply said, "Welcome home, sis, welcome home."

18. Lord İllyrius

O n the evening Father and I were to leave for Slovakia to meet with Lord Illyrius, the entire family was waiting for me at the foot of the stairs.

"What's this?" I asked.

Sara hurried up the steps and took me by the arm. "We wanted to see you off," she said, guiding me down to the others. Even Randolph was there, holding a tray with eight glasses of blood and one of champagne. Everyone took a glass, and Father raised his in a toast.

"To Sophia," he said. "With the blood that gives us life, we say good-bye to any part that remains of Sophia Dobre and expect her return as Lady Sophia Manori."

"To Sophia!" the others echoed. They lifted their glasses and drank.

I felt myself blush. "Thank you," I said. "I'll do my best to make you all proud."

"You've already done that," said Sara, smiling at me. "We just need to make it official."

"And then Father will throw you a ball," said Vanessa. "And there may even be some passably interesting men there this time, if he lets me manage the guest list."

"We're getting ahead of ourselves," said Father. "Sophia still has to meet with Lord Illyrius's approval—although I have no doubt she will." He turned to me. "Now drink up, my dear. We don't want to delay our flight."

We flew first-class to Budapest. From there we took a private jet to the small town of Hlohovec, where a limousine waited to carry us on to the final stage of the journey.

It was early evening as the limousine wound through a thickly forested countryside and a nearly full moon cast a blue light over the hills. After we drove for several hours, Lord Illyrius's castle finally came into view. A tall hedge separated the castle grounds from the surrounding forest. We passed through the gate, and I was surprised by the beauty of the estate.

Carefully tended shrubs and flowerbeds studded the green lawn, and majestic marble statues presided over the landscape. It was so inviting that I hoped I would have a chance to explore the grounds at some point during our stay.

The castle itself was massive, constructed of ancient gray stone bricks. Its medieval towers, high walls, and grotesque gargoyles brought to mind a place one would find in a scary novel. At the same time, I couldn't help but admire its architecture.

As we entered the castle, we passed through a set of huge oak doors and were greeted by a robed servant. My gaze was immediately captured by the vaulted ceiling and ancient tapestries. I had seen European castles while traveling with Sara, of course, but it was different to see such an ancient one that was still being lived in.

The servant led us through the great hall to a small room, like a parlor. "Please have a seat and make yourselves comfortable," he said. "Help yourselves to a drink if you wish. Lord Illyrius will be with you shortly." He bowed and left us there.

When he had gone, Father went to the bar and poured two glasses of blood. He clearly knew his way around.

We sat there for about fifteen minutes, sipping our drinks in companionable silence, before Lord Illyrius arrived. We leaped to our feet as he swept into the room. I must admit the nineteenth-century-style attire he was wearing, complete with a regency style neckcloth tied in a bow and a silk waistcoat, surprised me. But what drew my attention most were his dark, piercing black eyes and pale, thick skin. "Forgive me for being late," he said. His voice was deep and as dry as old bones. He shook Father by the hand. "As always, it is good to see you, my friend," he said. "And is this the newest addition to your family whom I have heard so much about?"

"It is my honor to present Sophia Manori, my lord," said Father.

The ancient vampire acknowledged the introduction with the barest hint of a bow, and I managed a curtsy in return. "It's an honor and a privilege to meet you, my lord," I said.

"The honor is all mine," he said, taking my hand. "You are very lucky, Marcus, to have such a beauty for a daughter."

"Indeed I am, my lord."

"Please sit down and make yourselves at home, both of you. You are welcome to come and go throughout the castle as you wish —with the exception of my library, of course. I'm rather particular about that."

"Of course, my lord," I replied, knowing from the warnings of my siblings that it was off limits.

But first, Sophia—May I call you Sophia?"

"I insist, my lord."

"Excellent, excellent—now if you don't mind, my dear, may I taste a little of your blood?"

I had been expecting this. I nodded and quickly rolled up the sleeve of my blouse. He sat beside me on the couch and bent over my proffered wrist, closed his eyes, extended his fangs, and sank them into my flesh. He took his time, drinking slowly for almost a full a minute, and as he finished I felt his rough tongue lap across my skin. Finally, he straightened again and stood perfectly still with his eyes still closed for several seconds. Then he produced a silk handkerchief from his pocket and used it to dab elegantly at the corners of his mouth. At last he said, "Very interesting. Thank you, Sophia." He fixed his unblinking gaze on me. "Would you like to know a little about how your dhampir bloodline began?"

"Yes, my lord, very much so." I said.

"Very well. I will tell you what your blood showed me just now. The memories are incomplete—fragments are often all that can be retrieved from so many generations ago. But I saw through the eyes of the woman who gave birth to the first dhampir in your bloodline." He closed his eyes again.

"It was a cold night," he said slowly. "I can see her breath in front of her face, and the mist is heavy on the ground. She is running through the woods with an infant child wrapped closely to her chest. She keeps looking behind her; she expects to be followed." He caressed his lips with his pale tongue. "Yes, I can taste her fear."

I stared at Lord Illyrius, utterly fascinated. I knew some vampires had the ability to discern a person's bloodline by tasting their blood, of course Father had first learned of my dhampir abilities by tasting my blood—but I had had no idea specific memories could be re-experienced so vividly.

"It is a new moon," said Lord Illyrius. "She can barely see the path. She stumbles, catches herself. She does not stop running. Finally, she sees the glow of a flame between the trees: a candle in a church window. A man runs to meet her. He must be a priest or a monk; he is wearing a habit. He takes the babe in his arms."

"The woman is weeping now. The man tries to console her. 'Take comfort,' he says, 'for your child will grow up in the light of God. As we planned, I will take the child to the old blind woman. Someone will then take the child from her. The boy will have a good home far away from here as I promised, and his father will never find him.' She sobs; she is not comforted. He seems about to speak again, but she turns and plunges back into the forest, distraught."

Lord Illyrius opened his eyes. "The memory ends there," he said. "I don't know what end she came to. But the priest must have been successful—I got a glimpse of the boy's life, and there were no memories that he knew what he was."

"Thank you, my lord," I said. "That was amazing."

"No, thank you, my dear," he said. His thin lips curved into a smile. "I have not tasted such an interesting bloodline this century. I wonder what became of the woman. Vadim Preda was not known for his kindness toward humans, and he would not have been happy to find that his son had disappeared."

The room was silent for a moment. Then Lord Illyrius stood up. "Well," he said, "now that my curiosity about your past is satisfied, I look forward to seeing how you respond to your test tomorrow. I'll have someone show you to your room so you can get some rest. Marcus and I have other matters to discuss."

Another of Illyrius's robed servants (perhaps the same one; I wasn't sure) guided me back through the great hall and then up a flight of steps to a long, narrow hallway. He stopped in front of an arched wooden door and pulled an iron key ring from the recesses of his robe.

"Excuse me," I said, "but are all the rooms in the castle kept locked?"

"No, my lady," said the servant, "only the rooms that Lord Illyrius feels some sentimental attachment to. This room was built in honor of Cadmus's daughter Ino, who was once the queen of Thebes. There is a legend that after her death, she married Poseidon, god of the sea, and some pagans still worship her. They now call her the white goddess or the queen of the sea. It is said that she was quite beautiful as a mortal." He opened the door and gestured for me to enter.

"Thank you," I said, peering into the room, which was lushly carpeted and hung with elaborate medieval tapestries in blue and silver.

"Is there anything else I can do for you?" asked the servant.

"No, thank you. I think I'll do a little exploring, if that's all right."

"Of course," he said. "I hope you enjoy your stay." The servant bowed and disappeared down the hall.

The room was beautiful, but I would have plenty of time to enjoy it later. I wandered aimlessly down one hall and then another until I found a spiral staircase, which I climbed down to a door that opened onto the castle grounds. It was a beautiful spring night, and the moon still cast its blue light over the lawn.

I followed a stone path and soon came to a bench next to a marble statue of the Greek god Zeus. White flowers bloomed nearby—I didn't know what kind they were but their scent perfumed the air. I sat there for some time, taking in the castle gardens under the moonlight.

"Sophia?" said Father as he approached from the castle.

"Over here, Father," I said.

He made his way to the bench and looked up at the statue. "Zeus, father of the gods," he said. "Does he have any particular meaning for you?"

"No, not really. I just like surrounding myself with powerful men." I grinned at him, and he rolled his eyes.

"Do you mind if I join you?" he asked.

"Of course not." I patted the bench beside me, and he sat down.

"You know, Sophia," he said almost hesitantly, "there is a gentle quality about you that is very rare, especially for a vampire with your strength. I would hate for you to lose it."

I looked at him in surprise. "What do you mean?"

Instead of answering my question, he said, "Lord Illyrius is quite impressed with you."

"What do you mean, Father? I have done nothing to prove myself to him."

"He drank your blood, Sophia. In some ways, he probably knows you better than you know yourself. He now knows of your abilities."

"I don't understand. Do I still have to take the test tomorrow or not?" I asked.

"It seems," said Father, "that Lord Illyrius has something else in mind for you. He wants you to take a different test, the one the council's assassins have to go through. It's a difficult test, and it's also dangerous." He looked at me with a serious expression.

"Do you want me to take this test?" I asked.

"The choice is yours," said Father. "On the one hand, it would bring great honor to the family and earn you the highest respect from Lord Illyrius. However, the last thing I want is to see you to get hurt—and I don't mean just physically." He sighed heavily. "Sophia, I hope you know that you don't have to prove yourself to me. Whether you take this test is entirely up to you."

"If I don't take this test, will Lord Illyrius still let me be a member of your family?" I asked.

Father leaned toward me and said, "Can you keep a secret?" I nodded. "He already told me you can stay with us."

"He did?" A grin spread over my face, and I threw my arms around Father's neck. "I'm so happy, Father."

He hugged me back. "So am I. And I'll be proud to introduce you as my daughter at the ball we'll throw for you when we get home."

I released him from my embrace. "So about this other test," I said. "How dangerous is it, exactly?"

Father's face became suddenly serious again. "I honestly don't know," he said. "The details of the test are a closely guarded secret.

I don't *think* your life would be in danger, but that's just a guess. Being that it is a test for assassins, I'm sure it will not be easy."

"When do I have to give an answer?"

"Before sunset tomorrow," he said stifling a yawn. "But now this old man needs to get some rest. I'll leave you to think about your decision." He rose from the bench and bent to kiss my forehead. "Welcome to the family, daughter." Then he turned and walked back across the moonlit lawn toward the castle.

I sat there for a long time, thinking about my decision. The moon sank slowly toward the horizon, and its last light lined the marble god's beard with silver. How bad could the test be? I had already defeated a vampire many times my age, and now that I knew how to use my venom, I shouldn't have any problem ending a fight quickly if I got into trouble.

But what would I have to do in order to pass the test? Would I have to do something so bad that it would change me in some way? I remembered clutching Vaine's bloody heart in my fist and shuddered.

Dew began to settle over the castle grounds, and a damp chill came over me, yet I still sat there on the bench and thought about what I should do. At last, as the first rosy blush of dawn bled into the eastern sky, I looked up at the statue of Zeus standing resolute in the darkness, and my resolve hardened. I decided I would take the assassin's test.

19. The Assassin's Test

I woke early the next evening and prepared myself for the test. Since I was not sure what to expect on this trip, I had packed for every situation I could possibly think of. I was ready for everything from a fancy dress ball to a fight with another vampire. I even brought my weapons with me. I had no idea what I would face during the assassin's test, but I wanted to be ready for anything.

I put on some comfortable clothes and packed as many shuriken as I could easily carry. Being that this is called "the assassins test," I had a feeling I might need them before the night was through. Shuriken were my favorite weapons: light, easy to carry, quiet, and very effective. Once I realized my venom could paralyze, I had come up with an idea to make my shuriken even more effective. I enlisted Randolph's help to find someone who could modify them just a bit. The final product was a shuriken that was hollow all the way down to its needle-like points; concealed inside was a tiny reservoir to hold some of my venom. The idea was to paralyze an attacker just long enough for me to run away or to get to my victim and inject a full dose of venom with my fangs. I got the idea when Lord Nemeth said that Nora and Michael had been hit with a hollow-tipped arrowhead. Thus armed, I could paralyze someone from a distance.

As I gathered my shurikens, I slipped a sharp, thin blade into my belt and slid a small dagger into my boot. I also made sure to bring a vial filled with Carmilla's potion to mask my scent.

One of Lord Illyrius's servants was waiting outside my door, and he led me through the west wing of the castle and out onto the grounds. There I found Father and Lord Illyrius waiting for me beside an impressive geometrical arrangement of flowerbeds.

"Good evening, my dear," said Father. "Have you made your decision?"

"I have. I will take the assassin's test."

"Excellent," said Lord Illyrius, rubbing his hands together. "The premise of the test is simple. In a few minutes, you will enter the forest through that gate." He nodded toward the hedge, and I noticed a small opening leading through it to the dark woods beyond. "There you will encounter a number of challenges. How you deal with them is up to you. There will be clues along the way to help you but they will not be easy to find. If you survive the night and complete all the challenges before sunrise, you pass the test."

"If I survive the night?" I asked.

The old vampire shrugged. "The whole idea behind this test is to see how you will do under the most extreme conditions. My assassins will hunt you while you are in the forest. But do not worry. They are under orders to report to me immediately if you are not up to the challenge, and I will end the test immediately. But understand, Sophia, they are trained killers. If you do not perform at your best, you will get hurt. Do you understand?"

I nodded.

"And you still wish to take the test?" asked Lord Illyrius.

I glanced at Father. He said nothing, but there was concern in his eyes. I knew that if I were to change my mind now, I would no doubt bring disgrace to the Manori family name, at least in the eyes of Lord Illyrius.

I looked at Lord Illyrius and simply said, "I do."

"Very well," said Lord Illyrius. "Follow this path to the hedge. As soon as you enter the woods, your test will begin."

Before I left, I grabbed Father's hand and squeezed it tightly. He squeezed back, and in that moment, I felt safe. It was just what I needed to take with me into the woods. No matter what happened, I knew my father loved me.

I trotted along the cobblestone path to the wrought iron gate, opened it, and passed through. The forest did not begin immediately. Instead, there was a little patch of lawn that held a few ornamental shrubs, a bench, and another massive statue of a Greek god. A moat of dark water about fifteen feet wide separated this little outpost of civilization from the dark shadows of the forest.

My nose twitched. An unsavory oily stench rose from the surface of the stagnant water. Something told me it wouldn't be a good idea to go for a swim. I looked down and noticed a little roll of parchment sealed with wax lying nestled in the grass, almost under my feet. I picked it up and broke the seal with my fingernail. Inside, two lines of verse were written in an ornate script:

Come across, but don't fall in.
Once you've crossed, your test begins.

I stood there for a moment and looked around. I thought to myself, *This is an assassin's test, and assassins kill by many methods. Assassins also make what may seem safe actually deadly. They are masters of misdirection.*

I knew I could make the leap across the water without any difficulty, but that seemed too obvious. A jump of fifteen feet is nothing for a vampire. I scanned the far bank of the moat for any signs danger but saw none. Of course, if I could detect danger so easily, it wouldn't be much of a test. Therefore, the question was, if the pool was so easy to jump, then why was it even there? It made no sense—unless it was there as a distraction from some true, hidden danger.

I knew I had to cross the water without getting wet, so I looked around for something I could lay across the water to use as a bridge. I knew the bench would be too short, but the statue might just be tall enough to reach the other side. It depicted Poseidon. The trident and the shellfish caught in the god's beard were a dead giveaway. Was it a coincidence that the god of the sea happened to be nearby to help me cross a body of water, or was it intentional? Either way it was all I had.

Even with my vampire strength, I didn't think I could carry a fifteen-foot marble statue, but fortunately the base was round.

I put my shoulder against the statue and pushed with my legs until I felt it reach the tipping point. It took some effort but I managed to tilt it just enough to roll it to the edge of the moat. Now all I had to do was give it a push, and with a little luck, I'd have a bridge. It fell, and I leaped back. There was a dull thud as the god's head hit the earth on the far bank. To my surprise, I heard the unmistakable snap of breaking wood, as a row of stakes sprang up from the ground under the impact. If I had jumped, they would have come up right under my feet as I landed.

Relieved that I had avoided a trap, I hopped onto the fallen statue and stepped lightly over the moat. Beyond the broken stakes on the other side was another scroll. I opened it and read:

With gentle might and piercing sight
Surprises wait in the woods tonight.
If you are not careful, your blood will spill
The forest has eyes, and the darkness kills.

This riddle didn't seem hard to figure out—traps and an assassin were within the forest. I peered between the tangled limbs of the trees into the shadows. There was no sign of any danger, but I knew danger was there. If there was an assassin in the woods, I could not detect his scent. That meant that I was probably upwind of him and he already knew where I was.

I decided my best bet was to get downwind of him quickly and catch his scent, but I wasn't going to go crashing madly through the trees. Quickly and quietly, I backtracked across my makeshift bridge and through the gate to the castle grounds. Once I was through, I sprinted with the wind along the inside of the hedge for a hundred yards or so, then turned and vaulted over the hedge back into the forest.

Had I gone far enough? I sniffed the air. I couldn't smell the assassin, but I noticed something else: the distinct scent of a birch tree. There were birch trees throughout the forest, but I didn't see any nearby, and in any case the smell was too strong. Someone would have had to cut deeply into a birch tree for the scent to be so strong. I was sure that my assassin was using the birch sap to mask his scent. Confident that I was downwind of my assassin, I took out the vial of Carmilla's potion, poured it onto my hands, and hurriedly rubbed it over my skin and clothes.

I had a feeling the assassin would be up in the trees, so I decided to level the playing field. I selected a large oak tree and swung up into its branches. About twenty feet up on the leeward side, I found a limb sturdy enough to support my weight. I stood on it with my back to the trunk and waited.

Slowly, the scent of birch grew stronger. I knew my assassin was close by. I guessed he was about twenty yards from the tree—but I heard nothing. I silently slipped a venom-filled shuriken into the palm of my right hand. I was breathing hard, but I told myself to be calm and wait. Finally, when the smell was very strong, I risked a peek around the trunk.

A dark figure stood on the forest floor no more than fifteen feet from my tree, hunched over a crossbow. We saw each other at the same instant, and he raised his weapon. I leaped for a branch on the next tree and heard the crossbow's twang behind me. The arrow grazed my arm as I flew through the air. Then my foot touched the branch. I pushed off of it into empty space, twisted in midair, and flung my shuriken at the assassin's back as he dashed away between the trees. I landed on the ground in a crouch. A moment later, I heard a heavy thud in the undergrowth, which told me my weapon had found its mark.

I sprang to my feet, dashed toward the sound, and found the assassin lying face down, my shuriken lodged between his shoulder blades. I wasn't sure how long the small dose of venom would last, so I quickly dropped to my knees and bit him in the neck to inject more. That would keep him immobilized for a good while. But I had no idea how long even a full injection of my venom would last, and I needed him out of my way all night.

I thought for a moment. I had nothing to tie him up with, but maybe I could make him so weak he wouldn't pose any threat to me. I picked up his crossbow, and stuck him with an arrow through each shoulder, each hand, and each leg pinning him to the ground. I hoped he wouldn't bleed to death before the night was over, but it was the only thing I could think to do.

Then without warning, a silver tipped arrow struck me in the stomach. I cried out in pain and doubled over, clutching at the shaft. The strong birch smell of the first assassin must have masked the scent of the second. I hadn't thought of that.

My attacker was on top of me in an instant. His fist smashed into my face twice in quick succession, and I flopped backward onto the forest floor. The assassin loomed over me, silhouetted against the moon, and stretched out a thin wire between his hands.

Even as I writhed on the ground in pain, a part of me realized that if I didn't do something fast, I was about to feel that wire jerk tight around my throat.

As he bent over me, I snatched the dagger from my boot and slashed desperately at the tendon just above his heel. He fell to one side with a muffled yell. I dropped my dagger, grabbed his right arm in both hands, and pulled it to my mouth. My fangs sank into the assassin's forearm, and my venom did its work.

When he stopped moving, I rolled onto my side away from him, gasping and coughing up blood. I knew I had to remove the arrow in order to heal, so I grasped it firmly in both hands, broke off the end, and pushed it through, out my back. As I did, my vision blurred, and I almost passed out from the pain.

I lay there for a moment, chest heaving, as my body started to heal itself back together. Gradually, the pain subsided, and I staggered to my feet. Then I pinned the second assassin as I had done with the first. This time, I didn't worry so much about whether he bled out. This one had pissed me off.

As I searched the vampire's paralyzed body for weapons, I came across another scroll of parchment. I held it up to the moonlight and read:

If you're reading this scroll, you must be alive,
But keep your wits sharp if you want to survive.
To the east of the castle look for a tomb,
But beware the death that waits in the room.
On a slab of stone a vampire lies;
If you fail this test, at sunrise he dies.

It took me a long time to work my way around the castle grounds through the forest. My senses were so heightened that I paused every few steps to sniff the air, and every time some sound rustled through the undergrowth, I froze. Once a shadow passed over the moon, and I dove into a thicket before I realized it was only an owl.

When I finally came to the east side of the castle, the tomb was easy to spot: a low, grassy mound devoid of trees rose into the moonlight at the edge of the forest. I circled it warily for a while, darting from tree to tree before I approached. On the west side of the hill was a stone door that I guessed led into the tomb, and another bench and a moss-covered statue stood in a recess cut into the southern slope.

The words of the riddle ran through my head. *Beware the death that waits in the room.* Clearly, there was some sort of trap guarding the burial chamber; strolling in through the front door was out of the question. *If you fail this test, at sunrise he dies.* That only made sense if sunlight could get into the chamber somehow, but I couldn't see any openings in the mound from where I stood.

I crouched low and sprinted up the hill, expecting another crossbow arrow to tear through my flesh at any moment, but it never came. When I reached the top, there it was. At my feet was a circular opening in the stone large enough to let the sun in at dawn. Through it I could see an elderly vampire lying with his arms crossed on a stone slab about twenty feet below me. He was completely still, and I wondered if he had been drugged. If he was, he would be burned to ash when the sun came up.

I thought for several minutes about how to lower myself into the tomb without triggering any traps before the obvious solution came to me in a flash: I didn't have to go into the chamber at all. I just had to close up the opening on top of the tomb so the sunlight couldn't get in. I laughed aloud at my own foolishness and began to search for something to cover the hole.

I thought of dragging branches from the forest, but I was worried they might not block out the light completely, and what if they shifted during the night? I needed something solid. As I looked around, my gaze fell on the statue on the side of the hill. I saw it was the god Apollo. Surely this wasn't a coincidence—the god of the sea had helped me cross the water, and now the sun god would help me keep the sunlight from entering the tomb.

The statue's base was big enough to cover the opening, but I knew I wasn't strong enough to get it up the slope and on top of the tomb. I circled the statue, trying to figure out how to move it. Then I noticed a network of fine, branching cracks that crisscrossed the statue's legs. That gave me an idea. "Sorry about this," I said, giving the statue a hard shove.

It toppled onto the nearby bench with a loud crack. The head rolled away from the body, and the god's legs crumbled below the knee. Feeling pleased with myself, I tipped the statue's base onto its side and rolled it up the hill. It covered the hole perfectly.

I wiped the sweat from my forehead and brushed the stone grit and moss from my hands. Then I realized I didn't know what to do next. I looked all around the tomb for another scroll but didn't find one. Finally, the broken statue caught my attention. It was hollow—that was why it had broken so easily. I walked over and began searching through the fragmented bits of stone. When I picked up Apollo's head, a slightly crumpled scroll fell out. *How long has it been in there?* I wondered. The statue didn't seem new; it was weathered and much of it was covered in moss.

However, I didn't have time to worry about that now. I quickly opened the scroll and read:

> *You're doing well if you're still alive.*
> *Live till the dawn, and your bloodline will survive.*
> *Your next task will test your fighting skills,*
> *So try not to get yourself killed.*
> *To the south of the castle, you will find a steel door.*
> *Go down into the dungeon. I can tell you no more.*

These riddles were starting to annoy me. The truth was I was getting tired and just wanted to get this test over with. So I picked myself up and headed toward the south side of the estate, where I found the steel door. I grabbed the handle and yanked it open. In front of me was a stone staircase that clearly led underground.

20. The Master of Pain

The stairs took me deep underground. Finally, I came to another door. It was made of iron-bound oak and was barred from my side; it was meant to keep something inside from getting out, not to keep people from getting in.

I listened at the door for a long while and heard nothing. I sniffed the air and smelled not only old iron, as I had expected, but also pungent smoke and the sickly sweet aroma of dried blood. I took a deep breath and lifted the bar, and the door swung inward with a loud creak as if it had not been used for years.

As soon as I crossed the threshold, the door slammed shut behind me, and I heard the bar slide back into place. *I won't be getting back out that way*, I said to myself.

I found myself in a large room with walls of dry-laid stone. Torches burned in wall mounts along the walls, and their red light glinted dully against the iron chains and implements of torture that hung on the walls. As I continued my way into the dungeon, I could smell the scent from old dried blood of humans and vampires alike that stained the floors.

I scanned the room. In the far corner sat a figure cloaked all in black, a hood covering his face. As I passed the flickering torchlight, he looked up and threw back his hood. The pale, wrinkled skin of his face was stretched thin over jutting cheekbones, and only a few wisps of thin white hair still clung to his spotted scalp.

Since he had already seen me and hadn't immediately leaped to attack, I thought I might as well introduce myself. "I am Sophia Manori," I said. "Who are you?"

With a slight cock of his head, he looked at me with black eyes and said, "You are a female. It has been centuries since a female has walked through that door. I wonder what makes you so special."

"I am no different than any other vampire. Maybe just a little smarter than most," I replied in a defense tone.

"That is a lie," he said sharply. "I can see in your eyes that you have a secret. How long have you been a vampire ... Sophia?"

I decided that if he wasn't going to answer my questions, I wasn't about to answer his. "This place stinks," I said. "Do you live down here?"

A low, croaking laugh issued from his throat. "In a sense," he said. "At least, this is where I feel most alive."

Anxious to see what my test would entail, I said, "So I assume you are my opponent?"

The old vampire smiled and said, "In a sense you will be your own opponent. You see, I am what many call the master of pain. You are in my domain, and I control everything within these walls. Shall I give you a demonstration?"

I took half a step back and peered warily around the room. The old vampire's finger twitched. I heard the grind of stone on stone, and before I could react, a feathered dart flew from the shadows and struck me squarely in the chest. The dart's tip was no bigger than a pin, but a searing pain spread out from the wound. I pulled it out and flung it aside.

"I see," I said levelly. "And do you have a name, master of pain?"

"I do have a name, but I will only tell you it if you can get past the fire pit."

"Never mind. I think for the moment I will stay where I am. I have no desire to be hit by more of your darts."

The ancient vampire seemed content to let me stand there for the moment, so I used the time to think hard about what to do next. I guessed he was using thin threads of some kind attached to his fingertips to control the darts, but I doubted that was the only danger in the room. I could paralyze him with one of my shuriken, but that would only last a few minutes, and who knew what traps I might set off trying to cross the room to bite him?

"It seems you have patience, young one," he said at last. "I, on the other hand, have things to do. Perhaps you need a little encouragement ..." Another finger twitched, and I dropped belly-down on the floor even before I heard the mechanism engage. Unfortunately, this time the darts came from the ceiling directly above me. I heard several darts strike the flagstones around me, and two sank into my back. The pain was excruciating.

I leaped to my feet. As I pulled out the darts, a growl formed in my throat. "I don't appreciate your games, old man. Let's finish this."

I whipped a shuriken from my sleeve and hurled it at the old man. It hit him hard in the gut, and he doubled over. A dozen traps around the room went off at once. Another dart hit me in the shoulder, and I rolled away just in time to avoid a blade that buzzed through the air at chest height.

As the blade thwacked into the oak door behind me, I was already up and running across the room toward the crumpled form of the vampire in the corner. I was only halfway across the room when I felt something puncture my right side, just below my ribs. I fell hard and sprawled on the flagstone floor, a silver-tipped crossbow arrow buried deep in my ribs.

I had just pulled it free when a dark figure emerged from the shadows. He had discarded his crossbow and now carried a long, thin sword in one hand and a dagger in the other. I looked up at him in confusion. How had I not sensed him before?

He kicked me in the face, and I fell onto my back. Before I could roll away, I felt the tip of his sword gently pricking the skin over my throat, and I froze.

The assassin loomed above me. He pushed the blade up against my chin so that I had to look him in the eyes. "I refuse to believe you made it past my companions on your own," he sneered. "Tell me who helped you, and I may let you live. Otherwise ... well, let's just say your last few hours won't be pleasant."

Even though I was still in pain, I managed to say, "So your plan is to bore me to death? Why don't you just shut up and cut my throat like the coward that you are?"

Out of anger, he thrust the sword through my right shoulder. I cried out in pain as the toxin on the sword invaded deeper into my flesh.

"Tell me," I managed to spit out, "did I miss any of your friends in the woods?"

My taunt must have struck a nerve. He brought his knee down hard on my stomach, knocking the wind out of me. He twisted the sword in my shoulder as he bent over me, and I felt it grate against cartilage and bone. I gasped in pain. He smiled cruelly and twisted it again, and I couldn't stop myself from crying out.

Suddenly, anger boiled up inside me, overwhelming the pain. For a moment, I thought I was going into bloodlust and I even welcomed it, but this was something different, something new. Perhaps the pain had awakened some other ability than had not yet come to the surface. Whatever it was, I barely felt the pain when the assassin continued to work his blade back and forth in my flesh. The pain actually became fuel for my rage, and my rage was what made me strong.

I smiled. A look of confusion passed over the assassin's face, and then I struck. I snapped my head forward, not caring that in doing so I impaled myself farther onto his sword, and sank my fangs deep within his throat.

After a moment, his body went limp, and I pushed him off of me and rose to my feet. Part of the sword protruded from my back, but I grabbed the hilt and pulled it out, still oblivious to the pain.

I looked down at the assassin and saw that his eyes were wide with confusion and fear. "Did you know that even when you're completely paralyzed, you can still feel pain?" I asked. I thrust the point of the sword through his shoulder until I felt it scrape on the stone floor. Then I gave it an experimental twist. The corner of the assassin's eye twitched.

I meant to torture him for a while, but something struck me in the back. I turned and saw that the venom from my shuriken had worn off, and the old vampire was once again up to his tricks. I pulled the dart from my back and flung it aside with contempt.

I strode purposefully across the room. A few more darts hit me in the chest, but I ignored them. When the vampire realized his darts weren't going to stop me, he tried to turn and run, but I was too quick for him. I lifted him by his neck with my left hand and slammed his back against the wall. Then I snatched a torch from the wall with my right hand and held the flame just close enough to his face to let him feel the heat.

"Look," I said softly. "I made it past the fire pit. Now tell me your name, or you will burn."

He swallowed, struggling to speak against my hand clenched around his throat. "Erebus," he managed to croak. "My name is Erebus. I am the guardian of the elders who sleep. If you kill me, they will be lost forever. Only I know where they are hidden."

I stared at him coldly. "I'm going to let you guess exactly how much I care about your elders right now," I said. "Now tell me, are my tests over?"

Shaking his head, he managed to say, "One more—there's a maze through that door. It's the only way out. Many have died inside. You have to use your wits to find the way."

"How about this?" I said, shaking him roughly. "You can either show me the way out, or I can burn you alive." I sensed a great deal of fear from him as I held him against the wall. I guessed that no one had gotten close enough to threaten his life in a long time.

"Doesn't staying alive sound better than burning to death?" I growled. He nodded, and I lowered him to the floor. "You first," I hissed still holding the lit torch in my hand.

He opened the door, and we entered a dark, narrow passage. After a few yards, it split into three directions. He took the middle path, and a few yards later, it split again. This time he took the passage to the left, which sloped steeply upward.

As he led me through the twists and turns of the maze, whatever burst of strength that had allowed me to ignore the pain of the assassin's sword and Erebus's darts began to wear off. I felt exhausted, and a dull ache in my shoulder told me my wounds hadn't completely healed.

As we turned the next corner, I staggered, and Erebus immediately took off at a run. I was too weak to keep up with him—it was all I could do to stay on my feet. I almost gave up hope, but then I caught a hint of his scent lingering in the air behind him, and I was able to follow it down one corridor and then another.

At last, I came to another wooden door. I stumbled through it and out onto the starlit lawn of Lord Illyrius's castle. I collapsed on the lush grass and lay there for several minutes, taking great gulps of the blossom-scented night air into my lungs, until I had gathered enough strength to struggle to my feet. The moon had set while I was in the dungeon, and the first faint glimmer of dawn was just starting to show along the eastern horizon. I had passed the test.

I made my way to the west side of the castle and the garden where my test had begun. To my surprise, Father was waiting for me there with a bottle of blood. I was so relieved when I saw him I almost laughed. He rose from the bench and helped me to sit down. Completely out of strength, I leaned up against him as he held me.

"Have you been here all night?" I managed to ask.

"Of course not," he said with a smile. "I got up once to get a bottle of blood." He held the bottle out to me. "Care for a drink?"

I was ravenous. I took the bottle in both hands, tipped it back, and drained it to the last drop. As I handed the empty bottle back to Father, I tried to stand. My legs buckled, and I almost fell, but he caught me.

"Can I go to bed now?" I asked, leaning drunkenly against him.

"Yes, my dear. You can go to bed now," he said quietly, and he helped me up to my room, where I immediately collapsed on the bed and fell asleep.

*   *   *

I slept late into the next evening—so late that Father had to knock on my door to wake me. I called out that I would be there in a moment and crawled stiffly from the bed. My whole body ached.

I peeled off my torn and bloody clothes from the night before and limped to the shower. The hot water eased some of the soreness from my limbs. Once I had dried off, I put on fresh clothes and poured myself a glass of blood. I almost felt fit to be seen in public again.

The events of the night before played through my mind as I combed my hair. The more I thought about the test, the angrier I became. Lord Illyrius had promised the test would stop if my life was in danger, but I was utterly certain his assassins had meant to

| 146 |

kill me. My blood boiled, but I knew I couldn't confront him about it without jeopardizing Father's position on the council. Before I left my room to go downstairs, I resolved never to trust that old vampire again.

Father and Lord Illyrius were waiting for me in the great hall. As I entered the room, Lord Illyrius stepped forward and bowed deeply. The gesture confused me, but I managed a curtsy and politely asked, "Lord Illyrius, why do you honor me with a bow?"

"Lady Manori, I must apologize for putting you through such a dangerous test. I tried to monitor your movements from high in one of the towers so I could call off the test if I felt you were in any danger, but you hid yourself extremely well. There were times I could not find you at all, and my assassins conveniently forgot to take their radio headsets," said Lord Illyrius with a bit of anger in his tone. "I should have never asked you to take such a dangerous test in the first place. I humbly ask for your forgiveness."

"Well, Lord Illyrius, as you can see I survived, so there is really nothing to forgive, but I do appreciate the gesture. It is most gracious of you."

"Lady Manori, few have accomplished what you did last night, and no one has ever done so at such a young age. You have brought a great honor to the Manori clan." He held out his hand, and I placed my hand in his, hoping he wouldn't be able to sense how furious I still was. He bent to kiss my hand, and as he rose, he pushed a small velvet box into my palm.

"What's this?" I asked.

"This is what all vampires receive who have completed the assassin's test. Please open it, my dear."

I flipped open the box and saw a gleaming platinum ring set with an oval moonstone encircled by a string of tiny diamonds. "It's beautiful, my lord."

"I had this ring specially made for you," he said. "It's been several centuries since a woman has passed the assassin's test, and the usual design seemed far too masculine for a hand as delicate as yours. However, it will still be recognizable to those who know its meaning."

"I don't know what to say. Thank you, Lord Illyrius."

"You're welcome, my dear. I must also ask that you tell no one that you took the assassin's test. If other vampires found out, some might seek to test their skills against yours, which could put you in danger. Only council members and others who have passed the test will recognize your ring for what it is, and you needn't worry that they will reveal your secret."

"I understand, my lord," I said.

"Good. Now I'm sure you'll want to spend some time with your father. If you'll excuse me, I have some other business to attend to." He bowed once more and swept from the room.

When he was gone, Father led me to the parlor where we had waited for Lord Illyrius on our first day at the castle and poured two glasses of blood. He raised his aloft. "To my daughter, Lady Sophia Manori." We both drank, and then he said, "I'm very proud of you, Sophia. And Lord Illyrius is very impressed. I think you've made a new friend."

I took another drink of blood to hide my disgust at the idea that I might consider Lord Illyrius a friend after what he had put me through. Father gave me a knowing smile, and I realized he could tell what I was thinking.

"We leave tomorrow," he said, "and as soon as we're home we'll throw a grand ball in your honor."

"Oh, Father, you don't have to do that."

"Yes, I do," he said. "It's tradition; you're Lady Sophia Manori now. You've been through a lot, Sophia, and you should have a chance to enjoy yourself. After the ball, I think you and Sara should do some traveling."

"It does sound nice to relax for a while," I admitted. "Thank you, Father."

"Good. It's settled then. Besides," he added with a wry grin, "Vanessa would never forgive me if I promised a ball and then didn't throw one."

21. Intrigue at the Ball

When we arrived back at the mansion, the family was gathered in the living room to welcome us home. Each of them congratulated me on my official initiation into the family with a hug. It was nice to see them again, but I desperately needed some time to come to terms with what had happened during the assassin's test. I was emotionally exhausted.

As soon as I could decently excuse myself, I grabbed Sara by the arm and guided her up to my room. When the door closed behind us, I threw my arms around her.

"What's wrong?" she asked, holding me tightly. "I thought you would be happy."

I know I promised Lord Illyrius not to tell anyone about the assassin's test, but I desperately needed Sara to know what I had been through.

"I need you to see something," I said, holding out my wrist. "I promised not to tell, but I need you to know what happened. I can't bear to live with this by myself, and to tell the truth I'm not sure I could even put it into words. Drink, please."

Sara sat next to me on the bed and hesitantly took my arm in her hands and brought my wrist to her mouth. Then she extended her fangs, bit down on my wrist, and began to drink my blood. When she had had enough, she sat still with her eyes closed.

"Oh, Sophia," she said softly, opening her eyes wide. "No wonder you're such a mess."

"Thanks," I said sarcastically.

"You know what I mean—it's just a lot to process. I can't believe you took the assassin's test! I thought vampire assassins were just a myth to keep the clan leaders in line."

"Apparently not." I said. "It was horrible, Sara. I was literally fighting for my life."

"I know. I saw," she said, looking at me gravely. She put her arm around me, and I leaned against her. After a moment, she said, "Can I see the ring?"

It was on my finger, so I held it up for her to look at. The diamonds sparkled brightly in the light.

"It's very pretty," she said.

"If you look at the design on the sides you can make out the Greek letter for *theta*," I said. "In Greek mythology, some people used this symbol to reference a minor god called Thanatus, whom many call the god of death. I guess the assassins adopted it as their own symbol for death. If you ever meet anyone with a ring with this symbol on it, I'd recommend staying the hell away from them."

"Don't worry. Bad boys aren't my type—well, not usually." Sara grinned at me wickedly, and I couldn't help laughing at her. As the smile slowly left her face she took may hand and said, "Sophia, I know what you just went through was horrible, especially for someone as young as you are, but I promise you will become stronger because of it. I know you have seen into my past and the countless people I have killed in battle. You will never get used to hurting or killing someone, but in a sense we vampires are like warriors. What you just went through was a battle, and you have to look at it like that. It was them or you, and you won." She smiled. "You are one amazing vampire, and I so proud to have you as my sister."

We sat there in silence for a moment. It felt so good just having Sara next to me. Perhaps it was the bond we shared—I don't know, but whatever it was, I always felt safe when I was with her, and her advice was priceless.

"Well, Lady Manori," Sara said in an exaggeratingly regal tone, "I believe we have some invitations to send out."

I shrugged and said, "I suppose. It's still weird to think of you guys throwing a ball just for me."

"Don't be silly. Father's an elder, and it's expected for a noble clan to have a ball to introduce a new family member. Besides," she added, "it'll be fun. You won't have to worry about a thing. We will make all the arrangements. Vanessa and I already picked out the most beautiful dress for you. You're going to love it."

She was right about the dress. Early on the evening of the ball, Sara and Vanessa appeared at my door with the most beautiful royal blue ball gown I had ever seen.

"Is that for me?" I gasped.

"Of course," said Sara. "We're here to help you get ready."

Vanessa sat me down in front of the mirror. "Let's see what we can do with this hair of yours," she said. "This is your ball, and we want you to look like royalty." Once Vanessa had finished with my hair and makeup, they helped me put on the dress. When they finally finished and let me examine the results in the mirror, I was astonished. I looked beautiful and felt like a royal princess.

A few minutes after Sara and Vanessa left, there was a knock at my door. When I opened it, there stood Father, already dressed in his black tuxedo and looking quite handsome.

"You look stunning, my dear," he said, kissing me on the forehead.

"Thank you. Do you like the dress? Sara and Vanessa picked it out for me."

"It's lovely," he said. "But I think it's missing something, don't you?" He placed a black velvet box on my dresser and beckoned me over to it.

I looked up at him and asked, "What's this?" He lifted the box lid and revealed a diamond-studded tiara and the most beautiful glittering necklace I had ever seen. I automatically put my hand over my mouth in awe.

"Is this for me, Father?" I asked.

"Yes, Sophia. Every female in this family has worn this tiara and necklace at their own ball as they were brought into my family. It is a tradition that my wife started many centuries ago. You are now a recognized member of a noble clan, Sophia, and at your ball you should look like one. Wear them with pride, my dear."

I stepped in front of the mirror, and Father gently fastened the necklace around my neck. A delicate string of diamonds supported a line of deep blue sapphires cut into teardrop shapes. It matched the dress perfectly. He then took out the diamond tiara and placed it on my head.

"Thank you, Father," I said softly as I turned from side to side in front of the mirror.

Father then held out his hand and said, "It's time, Sophia. May I have the honor to be your escort, Lady Manori?"

"Of course, Father. I would not have it any other way."

Wearing white gloves, Father held out his arm with his hand palm down and I placed my hand on top of his. We then walk to the top of the ballroom stairs.

I had been so busy getting ready that I hadn't had a chance to see the decorations. Silk ribbons stretched from the crystal chandelier in every direction across the ceiling, and rich tapestries depicting the symbols of the various noble families that had been invited hung from the walls. There were flowers everywhere; red roses wrapped around the banisters, and tall vases and urns with spectacular explosions of exotic blossoms were positioned artfully about the room. There was even a small orchestra at the back of the ballroom.

Standing at the top of the stairs, Father made a gesture to the conductor, and the orchestra stopped playing. Trumpets began to sound a herald to get everyone's attention. All eyes in the room then turned in our direction. As we descended the staircase, I noticed Randolph standing at the foot of the stairs.

"Ladies and gentlemen," he said in a loud, clear voice, "the Manori family would like to thank you all for joining them to celebrate this very special occasion. It is an honor to have you all here. Now, without any further ado, it is my great pleasure to introduce the newest member of the esteemed Manori family, Lady Sophia Victoria Manori."

We walked slowly down the stairs and out into the ballroom. Men bowed and women curtsied as we passed, and they shuffled aside to make a space for us on the dance floor. The orchestra struck up a waltz, and Father bowed low over my hand.

"Will you do me the honor of having this dance with me?" he asked.

I curtsied and said, "It would be my pleasure."

As we began to dance, I said a silent thank-you to Sara for taking me to so many fancy parties over the past months. She was the only reason I made it through the waltz without stepping on my dress and falling flat on my face in front of all the guests. Out of the corner of my eye, I saw Sara and the rest of the family smiling at Father and me as we glided across the marble floor.

When we finished our dance, everyone clapped and cheered. We both bowed to the crowed and then walked off to the side of the dance floor. I was grinning from ear to ear.

Then the orchestra struck up a livelier tune, and the guests who wanted to dance flooded onto the dance floor. Father guided me to a table of refreshments in the parlor and introduced me personally to several of the more distinguished guests before giving me a peck on the cheek and sending me off to enjoy myself. Because vampires live for such a long time, they can be slow to adapt to new social customs; the etiquette of the ball was strictly Victorian. Everyone treated everyone else with polite respect but also with a keen regard for the social hierarchy. As soon as Father left my side, several young men hurried up to me, and in just a few minutes, my dance card was full.

After more than an hour on the dance floor, I took a break and went to the parlor to find something to drink. Almost all the guests were vampires, of course, but Father had spared no expense to create a balance of a culinary variety for those who were human. I got myself a glass of warm blood and went looking for Sara.

She was dancing with a strikingly handsome young man with a chiseled jaw and dark, curly hair—I made a mental note to ask her to introduce me. As I looked around the room, I caught sight of Father standing with Vladimir Németh in a corner. Father's back was to me, but the look on Vladimir's face suggested he wasn't enjoying himself. Curious, I sidled closer and strained to make out their voices over the noise of the crowd.

"—resent the implication," Vladimir was saying. "Just because this *alleged* vampire hunter works at my mortuary doesn't mean—"

"Calm yourself," interrupted Father. "If I didn't ask these questions, I wouldn't be doing my job as an elder. My daughter was attacked while under your protection. I need to know how it happened."

"My son was also attacked, Marcus," said Vladimir coldly. "Please remember that."

"I do. I have a very good memory. For example, I remember that Nora's casket was sealed shut when I arrived at your home. Why was that, Vladimir? It almost seemed as if someone wanted us to believe she was dead, when in fact she was not."

Vladimir's eyes widened, and then his eyes darkened with barely restrained anger. "How dare you say such a thing," he hissed.

"I am your elder and a member of the council. I will decide what needs to be said," said Father. The two men locked eyes for a moment. Vladimir was the first to look away.

"Of course," Vladimir said stiffly. "Please forgive me."

Father waved his wine glass dismissively. "Now that I have alerted you to the presence of this vampire hunter, I trust you will deal with him appropriately," he said.

"Consider it done, my lord," said Vladimir. "I would pay my respects to your daughter Sophia, but apparently there is some business that requires my immediate attention. Please make my apologies for me." He bowed just deeply enough to avoid open insolence and then spun on his heel and stalked away.

Father shook his head and turned around. He caught sight of me looking at him from across the room, and the angry look on his face dissolved into a smile. He raised his glass in a silent toast.

I returned his smile and raised my glass, but as I began the next dance, my mind raced. Could Vladimir Németh be the one plotting against the Manori clan? Father certainly seemed to suspect him. But if that were true, why had Vladimir's son Michael also been attacked?

My dance partner, a stocky young vampire from a minor clan who was several inches shorter than me, must have noticed that my mind was elsewhere. "Is everything all right?" he asked.

"Sorry," I said. "I was just spacing out there for a second. Let's dance."

I decided to put all sinister plots out of my mind for the rest of the night; this was my party, after all, and I was allowed to enjoy myself.

I danced late into the morning. Finally, out of exhaustion and very sore feet, I headed up the stairs and into my room.

I've heard it said that every little girl dreams of being a princess one day. I'm not sure about that, but I certainly felt like a princess tonight, and apart from the conversation I overheard between Vladimir and Father, it was one of the most wonderful nights of my life.

22. THE BALANCE OF POWER

A week after the ball, Sara and I took Father's advice and decided to take a trip together. We were in the VIP lounge at Logan International Airport in Boston waiting for our flight when Sara's phone rang. I could tell by the look on her face that it wasn't good news.

"What?" she exclaimed. "But is he's okay? Are you sure? All right, we'll get a taxi and be home soon."

As she hung up her phone I asked, "What's going on?"

"Father was attacked. He's all right, but it was close. He was hit by an arrow—the same type of poisoned arrow that was used on Nora. Luckily, the arrow missed his heart. Nikolai and the rest of the family are giving him a blood transfusion, as we did with Nora. Nikolai said he is responding well and should make a full recovery."

"How did this happen?" I asked. "I mean, he never leaves the house."

"I don't know all the details, but someone called and said Dante was hurt. Father had Randolph drive them to where Dante was said to be. While they were searching for Dante, someone shot Father in the back. Randolph managed to get him back in the limo and bring him home, where Nikolai immediately started a blood transfusion. He's awake now but still weak."

Sara spoke matter-of-factly, and her face was like stone, but I could see concern in her eyes. As I heard what had happened, anger ran through my body. The muscles in my shoulders tensed, and I had to make a conscious effort not to extend my fangs right there in the airport lounge.

"Vladimir Németh," I growled.

"Vladimir Németh—you think the Németh clan did this?" asked Sara suspiciously.

I quickly explained about the conversation at the ball that I had overheard between Vladimir and Father about the vampire hunter working at Vladimir's mortuary.

"He has to be the one behind this," I said. "I know he's hiding something, and it was exceedingly obvious he was furious with Father."

"Interesting," said Sara. She paused for a moment, deep in thought. "Let's say Vladimir is behind these attacks. But why? Why would he want Nora or Father killed? We have done nothing to their clan. In fact, the marriage between Nora and Michael would bind our two clans and make us all more powerful."

"I wondered about that myself, and I have a theory. Back on the farm, we had a chicken house that held ten chickens and one rooster. Everything seemed fine, but we were not getting as many eggs as we expected. Thinking that we had too many chickens for one rooster, we decided to get another rooster. The day after we put the new rooster in the chicken house, we found him dead. It seems the old rooster had killed him."

"So what's your point?" asked Sara.

"My point is that sometimes there can only be one rooster in the chicken house. If Nora and Michel were to get married, it would bind our two clans together. Being the elder, Father would be seen as the clan's leader, and Lord Németh would always be in Father's shadow. If Nora were to die, then there would be no wedding, and things would stay the same. But that plan failed, and the wedding is still on. If Father were to die, then that would mean that the vampire council would need someone to fill his position, and Lord Németh would be the obvious choice. This would give him more power and respect within the vampire community, and he would take over as leader of both clans."

"Wow, I never thought of it like that," said Sara. "Now things are starting to make sense. You're pretty smart for a farm girl," Sara said with a smile, "but we can't just act on a hunch. We need some solid proof. Got any ideas?"

"Actually, I do," I said with a grin. "You go back to Father, and I'll catch a flight to New York and see what I can dig up at the Németh's mortuary. That's where Father said that this vampire hunter works. Maybe I can find some clues there."

"You're crazy," exclaimed Sara. "I'm not going home while you have all the fun." She laughed, but her eyes were grim.

"Very funny," I said. But before I had a chance to say anything else, Sara was already on her cell phone, making arrangements for a private jet to take us to New York.

Just before Sara hung up, I overheard her say, "Thanks, Sam, I owe you one. How does a case of your favorite scotch sound?"

I smiled and shook my head. Although I was starting to get used to some of the benefits that came with being a member of a noble family, occasionally the influence of the Manori clan still caught me by surprise.

Thirty minutes later, Sara and I were taxiing onto the runway in a private jet, on our way to New York.

Suddenly Sara became very serious and took my hand. "Sophia," she said, "if we do find evidence that Vladimir is somehow involved in the attacks against our clan, you know that this means that our two clans will go to war, right?"

"To be honest, I had not thought that far ahead," I said. "But I suppose we would have no other choice but to go to war."

"I know you've been through a lot lately, and you're an extremely gifted vampire. But a war between two clans—it's horrible." A look of deep pain passed over Sara's face, and I wondered what she was remembering. "It's bloody and violent, and vampires die. They die on both sides, sis," she said softly. "I know you love our family, but you have to prepare for the possibility that some of us may die."

A lump formed in my throat, and I tried to imagine what I would feel like if Nora or Dante—or, God forbid, Sara—were killed. I gripped Sara's hand tightly.

"Remember how you were able to ignore the physical pain you felt during the assassin's test?" she asked.

I nodded.

"Well, in a war, you have to be able to do that with your heart. If you hesitate for even a second during a fight, it could cost the life of one of your brothers or sisters. Are you up to this, Sophia?"

I looked Sara in the eyes. "Of course," I said. "This family is all I have left in world. If we go to war, I'll protect it with my life."

"That's what I wanted to hear," she said, squeezing my hand. We sat in silence for a few minutes, and then Sara said, "If we do go to war, we'll have to make the first strike, and it will have to be swift and deadly. If Vladimir dies, the rest of the clan will most likely lose their will to fight." She shook her head, waved her hand in the air. "But I'm getting ahead of myself. We can talk about that later. Right now we need to concentrate on finding something to tie Vladimir to this vampire hunter."

We landed in LaGuardia airport, and to avoid attention, we took a taxi instead of a limo to the mortuary. We got out a few blocks short of our destination. "We'll be back in an hour or two," Sara said to the driver. "Leave the meter running. If you're still here when we get back, I'll give you a five hundred dollar tip on top of the fare." Sara tossed him a hundred dollar bill to prove she had the money.

The taxi driver snatched up the bill and said, "Yes, ma'am. I'll wait right here."

Sara started walking down the street, and I trotted along behind her.

The mortuary turned out to be a large, single-story building conveniently located next to a cemetery. I could tell that the building had been there a while because it was entirely constructed of wood. The grounds around it were kept immaculate.

"This way," Sara said. She took off running and leaped over the wrought-iron fence surrounding the cemetery grounds. I followed, and we approached the building quietly from behind. Outside the back door, we stopped and listened. I sniffed the air and could not detect anyone else inside. We were alone.

Sara produced a dagger with a long, thin blade from her purse and wiggled it into the lock. There was a click, and it swung open. A warm gust of air rushed out to meet us, carrying the smell of various flowers and a strong scent of chemicals. I felt dizzy and had to take a few steps back for some fresh air.

"Are you okay?" asked Sara in a low whisper.

"Sorry," I said. "I just need a minute to get used to the smell." I took a deep breath of fresh air and stepped cautiously back toward the open door. This time it was less overwhelming, and I managed to pick out more individual scents. I recognized one in particular immediately. I nodded at Sara.

"What is it?" she asked. "Can you smell something?"

"Yes, I can smell the exact same chemical that was in Nora's blood. Can't you smell it?"

She shook her head. "Your sense of smell is more sensitive than mine." She held the door open and gestured for me to go ahead. "Lead the way, sis," she said. "I'll be right behind you."

I followed the scent down a carpeted hallway, through a metal door, and down a flight of stairs that opened to a rather large basement. The floor was concrete, with various stains splattered here and there. A bare metal table stood in the middle of the room. Shelves stacked with bottles and jars and other supplies lined three of the walls, and the fourth held rows of steel doors that I guessed led to the refrigerated compartments where they kept the cadavers. It was obvious we had found the embalming room.

I sniffed all around the room, paying particular attention to the various bottles on the shelves, but I couldn't figure out where the specific chemical I was looking for was coming from. "I don't understand," I said to Sara. "The scent seems to be coming from over by the cadavers somewhere, but there's nothing there."

Sara smiled. "I may not have your nose," she said, "but I do have some common sense." She pulled out one of the empty cadaver drawers and laid down on it. "All right," she said. "Slide me in and shut the door."

I did as she asked. A few moments after I shut the door I heard a faint knocking sound. I opened the compartment. To my surprise, it was empty. I looked inside; on the opposite end, I saw Sara peering back at me through another open door.

"Come on," she said. "You're not going to believe this."

I slithered through the cold steel compartment and out the other side. As I looked around the hidden room, I couldn't believe my eyes. Along the walls were crossbows and arrows of all kinds. Over to the side of the room was a machinist drill, and on a table next to the drill, lined up one after the other, were dozens of hollowed-out arrowheads. But the room's most striking feature was a large terrarium. Inside, staring back at us must have been half a dozen snakes coiled around one another in a hissing, writhing knot.

As I stared at the snakes in amazement, Sara was already taking pictures of everything in the room with her cell phone. "What do you think the snakes are for?" she asked.

"I'm guessing their venom is one of the ingredients in the vampire hunter's toxin," I said. "As you know, a snake bite alone would not harm us. But I'm guessing he found a specific chemical to mix with the snake venom that can cause paralysis in vampires."

"Wow, this vampire hunter must be pretty smart to be able to create such a toxin," she said, snapping a final picture of the terrarium. "I think that's all the evidence we need. Now let's get the hell out of here."

"Wait," I said. "What if Lord Németh just denies knowing about this room?"

"I see your point," said Sara. "He would just set up shop somewhere else." She thought for a moment, and then an evil grin spread across her face.

"What?" I asked.

"We'll just have to get a sample of Vladimir's blood. One sip will tell us everything we need to know."

"Sara," I said. "Tell me how exactly you plan to get some of Vladimir's blood?"

"We'll lure him out, just like they did to Father," said Sara. Her gaze swept over the collection of crossbows arrayed on the wall and came to rest on the hollow-point arrowheads on the workbench. "Nikolai is a crack shot with a crossbow. We'll poison an arrowhead with some of your venom. Once Vladimir is paralyzed, one of us can cut him and collect a sample."

"Do you really think we can pull something like this off?"

"Sis," said Sara, "I have lived a very long time and have learned a thing or two about war and strategy. I will come up with a plan that will work. Trust me."

Seeing the conviction in her eyes was all I needed. "I trust you, Sara," I said.

"Good. We can work out the details later. Let's get out of here. This place gives me the creeps."

We left the secret room exactly as we had found it, except for two hollowed-out arrowheads that Sara took. We locked the door behind us and headed back to the taxi. The taxi driver was waiting for us right where we left him. On our way home, Sara and I said nothing to each other. I guess we were both still processing what we had discovered. Once we reached the mansion, Sara handed the driver a stack of crisp bills from her purse.

He let out a low whistle. "Damn," he said. "If you ladies ever need a ride again, you give Jose a call, okay?"

*   *   *

Father called us into his bedroom as soon as we walked in the door. He was sitting up in bed, but he seemed a bit paler than usual. When he saw us, you could see the relief in his eyes.

I perched on one side of the bed, and Sara took the other. "How are you doing?" asked Sara, clasping his hand in hers.

He waved away her concern with his other hand. "I'm fine. The poison is out of my system, and my wounds have already healed. I just need a little rest and a little blood."

I refilled the glass on his nightstand with blood from the decanter, and he took a sip.

"Thank you," he said. "It's nice to have you two home safely. I'm afraid you'll have to postpone any more travel plans until we've dealt with this vampire hunter."

Sara threw me a significant look from across the bed.

"Of course, Father," I said smoothly. "Have you found out anything more about who might be behind the attacks?"

"I have my suspicions, but nothing substantial," he said. "Until I have something I can act on, we all need to be on our guard."

After a few more minutes, we left Father to rest and went upstairs to talk to Nikolai. It was after dawn, but he was still awake.

"Come in," he said. "I'm glad you're home. Father was worried about you."

"We need to talk," I said in a low tone. We pushed past him and sat on the edge of his unmade bed.

He tightened the belt of his robe and found a seat in an easy chair. "Okay," he said. "What's going on?"

I explained what we had found at the mortuary, and Sara showed him the pictures on her cell phone and quickly outlined our plan to get some of Lord Németh's blood.

When we were done, Nikolai asked, "Have you told Father about this?"

"No," said Sara. "You know he'd never let us do something as dangerous as this. Besides, if it turns out we're wrong, we're the only ones to blame. Father can honestly say he didn't know about it, which could mean the difference between going to war or not."

Nikolai rubbed his chin with his thumb and forefinger for a moment. "I don't know, Sara. This is a dangerous plan." He turned and looked at me. "No offense, Sophia, but I don't know if you're ready for something like this. I know you can fight, but how will you react under pressure if this plan falls apart?"

I glanced at Sara.

"Are you going to tell him, or do I have to?" she asked me. "I know it's supposed to be a secret, but this is a matter of life and death."

Nikolai looked from me to Sara and back again. "What are you talking about?" he asked.

"Fine," I said. "But you have to promise you'll never tell anyone what I'm about to say, ever. Understand?"

Nikolai nodded.

I looked down at my hands, took a deep breath, and said, "When I went to see Lord Illyrius, I didn't take the test that the rest of you took. I took the assassin's test."

His eyes widened. "You did what?" He quickly sat up in his chair. "So it really does exist. But still, it's just a test. I'm sure there wasn't any real danger."

The memory of the assassin's sword twisting in my shoulder flashed through my mind. A growl formed at the back of my throat. My eyes darkened, and my fangs extended of their own accord.

Sara put a hand on my shoulder. "Calm down, sis. You're going to have to show him," she said. "Otherwise he'll never believe you."

I got up and shoved my wrist in front of Nikolai's face. "Drink, damn it," I said in a condescending tone. He looked up at me and then back to Sara.

"Go ahead, Nic. It's the only way you will truly understand what she went through," said Sara.

He slowly reached up and took my arm. He then extended his fangs, bit down on my wrist, and drank. After a moment, I pulled away and rejoined Sara on the bed. Nikolai sat silently in his chair, obviously stunned.

"You can't tell anyone about this, not even Father," I said. "If Lord Illyrius ever found out how much you know, he might go as far as sending one of his assassins after us. And no offense, Nic, but you're no match for them. Got it?"

He nodded slowly. "I'm sorry. I had no idea," he said. "All right, I guess I'm in. So how do we get Lord Németh to leave his estate?"

"Arson," said Sara.

We both looked at her.

"The last thing he would want is someone finding his secret room," she explained. "If we set the mortuary on fire, I bet he'll show up in person to tell the firefighters what to save and to keep them from poking around in the basement any more than necessary."

"Good idea," said Nikolai. "When do we move?"

"Soon," I said. "There was quite an arsenal in that hidden room, and the most recent attack on Father almost killed him. I don't want to give them time to try again."

"Tomorrow night then," said Nikolai. "That should give us enough time to rest and make our preparations. We should leave just before sundown."

23. An Unintentional Diversion

The next afternoon, Sara, Nikolai, and I prepared for our trip to the mortuary. Luckily, Nikolai had a cooler large enough to hide his crossbow and a gallon of gasoline so that Randolph wouldn't get suspicions. It seemed Nikolai had smuggled his crossbow out a time or two before. As for me, I wasn't going to take any chances, so I armed myself heavily, just in case there was trouble.

Once we had everything set, Sara, Nikolai, and I got into the backseat of the limousine. I had told Randolph that we were going to see some old friends of mine and that showing up in a limousine would just raise a lot of unwanted questions. So the plan was for him to drop us off about ten miles from our destination; I had arranged for a taxi to take us the rest of the way.

Sara and Nikolai fell asleep during the drive, but I was pumped too full of adrenaline. I guess I was still a little jumpy from the assassin's test. I kept flipping the matchbook over and over again inside my pocket.

It was well after sundown when we reached our destination. Our taxi was waiting for us as planned. Randolph parked the limo just behind it as I shook the others awake and jumped outside.

It was a warm night. The blue lights of television screens glowed in a few windows, but no one was around. Sara and Nikolai retrieved the cooler from the trunk, and we waved good-bye to

Randolph and hopped into the taxi. A few minutes later, we had the taxi driver drop us off about a quarter mile down the street from the Németh's mortuary.

Retracing the path Sara and I had used on our first visit, the three of us hopped the cemetery fence and made our way toward the rear of the building. Nikolai pulled his crossbow out of the cooler, and I retrieved the can of gasoline. We left the cooler behind a large tombstone. I approached the back door with the gas can and my book of matches. Just as before, all the windows were dark, and the door was locked.

I looked back at Sara and Nikolai, who were crouched in the shadows beside a white marble crypt. Sara gave me an encouraging nod, and I proceeded to uncap the gas can.

The sharp scent of petroleum filled my nostrils as I slopped the semiclear liquid all over the building's back door and wooden back wall. With the last little bit of gas, I made a trail along the sidewalk toward the cemetery. Then I tossed the empty can into the tall grass across the street. I lit a match and dropped it on the ground. Flames darted along the trail of gas to the mortuary's back door. A bright orange ball exploded out from the gasoline-soaked wall as the fumes caught fire.

I ran back to Sara and Nikolai. By the time I got to the crypt and looked back, the whole back side of the building was on fire. The flame groped and spread up the side to the roof. Black smoke billowed into the night sky, and the odor of burning wood filled the air. After a while, lights began to come on in the windows of the townhouses across the street. A minute later, the first siren blared to life in the distance. I asked Nikolai for the hollow arrowheads, and I filled each of them with my venom. He attached them to the ends of two arrows and waited.

We watched as first one fire truck and then another pulled up, sirens blaring and lights flashing. The first crew hooked up a hose to a nearby fire hydrant and tried to control the blaze, while the second extended a ladder and lowered it over the roof.

There was still no sign of Vladimir or the other members of the Németh clan. Nikolai peered along his loaded crossbow in the direction of the blaze. The blue and red lights of the fire trucks played across Sara's face as she returned my look of concern. Would Lord Németh come?

Finally, a black SUV pulled up behind the trucks, and Vladimir Németh stepped into the firelight, two of his sons behind him. I recognized them from our visit to the Németh mansion; neither was Nora's fiancé. Two firefighters tried to wave Vladimir back from the area, but he pointed at the burning building and shouted something. I couldn't make out what he was saying over the roar of the fire but they then let him through.

I glanced over at Nikolai. He was still sighting along his crossbow, waiting for a clear shot. But Vladimir wouldn't stop moving. He was filled with a nervous energy and bounced from one foot to the other while speaking to the fire chief, shouting orders all the while. To make matters worse, a constant stream of firefighters rushed back and forth between us and him. Nikolai shook his head in frustration.

I knew if I didn't do something soon, our plan would fail. Motioning for Sara to follow, I sprinted to the edge of the cemetery and vaulted over the fence. A small crowd of civilians had gathered to watch the fire, many of them still in pajamas or bathrobes. I used them to mask my approach until I was about fifteen feet from the nearest truck. Vladimir was still lecturing one of the firefighters, and his back was to me. I darted out from the crowd and dashed toward him. All around was chaos—firefighters rushing in all directions, flashing lights, the roaring heat of the blaze. I was still several feet from Lord Németh when he turned abruptly and saw me. His eyes widened, and he froze.

He stepped forward again just in time for Nikolai's arrow to pass inches behind his back and slam into the side of a fire truck. He flinched at the sound of crumpling metal, and before he could recover, he felt one of my shuriken sink into his chest. He looked down at the wound and staggered, trying to fight the effects of my venom. Then Nikolai's second arrow struck him in the shoulder, and he crashed onto the sidewalk.

As he went down, I heard a scuffle behind me and whirled to see Sara squaring off with one of Vladimir's sons. Almost before I knew what I was doing, another shuriken left my hand. It hit Sara's assailant in the back of his leg, and he went down almost immediately. She hurried toward me with a dagger in one hand and an empty vial for Lord Németh's blood in the other.

Before I could look around for Vladimir's other son, a knife plunged into my lower back. Compared to the pain I had experienced during the assassins' test, it barely hurt at all. I turned, snarling, to face my attacker, and his contemptuous sneer turned to a look of horror as I lifted him off the ground by his neck, pulled him between two fire trucks, and sank my fangs deep into his throat. As soon as I felt him go limp, I flung his body as far as I could over the fence into the cemetery.

I looked around for Sara and saw her crouched over Lord Németh's motionless body, her dagger between her teeth. She replaced the cap on the vial and looked up at me, nodding and grinning around the blade. I nodded back, and she took off into the darkness. Before I followed her, I stooped and hissed into Lord Németh's ear, "I should tear your heart out now, you piece of shit. Next time we meet, maybe I will." I raked my nails across his face and sprinted away, leaving three paralyzed vampires, a crowd of confused firefighters, and the smoldering ruins of the mortuary behind me.

I caught up with the others. Nikolai had already retrieved the cooler and placed his crossbow back inside. Sara held Vladimir's blood aloft for Nikolai and me to see, and we all exchanged high fives, giddy at our success.

Sara then called for another taxi to pick us up and take us back to Randolph and the waiting limousine. It was all we could do to contain our excitement and not give away the real reason for our trip.

Once we got back to the mansion, we stopped dead in our tracks in the entryway. Our triumphal grins vanished. Father was standing in the foyer, and he did not look happy. Somehow, he already knew what we had done. "Hand it over right now," he said, holding out his hand.

Sara sheepishly retrieved the vial from her jacket pocket and placed it on his waiting palm.

"What on earth were you thinking?" he demanded. "You could have been killed!"

Sara and I stumbled over one another in our attempts to explain about the mortuary and the secret room, but Father was having none of it.

"I have known that Vladimir was behind the attacks for some time," he said sternly. "I have known it since the attack on Nora."

"Then why didn't—" I began, but Father held up a hand to silence me.

"It was not yet time," he said. "Your stunt tonight may have put my informant's life in danger. It may also have jeopardized my position as an elder." He sighed and closed his eyes.

"We never thought this would get you into trouble, Father," said Sara. "We'll tell Lord Illyrius it was our idea and you had nothing to do with it."

His eyes snapped open again. "As head of this family, I am responsible for your actions. Surely you must know that."

The three of us looked at the floor.

After a moment, I looked up and met his gaze. His disappointment showed clearly in his face. "I'm sorry," I said. "Truly, I am. But will you at least taste the blood? He's already tried to kill three members of this family, Father. He's going to try again."

"I understand your concern," he said. "I share it. It's your methods I disapprove of." He sighed again and held the vial up to the light. The dark, viscous liquid sloshed back and forth inside the glass. "I will taste the blood. As an elder, it's my right. I just wish the three of you had come to me first. Did any of you taste it?"

We shook our heads.

"Good," he said. "Vladimir is still the head of a powerful clan, and we don't yet have the concrete evidence we need to justify this kind of action. However, I'm his elder, and given the circumstances ..." He removed the top of the vial and lifted it to his lips.

He stood with his eyes closed for a moment. "Well," he said at last, opening his eyes, obviously angered by what he had seen, "It seems the Németh clan had intended to attack our home in force tonight. The fire at the mortuary caused Vladimir to postpone his plans. I dare say your recklessness may have saved our lives. Nikolai, get your brother and sisters from upstairs, now."

Nikolai hurried up the stairs. Father put the empty vial down on an end table, clasped his hands behind his back, and began to pace back and forth across the room, a grim expression etched across his face. I glanced at Sara, but she was still gazing at the floor.

After a moment, Nikolai returned with Vanessa, Carmilla, Nora, and Dante in tow. Father's gaze swept over us. "As of this moment," he said, "we are at war with the Németh clan."

Nora gasped, and Vanessa put an arm around her; the rest of us remained silent.

"A fortunate coincidence is all that saved us from a devastating attack tonight," Father continued. "They will try again, and we are not prepared. So we're going to attack them first. Dante and Sophia, I want you to take the first watch from the second-floor balcony. Nikolai, make an inventory of our weapons and bring whatever you think might be useful up here to the living room. Vanessa and Sara, help Nikolai. Carmilla, we'll need some smoke grenades and a way to hide our scent. Nora can help you."

Each of us nodded curtly as we received our instructions.

"Now," said Father, "if they don't attack tonight—I don't think they will after your little diversion—we will attack tomorrow at sundown."

"What about Michael?" Nora asked. She was obviously trying to be brave, but her voice shook.

"I don't believe Michael has been party to any of this," Father said gently. "I know he truly loves you, Nora. No harm will come to him as long as he doesn't attack us first."

As everyone hurried off to prepare for battle, I noticed the empty vial lying on its side on the end table where Father had left it. A few drops of blood had fallen onto the table's marble top, and my curiosity got the better of me. I glanced cautiously around the room to make sure no one was looking, swiped my finger through the dark liquid, and brought it to my lips.

I closed my eyes, and a confused jumble of images swirled into my mind. Most of what I saw was too fragmentary to make sense out of—faces I didn't recognize, images of events from far in the past. Strangely, one image seemed to draw my attention. I watched as one of Vladimir's ancestors took a crying child from an old blind woman, pricked his heel, and took a small amount of the child's blood. The image then faded.

Before I could digest this information, more images flooded my brain, rushing forward in time. A face I recognized jumped out to me from all the others: it was Devin Johnson, my former fiancé. Through Vladimir Németh's eyes, I saw him standing in the secret room of the mortuary milking the snakes for their venom. Then the image changed, and there was Devin, using a needle and syringe to carefully fill hollow-point arrowheads with a milky liquid.

I opened my eyes in shock. I could not believe it. Devin was the vampire hunter!

Without thinking, I ran after Father and stormed into the library. "Why didn't you tell me Devin was the vampire hunter?" I demanded.

Father spun around with a scowl on his face. "I told you not to drink any of Vladimir's blood," he growled.

I pressed on, undeterred. "How long have you known, Father? And how come you didn't tell me?"

"Honestly, Sophia, I was trying to protect you," he said in a fatherly tone.

"Protect me how? What do you mean?"

"I first learned about Devin Johnson's involvement just before our trip to the old country. I didn't think the best time to tell you was while you were preparing for your test. You needed to stay focused. The last thing you needed was a distraction from your old fiancé. Since then, so much has been going on. I was going to tell you—I was just waiting for the right opportunity." He sighed. "Well, now you know."

The anger drained out of me as I heard Father's explanation. "All right," I said. "But Devin, a vampire hunter? How is that even possible?"

"I don't know much more than you do," said Father, "but I can guess how it happened."

I slowly sat down, never taking my eye off Father as he began to explain.

"He loved you, Sophia," said Father, "and you left him without even saying good-bye. He felt betrayed, and the obvious place for him to put the blame and focus his anger on was the vampire family who took you in."

"But how did he even know where I was?"

"Veterinarians sometimes supply animal blood to the less civilized vampires," said Father. The look on his face suggested that this was the vampire equivalent of digging a half-eaten cheeseburger out of a Dumpster. "He must have known enough to at least suspect vampires were involved, especially after Sara bit you. Anyway, it seems Vladimir found him and decided to take advantage of his hatred for our family."

I didn't know what to say. Competing emotions struggled for my attention. I felt guilt for hurting Devin by agreeing to marry him when I didn't love him; guilt that my relationship with him had put my new family in danger; rage that he had dared to attack the vampires I had come to love.

Father put his hand on my shoulder. "Will you be able to face him in battle?" he asked gently. "He is still working for Lord Németh, and he has tried to kill both me and your sister Nora."

"Yes, Father," I said. "I will do whatever needs to be done to keep this family from harm. Now more than ever."

"Good," he said, smiling grimly. "That's what I thought you would say. Now go find Dante. He shouldn't have to keep watch alone."

There was no attack that night; our unintentional diversion had saved the family. If the Németh clan had attacked while Sara, Nikolai, and I were away, it would have been a massacre. Maybe it was luck, or maybe an angel was watching over the family, as strange as that may sound coming from a vampire. Whatever the case, war was finally upon us. Tomorrow there would be a battle. I could only hope that the blood spilled would be theirs and not ours.

24. BATTLE OF THE CLANS

It was a sleepless day as we all prepared for battle. Vanessa, Sara, and Nikolai gathered and prepared as many weapons as they could find, while Dante and I tested each one and separated them for each person. Nora was not much help to Carmilla, but she did the best she could while trying to hold back her tears. Even Randolph was preparing for battle; he carefully pressed rounds into the small arsenal of guns.

Even with all the modern weapons we have today, the crossbow is still a vampire's main weapon of choice. It was silent, easy to use, and could propel a silver-tipped wooden arrow into the heart of a victim from a distance. As for me, I preferred my shurikens.

I gathered as many venom-filled shurikens as I could carry and placed them in the leather pouch strapped to the small of my back, sliding a dagger into one boot and a wooden stake in the other. My goal was to be as fast and light on my feet as possible.

The sun was still well above the western horizon as we loaded up the limousine. We all stood around the limo in silence as we waited for Father. At last, Father walked into the garage and stood at the front of the limo.

"Listen up," said Father. "The plan is simple. We will enter the mansion by the servant's entrance. Once inside we will split into pairs and search every room. You are to kill each member of the Németh clan as we search the castle. They had every intention to kill us last night, but we got lucky. Remember, we are vampires, and tonight we will fight as we have for centuries. There is to be no mercy. This is a kill-or-be-killed battle. If we do not destroy them, they will try to destroy us."

Father then looked at Nora. "Nora, you are not yet ready for a battle such as this. You are to wait inside the limo during the battle. Whoever finds Michael, tell him where the limo is parked and that Nora is waiting for him. He is not to be harmed. Does everyone understand?"

Each of us gave Father a nod.

"All right, let's go," said Father, and without hesitation, we all piled into the limousine and headed toward the Németh estate and into battle.

As we neared the Németh's estate, our timing was perfect. The sun had just set over the horizon. Father gave Randolph instructions to park the limo about a mile from the mansion.

The moment we came to a stop, we all jumped out of the limo and gathered our weapons while Carmilla passed around a bottle of one of her potions to mask our scent.

It was only a short walk down the main road to the tall fence that surrounding the estate. We crouched beside the fence in the darkness. I sniffed the air and smelled only pine needles, freshly turned turf, and rust on the iron fence. There were no guards.

I nodded to Father, and he whispered, "All right, you all know what to do. Once we're over the fence, Sophia and Nikolai will take point; the rest of us will follow behind."

As I leaped over the fence, my apprehension disappeared. A fierce exhilaration filled me. I landed softly on pine needles ahead of Nic and sprinted silently between the trees.

The forest was empty. There was no one lurking in the trees, and no traps sprang up to meet me. I stopped when I came to the edge of the trees. Ahead of us was a wide lawn that stretched out between the forest and the mansion. A few lights glowed in the windows, but I didn't see any movement.

Father then trotted up behind me, the others in tow.

"There is no cover once we leave the trees," I whispered, "but I don't see anyone keeping watch, nor do I smell anyone outside."

Father nodded. "Sara," he said softly. "See if you can get to the back door."

Without hesitating, Sara sprinted across the lawn, her footsteps silent on the soft grass. She covered the distance in a couple of seconds, but the time seemed to stretch into an eternity. She reached the back door unharmed, and I let out a long sigh.

Crouching low beside the house, she reached up and tried the door. It was unlocked. She motioned for the rest of us to come forward.

Now it was our turn to make the nerve-wracking dash. One after the other, we each made it safely to the back door. We took up positions around Sara, and Father pointed to Nikolai and me and then to the door. Sara snapped the door open, and Nikolai charged through, loaded crossbow at the ready. I was right behind him.

The back door led to the kitchen, a long, rectangular room, dimly lit except for a lamp on a wooden table just inside the door. Three women and one man sat around the table playing cards. A quick sniff told me they were human. Most likely, they were servants.

They looked up in alarm, but Nikolai trained his crossbow on them and raised a finger to his lips. I pointed toward the door, and they rose and filed quickly through it, eyes wide, not saying a word.

Straight ahead through the kitchen was a set of French doors that led deeper into the mansion. At the east end of the room was a narrow staircase that led to the upper floors.

As soon as the servants were gone, Father came in, followed by the rest of the family. He motioned for Dante and Nikolai to take the stairs, and the rest of us followed him through the French doors into a formal dining room. To our surprise, it was deserted.

We continued forward into the living room and on to the front entryway of the mansion. The gleaming marble floor gave way to the grand staircase leading to the second floor. Still we saw no one and heard nothing. Father then motioned for me to stay downstairs while the others followed him up the stairway.

Where was the Németh clan? I wondered. I sniffed the air. We definitely weren't the only ones in the mansion. Could they be hiding? I followed the strongest scent through a doorway on the south side of the entryway. A wide set of stairs led down to a lower floor, where I found a sort of den. A bar ran along one wall and a billiard table stood in the middle of the room, but otherwise the room was empty.

As I turned to walk away, I heard the unmistakable sound of a crossbow cord being drawn behind me. There was a twang, and I dodged to the right just in time; the arrow whizzed past my ear. I spun around and noticed a rectangular hole in the wall behind the bar.

"They're in the walls!" I shouted at the top of my lungs, hoping desperately that the others would be able to hear me two stories above. "They're hiding in the walls!"

Somehow, they had known we were coming, but there was no time to think about that now.

I somersaulted toward the slit in the wall. As I regained my footing, I pulled one of Carmilla's smoke canisters from my belt and thrust it through the hole in the wall. Smoke streamed out, and a moment later there came a sound of muffled coughing. A hidden door at one end of the bar slammed open, and a vampire stumbled out in a cloud of smoke. He fired his crossbow a second time as he came into the open, but his aim was wild, and the shot went wide. Before he could reload, I lunged across the room and sank my fangs into his neck.

His body fell limply to the floor. I pulled a wooden stake from my boot and raised it for a killing blow. I hesitated. Then I thought of Sara bound and gagged in a chair, of Nora sealed in a glass coffin, of Father looking weak and pale in his bed. My visions filled me with rage, and I plunged the wooden stake through the vampire's heart. His body heaved, and blood welled up in his mouth and down his cheek. In a few moments, he would crumble to ash and there would be nothing left of him.

I quickly retrieved my weapon and made for the stairs, yelling as I ran. "They're in the walls! Flush them out with smoke!" The entryway was still empty, but the sounds of a battle reverberated from the second floor.

With a shuriken clutched tightly in each fist, I charged up the stairs and into a wide hall. Smoke filled the air and burned in my throat. Somewhere up ahead, I heard shouts and the sound of clashing blades. I started toward the noise, but a huge shape bore down on me out of the fog. He was built like a linebacker. Before I could react, he tackled me into the wall. There was a crunch, and plaster crumbled down around us as we both fell to the floor. I brought my hands up, and made two long slices across his big belly with my poisoned shuriken as he wrapped his large hands around my throat. After a moment, he stopped struggling, and I heaved his massive body off me, only to find myself staring into the business end of a loaded crossbow.

My gaze traveled down the weapon to the face behind it. It was Devin. He hesitated but I didn't. I lashed out with my foot, sweeping his legs from under him, and his arrow thudded into the ceiling. I was on my feet before he hit the floor, and I dragged him up by his shirt. "You just tried to kill me, you little shit," I growled. He tried to stammer a reply, but his words trailed off in a terrified gurgle as my fangs latched onto his jugular. A moment later, I tossed his paralyzed body to the floor and said, "I will deal with you later."

I then turned toward the large vampire still lying on the floor, covered in plaster dust. One of his fingers began to twitch, and I knew the venom from my shuriken was wearing off. I had to act quickly. I pulled the wooden stake from my boot and leaped through the air toward him. He let out a low moan as my stake cut through the air on the way to his heart. A moment later, he was dead.

As I continued down the hall, I heard screaming coming from downstairs. I ran back to the staircase. Once I reached the bottom, I saw a male vampire running toward the front doors. I ran quickly and reached the doors before the vampire. He did not try to fight me. It seemed all he wanted was to get out. He smelled as if he was burning, yet there was no sun. Then from around the corner walked Carmilla. I cocked my head, puzzled as to what was going on.

I kicked him back with my foot and watched as he fell to the floor. He screamed and crawled back toward the door, begging me to let him pass.

"You will find no mercy in me, vampire," I said.

Then Carmilla looked at me and said, "Sister, help me by holding this one down."

I placed my hands on his shoulders and held him down on the floor. The smell of his burnt flesh was disgusting, but I made sure he was not going anywhere. Then Carmilla walked up to the vampire, opened up a small bottle, and poured its contents over his heart. His screams immediately became louder. I watched the liquid eat through the vampire's clothes, through his skin, and into his body.

I looked at Carmilla and said, "I'm glad I'm on your side."

"This is no time for jokes," barked Carmilla. "Go help the others."

I hurried back upstairs and down the hall. The sounds of the fight had moved to other parts of the mansion, but I smelled blood up ahead of me.

As I got closer I saw Dante lying on his back in a dark pool of blood—his blood, and there was far too much of it. His shirt was torn in a dozen places, and a dagger was buried to its hilt in his throat. I dropped to one knee beside him and pulled it out. His eyelids fluttered, but the wound didn't heal. He had lost too much blood. I bit my right wrist, held it to his lips, and covered his wound with my left, but there was no response; he couldn't swallow.

I felt myself begin to panic. I didn't know what to do. I cradled him in my arms, trying to lift him enough to get some of my blood to flow down his throat, but it was no use. I sensed the life draining out of him and knew there was nothing more I could do.

I hugged Dante to my chest and kissed him gently on the forehead. "Sleep now," I said, fighting back tears. "Sleep now, my brother, and find peace." As I held him in my arms, I sensed the life leave his body. I laid him gently on the floor and rose to my feet, shaking with grief and anger. There was no time for mourning; that would come later. I embraced my anger. Fire coursed through my veins, and the emotional pain drained out of me. In its place, there was only rage.

My rage sharpened my sense of smell, and I followed a scent that was suddenly as clear as a glowing beacon pointing the way. There was a vampire hiding in another hidden passage in the next room. I kicked in the wall and hauled her out by her boots.

I didn't bother using my venom. I quickly grabbed a piece of splintered two-by-four and thrust it into her heart. I was already out the door and hunting my next victim before she was dead.

I had taken only a few steps down the hall when a shotgun blast shattered the smoke ahead. I saw an orange flash and felt the sting of buckshot slamming into my right shoulder and chest. I landed hard on my back on the wooden floor, ears ringing. A cough wracked my lungs, and I tasted blood at the back of my throat. I looked up and saw my attacker striding toward me through the smoke. He pumped another round into the chamber, and the empty plastic shell ricocheted off the wall.

My feet scrabbled on the wooden floor as I tried to stand up. Then the barrel's black mouth swung toward me. I flinched, waiting for the inevitable, but the second shot never came. I heard the shotgun clatter onto the floor, and when I looked up, I saw the silver tip of a blade protruding out of my attacker's throat. Next, I saw the pointed end of a wooden stake extending beyond his chest. He toppled forward, and behind him stood Sara, a dagger in one hand and a wooden stake in the other.

"Are you okay?" she asked.

I tried to get to my feet, but the effort made me cough again, and more thick blood welled up into my mouth. I turned my head to the side and spat.

"You are not healing, sis," said Sara. "The buckshot must be made of silver. Let's get you someplace safe."

"No. Cut them out," I demanded. "You have to cut the pellets out of me."

Her eyes widened, but she only hesitated for a second. She knelt beside me and slipped her dagger into one of the holes in my chest, probing for the shot. The pain was excruciating. I tried to block it out as I had during the assassin's test, but I couldn't. There was a soft clink, and the first pellet plunked onto the floor. I gasped for air.

"How many more?" I asked.

She quickly scanned my shoulder and side. "Three. The rest must have missed you."

"Crap," I said. Then the sound of gunshots echoed from the first floor, followed by a long, gurgling scream abruptly cut short. I gritted my teeth and nodded at Sara to continue.

The next pellet was lodged against a rib. I felt the point of Sara's dagger scrape against bone as she worked to pry it out. I screamed and grabbed her arm. Then the pain overwhelmed me and everything went dark.

25. The Reckoning

Although I was unconscious, I saw visions within my mind. A woman running through the dark, an infant wrapped in a tattered cloth, an open wound. In my delirium, I couldn't be sure which memories were my own and which were those of my ancestors, carried in my blood. Then a gaunt, pale face swam toward me out of the blackness. It was Vadim Preda, the vampire who had fathered my dhampir ancestors. His features were twisted with fury. "The offspring of the traitor who stole my son, Merek, is in this very house," he hissed. "Avenge me." The ancient vampire's rage burned like a red coal in my chest. Then, as the vision faded, the rage exploded into flames of fury.

My eyes snapped open. Sara was leaning over me with a look of concern on her face. "Sophia," she was saying. "Are you all right? Sophia!"

I got to my feet and pushed past her. She called my name again, but I didn't look back. I marched down the hall to the top of the main stairs. In the entryway below, Father and Vladimir circled one another warily, growling and hissing. The ashes of several vampires littered the floor. I made my way down the stairs.

"Stay back, Sophia!" said Father. "This is my fight."

"No," I said with a growl. "It's mine."

Father thrust out an arm to hold me back, but I grabbed it with one hand and slid him across the floor out of my way. He and Vladimir both stared at me, surprised at my strength.

"Gather everyone here," I said firmly. "Let them see what happens to traitors. Do it now, Father, or more of our family will die today."

He looked at me sharply.

"Dante is dead," I said. "I want no more deaths to come to our family because of this traitor. It ends now."

Father didn't understand what was going on, but he knew something was different about me. He stood there for a moment and then walked to the foot of the staircase and called out, "It's over! Everyone put down your weapons and come downstairs! The fighting is over." His deep voice filled the room and resonated through the passageways of the mansion.

An eerie silence fell. One by one, members of both clans began to appear. Sara descended the stairs, and Carmilla and Nikolai entered the foyer from the dining room together. Three members of the Németh clan had already gathered by the front door. Finally, Vanessa appeared from downstairs, supporting the bloodied but breathing form of Michael Németh.

Vladimir looked from Father to me and back again. "What the hell is this, Marcus? Call off your child and let's finish it. Or should I tear her apart?" He took half a step toward me, fangs bared.

I lunged to meet him, lifted him off the floor with one hand, and flung him into the wall. He slammed into it sideways and slid to the floor, his feet splayed awkwardly above him.

I laughed as he righted himself and scrambled to his feet. "Do you really think you can tear *me* apart? The blood of Lord Vadim Preda flows within my veins."

As soon as I mention the name Vadim Preda, I sensed anxiety within Lord Németh. He started to pace back and forth.

"What game are you trying to play, Marcus? Stop this foolishness. This is between you and me. Get this girl out of my way before I rip out her heart!"

"Look at me, Vladimir, not my father," I said. "Oh, is it all right if I call you Vladimir? It's just I feel I know you so well. You see, I have tasted your blood."

A vein throbbed in the old vampire's neck. "How dare you?" he spluttered.

"How dare I?" I screamed, baring my fangs. "Look around you! How many of your children are blood and ash? You killed them, Vladimir—you and your *ambition*."

Glaring around the room at the members of the Németh clan, I said, "Hear me now and learn the truth. The leader of your clan is a traitor and the son of a traitor. Centuries ago, it was his sire who kidnapped an infant named Merek, the only son of Vadim Preda."

A low growl issued from Vladimir's throat, and he charged. With a contemptuous flick of my wrist, I sent a shuriken spinning toward him. It stuck just under his collarbone. A look of confusion came over his face, and he toppled backward like a freshly cut tree.

Seeing their father paralyzed, the surviving members of the Németh clan surged forward, but I was already kneeling on the old vampire's chest with my dagger at his throat. "Another step and he dies," I growled, and they fell back.

"I think it's time for your family to learn the truth," I said looking down at Vladimir. There was a goblet on a table to one side of the entryway. I nodded toward it. "Sara, please hand me that cup."

She carried it over to me in both hands, as if in a formal procession. I nicked Vladimir's jugular with my dagger and held the cup under the wound. When it was full to the brim, I held it aloft toward the nearest member of the Németh clan, a young woman with dark, curly hair and a heart-shaped face. "Come have a drink," I said. "See the truth of your father's past."

Hesitantly, she stepped forward and brought the chalice to her lips. Her eyes widened, shocked by what she had seen.

"You see?" I said. "Now pass it around."

One by one, the members of the Németh clan drank from the cup. Shock was clearly visible on each of their faces as they learned of their father's crimes.

"Now your eyes are open," I said. "I know it's not what you expected, but you now know the truth. What happens next is the law. If he doesn't pay for his crimes, the price will fall on each of you in turn. Leave now and you will all live, but heed this warning: if any of you come looking for revenge, I'll see to it that your entire bloodline ceases to exist. Now go!"

They hesitated in the doorway, still trying to come to grips with their father's greed and treachery.

"I said go!" I yelled. They all scattered out the front entrance. When they had all left, I looked down at Vladimir, pulled the wooden stake from my boot, and with firm conviction in my voice as if I was carrying out the sentence of a crime, I said, "I Sophia Manori, carry the bloodline of Vadim Preda; I also carry the blood of Marcus Manori. Since both bloodlines run through my veins, I claim the right of blood vengeance for the killing of Dante Manori, as well as the attempted murder of Nora, Sara, and Marcus Manori, and for the kidnapping of Merek Preda, son of Vadim Preda, a crime committed buy your ancestor."

"Vladimir Németh, your life is forfeit."

I kneeled over him and placed the point of the stake against his chest over his heart. I cradled his head in my other hand, forcing him to look into my eyes. He managed to let out a slight moan as I shoved the stake home.

I rose slowly to my feet as his body began to disintegrate. My shoulders slumped, and Sara rushed to my side. I put my arm around her. "It is finished," I said weakly.

"Hold it right there!" a familiar voice yelled from the top of the stairs. I looked up and saw Devin holding a compound crossbow trained directly at Sara. The arrow's tip gleamed in the dim light, and I knew in a flash that it was filled with poison.

I had completely forgotten about him. Apparently, my venom had worn off and he still wanted to fight. I turned to face him and said as calmly as I could, "Look around, Devin, It's over. Vladimir is dead."

"It may be over for you, but I still have a score to settle."

"Don't be stupid. If you shoot any of us, you will die. It's not worth it. Go home Devin, please."

"No, *you* don't be stupid, Sophia," he said sarcastically. "Vladimir told me how you saved Nora, so I created a new poison. It will kill any of you damn vampires much quicker than before, and you won't be able to flush it out by a blood transfusion. Tell me again, Sophia, that I'm stupid." He glared at me with a wild light in his eyes.

"Now I want everyone to leave except for you and the blonde. Otherwise, I'll kill her right now. And don't think I can't see you trying to flank me!" he shouted at Nikolai, who had started edging toward the shadows.

"Okay, Devin," I said. "We'll do it your way. Everyone will leave except me and Sara." I nodded at Father, and the rest of the family backed slowly out through the front door. "There," I said. "Are you happy now?"

He laughed a horrible laugh. "Happy? Am I happy? Do you have any idea what you did to me? You don't, do you?" The insane grin faded from his face. In a strangely dead voice, he said, "I want you to feel the same pain that I felt when she took you away from me. You see, I was there in the barn the day she attacked you, and I know she was in the rafters watching." With anger in his eyes he looked at Sara. "You were the one who turned Sophia against me. So now, you are going to die."

Before I could react, the crossbow twanged, and his arrow sliced through the air. It struck Sara's left side with a dull thud, and she doubled over.

I let out an incoherent scream and leaped from the first floor to the top of the stairs in a single stride, mouth gaping wide with fangs extended. My teeth snapped shut on Devin's throat. I jerked my head back, tearing free a large piece of flesh. Devin gasped for breath, but it was no use. I had crushed his windpipe. His body stayed upright for a moment, staring at me with dead eyes, and then fell to the floor.

Sara was already unconscious when I reached her side. She let out a low moan as I rolled her over to examine the wound, but her eyes didn't open. The barbed arrow was lodged firmly between her lower ribs. I had to twist it horribly before I could ease it free.

I cradled the limp body of my sire and sister in my arms and cried out, "Oh no you don't, Sara. You can't do this to me. Come on, sis, wake up. We still have to take our trip to Hawaii, remember? Come on. I need you.

"Father!" I screamed. "Father!"

Father rushed into the room, the rest of the family behind him. "We need the IV kit. Sara has been shot with a poison arrow."

Nikolai wasted no time. He ran back to the limousine, drove it up to the front of the mansion, and grabbed the medical kit out of the trunk.

We found a bedroom upstairs with two beds and moved Sara there to begin the process of purging the poison from her blood. When it wasn't my turn to give blood, I held Sara's hand and talked to her.

Hours passed, but there was no sign that Sara was responding to the transfusion. Her face was paler than I had ever seen it, and her breathing was shallow.

"I don't know what more we can do," said Father. He secured the curtains over the window on the room's east wall as he spoke. Pink light was bleeding into the eastern sky; the sun would be up soon.

"You can't mean you're giving up hope," I said.

"Of course not," said Father. "I just don't know what more we can do, that's all."

"We keep going, that's what we do. We keep going."

I lay back on the bed next to Sara and brushed a stray strand of hair out of her face. The gesture sparked a memory of lying on another bed next to my brother Josh one summer when he was just four years old and had been bitten by a copperhead. The doctor had come and—I slapped my hand to my forehead. "Antivenin," I said.

"What?" said Father.

"Antivenin!" I sprang up from the bed. "I'm such an idiot. The main ingredient in Devin's poison is snake venom. No vet would work with poisonous snakes without having some antivenin around. Devin must have had some at the mortuary," I said. "If it survived the fire, there has to be some there—it's where the snakes are."

It was daylight outside, so none of us would be rummaging through the burned ruin of the mortuary any time soon.

"Randolph!" shouted Father.

After a moment, he appeared at the top of the stairs. "Yes, sir?" he replied.

"I need you to go to the Németh mortuary and see if you can find any antivenin in a secret room there. Sophia will tell you where to look."

"Right away, sir." Without any hesitation, Randolph hurried down the stairs. I quickly drew him a diagram showing where the secret room was and explained what to look for concerning the antivenin. He then grabbed the piece of paper and ran out the front door.

"I must give that man a raise," muttered Father.

It was a nerve-wracking wait. Sara's breath grew shallower and shallower as the minutes ticked by. I sat on the edge of her bed, clasping her hand, hoping desperately that Randolph would find what we needed. Carmilla met my gaze over our sister's body, and I could tell she was almost as worried as I was.

A little over an hour passed before we finally heard footsteps running up the stairs. Randolph appeared a moment later with a bottle clutched in his hand. He was out of breath, and his face was red. "This was the only thing I could find," he said. "I hope it works."

I examined the bottle and exclaimed, "This is it." I then kissed Randolph on the cheek and said, "You may have just saved Sara's life."

I gave the bottle to Carmilla, who filled a syringe with the yellow liquid and injected it into an IV bag full of human blood. We waited until the bag was empty, but there was no response. She them doubled the dosage in a new bag of blood, and again we waited.

Finally, after almost two hours, Sara groaned. I took her hand, and I felt her squeeze back.

"It's working," said Father. "Keep it up!"

About twenty minutes later Sara's eyes fluttered open. "Did we win?" she asked. Her voice was slurred, but it was the most beautiful sound I had ever heard.

I threw my arms around her and wept.

"What's the matter, silly?"

"I thought I'd lost you," I said through my tears. "Don't you ever do that to me again."

She smiled weakly and simply said, "Okay."

26. Nightmares

S ara recovered quickly once we got her back home. Within a week, she was back to her old self. Then one evening while we were sitting in the living room enjoying a glass of blood, Sara turned to me and said, "How are you doing, sis? We haven't talked much since the battle."

"I'm okay—I guess."

"You put on quite a show back at the Németh mansion. Do you remember everything you said to Lord Németh?"

I looked down. "Yes, I remember everything." I said softly.

"I can't believe you went against Father's wishes and tasted Lord Németh's blood."

"Yeah, I can't either, but I just couldn't help myself. I saw the vial there on the table and it was as if I was compelled to do it. But after I saw Lord Németh's memories, everything began to make sense."

"Well, it probably saved our lives," said Sara.

I slowly looked up at Sara. "You know, ever since the battle, I have been having nightmares."

"Do you want to talk about it?" asked Sara.

I shrugged. "I don't know. I guess."

Sara walked over and sat next to me on the couch.

"Are they nightmares about the battle?"

"No, and that's what's bothering me. I have been having horrible nightmare about things I have never seen or heard of before.

"Last night, for instance, I dreamed I was wearing armor and riding a horse, along with about a dozen other vampires. We stood on a hill that overlooked a village of humans. We rushed down upon the village and mercilessly fed off the humans there. I heard their screams as clearly as I'm talking to you now, Sara. I could even smell the warm blood in the cold night air as it poured from their veins.

"Then a young man—a boy, really—lunged at me with a wooden pitchfork. His face was pale in the starlight, smudged with dirt and soot. I could feel his fear, yet I felt joy, like it was nothing more than a game. I snatched the weapon from the boy with one hand and lifted him off the ground with the other. My fangs sank into his neck, and I drank until the life left his body. I carelessly tossed him aside and then rode off laughing. That's when I woke up."

"This may sound a little strange, but maybe your dreams are the memories of this Vadim Preda," said Sara. "You have acquired most of his abilities, so it would only make sense that you would share some of his memories as well."

"I suppose that could be it. I don't really care where they're coming from. I just want them to stop."

Sara put her arm around me, and I leaned against her shoulder. After a moment, I asked, "Do you think I'm a bad person, Sara?"

"What? Why would I think that?"

"After you were shot, I killed Devin. I didn't even hesitate. I was so filled with hate that nothing could have stopped me from killing him."

Sara grabbed me by the shoulders and looked me in the eyes. "Listen to me, Sophia," she said. "He tried to kill me, and I'm sure he would have done the same to you. He was insane, and there was no other way to stop him. You did the right thing. You have nothing to feel guilty about."

"I guess," I said. "It's just—in these dreams, I'm killing many people, and I'm enjoying it. I don't want to be like that."

"They're just dreams," said Sara. "They may be unpleasant, but they have nothing to do with whether you're good or bad. What you do in this life determines that."

I leaned against Sara's shoulder again. "Thanks," I said. "I needed to hear that."

After my conversation with Sara, I hoped the nightmares would go away, but I woke up screaming twice more that week. Both times, Sara heard me and rushed to my room, and her face was the first thing I saw when I opened my eyes.

Then one night, the unthinkable happened. In my dream, I was in a feeding frenzy. I chased a teenage girl down a hallway and into a room. The window was open, and moonlight streamed into the room. She dived for the window, but I caught her by the hair and dragged her back into the room. She struggled wildly, kicking and flailing her fists at me, but I overpowered her easily. Her head fell back, and my fangs pierced the soft skin of her throat. When I was done, I tossed her against the wall and walked out of the room laughing.

When I woke up, the first thing I realized was that there was still blood all over my chin and chest. The second was that I was strapped down tightly on the bed with thick leather restraints. I pulled and tried to wriggle free, but the leather was too strong, and the straps were pulled so tight that they dug into my flesh.

There was movement to my left, and Nikolai stepped out of the shadows. He was holding a crossbow.

"What the hell is going on?" I said.

"Good," he said. "You're awake. How are you feeling?"

"Okay, I think. Why am I tied up?"

"You almost killed Sara."

"What?" Panic gripped me, and I pushed against the restraints. "Is she all right?"

"She will be, no thanks to you," said Nikolai. "You fed off her and threw her against the wall. You mean to tell me you don't remember anything?"

"I was dreaming," I said softly. "There was a girl, and I fed, and …" The words trailed off into nothing. How could I have hurt Sara? I loved her. "She's really okay?"

"Yeah." Nikolai put the crossbow down on my dresser and started to unbuckle the restraints.

"How did it happen?" I asked.

"She heard you screaming again and came to check on you." He shrugged uncomfortably and glanced at me sideways as he freed my ankles. "You were still latched onto her neck when Father and I got here and managed to pull you off. She's in her room. You should probably go talk to her once you're cleaned up."

I found Sara sitting up in bed. Her face was pale, and she was still hooked up to an IV bag of blood. I was in shock.

"Oh God," I said as I covered my mouth. "I'm so sorry."

"It's okay," said Sara. "You were having another nightmare. I know you wouldn't ever hurt me on purpose." She held out her hand to me, and I stepped forward and took it in both of mine.

"I can't believe I did that," I said softly.

"It's okay, sis. I forgive you."

"No, it's not okay," I said, squeezing her hand tightly. "Promise you'll strap me down before I go to sleep from now on. I don't want to hurt anyone, especially not you."

"Father had the same idea," said Sara. "Since you're so much stronger than the rest of us, it's probably safest to restrain you during the day while you're sleeping, at least until you get over these nightmares."

I nodded. I felt so guilty that I wanted to go hide in my room.

"I'm so sorry," I said again.

"I said I forgive you," said Sara. "It's been a while, but I've been hurt much worse than this. You just caught me off guard."

"Sara," I said, "I want you to promise me something. If you ever think I'm a danger to anyone, I want you to do whatever it takes to stop me, okay? Even if you have to kill me."

"Oh, shut up," she said, smiling at me. "Come give me a hug, and then I want to try and get some sleep."

When I got back to my room, I sat on the edge of my bed and buried my face in my hands. What was happening to me? I felt like I was losing control and had no idea how to stop it.

I stayed in my room all night, too embarrassed to face the rest of the family. Then just before sunrise, Sara came and strapped me into my bed. I knew it was necessary—I even wanted her to do it—but it made me feel like some rabid animal that had to be locked away each night. I stared at the ceiling as she tightened the restraints, and a single tear rolled down my face. When all the straps were secure, she kissed me on the cheek and silently left the room.

It took me a long time to fall asleep, and I prayed that I wouldn't have another nightmare. Unfortunately, that didn't happen. I dreamed I was in a torture chamber and saw a young man tied by his hands and feet, stretched out on a rack. With a shock, I realized it was Devin—my nightmares were now beginning to merge with my own memories. At my command, the dungeon master turned a wheel that pulled Devin's body taut. Devin's screams and sobs echoed throughout the dungeon while I stood over him, smiling.

Long before sunset I woke up, weeping. I lay there in the darkened room, and my thoughts chased one another around in circles. I knew that these nightmares weren't going to go away on their own. I had to do something. Then I remembered the image of Vadim Preda in the old leather book Father had shown me when he first told me about my bloodline. If these really were Vadim Preda's memories I was dreaming, maybe learning more about him would help them go away. Psychiatrists sometimes cure nightmares by helping patients recover repressed memories of traumatic events from their childhood. Maybe this would work for me in the same way. At least it seemed worth a try.

When Sara came to undo my restraints, I was still awake. "Did you sleep at all?" she asked.

"A little," I said. "I had another nightmare."

She stroked my cheek before she undid the last leather strap that bound me to the bed. "Oh, Sophia," she said gently. "What are we going to do with you?"

I was famished, so I left Sara and went to find some blood. No one else was in the parlor, and I wondered if the rest of the family were avoiding me. I couldn't blame them. Every night my screams echoed through the house, and then there was what I had done to Sara. Clearly, I wasn't easy to be around.

When my thirst was satisfied, I trotted off toward the library to ask Father if I could borrow his book. When I was still several paces down the hall, I heard voices. I stopped and listened.

"—but what else can we do?" Father was saying. "Both you and Nora would probably be dead without Sophia, and you know I love her dearly, but if we can't figure out how to control these nightmares—"

"I understand, Father, but it isn't her fault," said Sara's voice. "She didn't choose this—she didn't even want to become a vampire! There must be something that can be done to purge these nightmares from her mind. Maybe it's just a myth, but I've heard of something called *kohinoor*—"

"Silence!" Father roared. Even out in the hall, I jumped at the intensity in his voice. "Never speak that word again. It is forbidden. Do you understand?"

"Yes, Father, but—"

"No, there is no *but*. By law of the vampire council created centuries ago, assassins have orders to kill any vampire that seeks the path of kohinoor. If Lord Illyrius hears that you have so much as mentioned the path of kohinoor, his assassins will hunt you down. Forget you ever heard the word. The last thing I need is to have to worry about you too."

"Yes, Father."

I decided I'd heard enough and backed quietly down the hall. Questions swirled through my head. What could possibly make Lord Illyrius so afraid that even saying its name was enough to get you killed? Whatever this kohinoor was, if there was a chance that it could stop my nightmares, I was willing to give it a try. *Lord Illyrius and his assassins can just go to hell.* My only problem was if it was forbidden to even talk about, how could I learn about it?

27. Fragments

Another day went by with me strapped to my bed, and with it came another nightmare. Since I had no idea where to find any information on the path of kohinoor, I decided to go with my first idea and learn as much as I could about Vadim Preda.

After Sara unstrapped me, I got dressed and headed to the library to ask Father if I could borrow any books with information about Vadim Preda. To my surprise, he wasn't there, and the grate in the fireplace was cold. That usually meant that he was away for the evening on business. I decided to try and find the old leather book myself.

As I scanned the shelves, a massive book on the top of one of the shelves caught my eye. It was obvious from its dried yellowed cover that it was far older than any of the other books on the shelves. I never could resist investigating something once my curiosity had been aroused, so I slid the ladder over to where the book was and climbed to the top shelf.

The book looked even older up close. The wooden boards of the covers were weathered and cracked, and it was fastened shut with dark iron bands and an iron lock almost as big as my fist. At some point, it must have gotten damp, because the iron was rusted, and ugly brown stains had tarnished the wood. A thick layer of dust covered the entire upper shelf; I wondered how long it had been sitting there undisturbed.

I gently lifted the heavy book from its place and climbed down the ladder to one of Father's wingback chairs. For a moment, I was concerned about the lock, but when I gave it a tug, it fell apart. The inner workings must have rusted away long ago. Carefully, I opened the book and began to turn the delicate parchment pages.

Many of the pages had intricate illuminations, and I guessed the writing was medieval. It was hard to make out, but I thought it looked like Latin. It was fascinating, of course, but it was not what I was looking for. I tore my eyes away from a drawing of a fox chasing a group of animals across the bottom of a page and shut the book. As it closed, three frayed and yellowed leaves of some fibrous paper fell from between the pages and onto my lap.

They were covered in a strange script scrawled in faded brown ink. Somehow, I knew at once that it was the language of the original elders of the vampire council; maybe having Vadim Preda's memories knocking around in my head was good for something after all.

Once I recognized the script, I had to know what it said. I pulled out my phone and photographed each of the ancient pages. I tried to be as gentle as I could, but even so, the edges of the leaves cracked and crumbled at my touch. I wondered how old they were and how long they had been tucked away in that medieval book. Judging from the paper, the leaves could have been in there for centuries. I'm sure they were much older than the book itself. When I was done, I put them back inside the book and returned it to the shelf.

I told no one what I had found—not even Sara. Somehow, I instinctively knew that there was something dangerous about what I had found. Whatever the reason, I felt a strong compulsion to keep my discovery secret.

I spent the rest of the night in my room trying to puzzle out the meaning of the text using Internet sources and the bits and pieces of Vadim Preda's memories I could dredge up from my subconscious. My curiosity soon became an obsession; I had to know what those three pages said.

At last, after almost a week of nights spent constantly on the computer, alone in my room, of days strapped down on my bed while nightmares wracked my mind, I came up with what I felt was an accurate translation:

It appeared to be a story about what happened to Cain after he killed his brother Abel in the book of Genesis.

(Page1)

... and so it came to pass that in the course of his wandering Cain met up with a demon. Cain begged the demon to slay him, for he had grown weary of his many years of suffering.
"Thou bears the mark of God, Cain, therefore I cannot sly thee."
Then was Cain sorely grieved, and he wept.
"Though I cannot slay thee, I can hide thee perhaps even from the eyes of God.
"If thee drink of my blood thou eyes will be open,
"If thee drink of my blood you will be have great power,
"If thee drink of my blood thou shall have dominion over all the creatures of the earth, thy suffering then may be abated."
Cain's heart was glad, and he agreed to drink the blood of the demon, and so the demon cut himself with a sharp stone and spilled his blood into a bowl made of wood of which ...

(Page 2)

... and the demon then laughed, saying, "Hearken unto thy blood: it cries out from within for more. How wilt thou replenish it? But truly, when thou hast drunk of the blood of man, which is the life of him, thy strength will be as the strength of a ten men and you will have all that I promised."
Cain was then wroth with great pain. He suffered greatly. And he became like a thing that crawled upon the earth. He shunned the light and cleaved to the darkness; and he drank of the blood of the sons of man to ease his pain but he ...

(Page 3)

... and when he saw the Angel, Cain was afraid.

The angel said, "Fear not, Cain, for the Lord has made a way out of darkness for thee, and the way will be called the path of kohinoor, the path to the mountain of light."
And Cain hid himself from the Angel's face, and he said, "But how can this be? For I am cursed with a great curse, and my sins weigh heavy upon me."
The Angel spoke unto him again, saying, "You speak the truth, Cain, but there is always hope for those who wander in the dark. Beware thou, for the path is hard, and the way is set about with sharp thorns that will pierce thy flesh and thy mind. Seek this path, O Cain, if thou wouldst be redeemed in the ..."

That was as far as the story went; the rest of the text had deteriorated to the point that it was unintelligible. I wasn't naive enough to take the text at face value, but it did seem obvious that the author wanted to document Cain as the first vampire. The mention of the path of kohinoor sent a chill down my spine. Could there actually be a way for vampires to find their way back to the light, to become human again? Maybe it was just a story, but then why was it against the law to even to speak the word? There had to be something to it.

I thought it strange that the day after I overheard Sara mention the work kohinoor that I find a story about that very thing. Was I somehow meant to find it? It just seemed too much of a coincidence. Nevertheless, I was surprised to find that the idea of becoming human again filled me with hope. How could that be? I loved my new family, and I was more powerful than I had ever dreamed possible. Even so, since becoming a vampire I had to fight for my life many times over. *Will my life always be this way? And now with these nightmares ... what more can I endure?*

Unfortunately, my research was at a standstill; I didn't know where to look for more information about kohinoor. If a person could get into trouble just by mentioning the word, I was sure there would be no books about it in Father's library. I had reached a dead end.

The next evening, I woke up screaming again. Tears streamed down my face as Sara unfastened the leather straps that held me to the bed.

"I can't keep living like this," I said.

Sara undid the last restraint and sat beside me on the bed, cradling me in her arms. "I know," she said. She tucked a stray strand of hair gently behind my ear. "Have you tried talking to Father about it? Maybe he'll have some ideas you haven't tried yet."

I wiped my tears and nodded. "I guess it can't hurt," I said.

When I was dressed, I went straight to the library. Father was seated in his usual place in front of the fire. I knocked softly on the open door.

"Come in," he said.

"Hello, Father. Do you have a few minutes to talk with me?"

"Of course, Sophia. Come in and have a seat.

As I sat down, Father asked, "How are you feeling, my dear? Still having nightmares?"

"Yes," I said. "That's what I came to talk to you about. I can't go on like this, Father." I felt a sense of despair creep into my voice and took a deep breath to calm myself. "None of the family speaks to me anymore, and even Sara does not know what to say to me. I don't blame them, but I do not want to live where I am not wanted. Please, Father, is there no one you know who can help me?"

Father reached over and took my hand. "Your brothers and sisters still love you," he said. "They just don't know how to comfort you. Each of them has come to me and asked what they can do, but I have no answers for them."

Tears filled my eyes. "Father, if there's nothing you can do for me, then send me away. There must be an asylum or ... or someplace where at least I won't be able to hurt anyone. I can't live this way anymore. Please just send me away." He offered me his handkerchief, and I paused to blow my nose.

"My dear Sophia," said Father, "I love you like my own flesh and blood. How can I possibly send you away? And besides, where would I send you?"

"I don't know," I sobbed, "but there has to be something you can do."

Father let out a heavy sigh and stared into the crackling fire for a long time. He then got up, walked over to the heavy wooden door to his library, and slowly closed it. As he took his seat next to me he said quietly, "There is ... someone ... who might be able to help," he said hesitantly.

"Who?" I asked.

"A woman. I don't know her name, but she calls herself the White Swan. I met her many years ago. She's very gifted, and she knows a lot about our kind, but she opposes everything the vampire community stands for. The question is will she want to help you. Also, if word got out that you were looking for her ..." He let the sentence dangle in the air unfinished and looked at me with a serious expression. "Sophia, this is not something I would recommend if you didn't seem so desperate. It's dangerous, for you and for the family."

I almost laughed through my tears. "More dangerous than me hurting someone else in the family if I were to break free in my sleep?" I asked.

"Yes," he said. "You would be killed." There was absolute conviction in his voice. "Knowing that, are you still willing to risk contacting her?"

On hearing that I could be killed, I instantly went numb. Father was serious, but I could see no other opinions. I had to take the risk. I wiped the tears from my face with my hand, and with conviction in my voice I said, "Yes, Father, I am."

"Very well," said Father. "It will have to be done carefully. All I have is an e-mail address. I don't know if it is still an active account or even how often she checks it. And it wouldn't surprise me if Lord Illyrius has spies monitoring her communications."

"Then how can we get her a message?"

"We'll have to word it carefully and send it from a public location." He thought for a moment. "How about, 'The noble lady seeks the White Swan.' That's not too incriminating, but it should be enough for her to find you. I know she has people that keep tabs on the vampire community and report to her."

"All right," I said. "Then what happens?"

"Then we wait. It could take some time, Sophia—maybe even months. I think it would be best for all of us if you were away from the family while you wait for an answer. If somehow it does get out that you're looking for the White Swan, your presence here could put your siblings in danger."

"Okay," I said. "Where should I go?"

"I have an apartment that I use in New York City when I am there on business. You could stay there while we wait for a return message from the White Swan. That way you won't feel like a burden to the family."

"I appreciate that, Father, but what about my nightmares?"

"I have thought about that as well. I own the apartment building, so I can easily have the basement there turned into a bedroom. Of course, you would still have to be strapped down at night, but at least we will be doing something to get you some help. Don't give up hope, Sophia," Father said. "I have not given up on you."

"What about my screams?" I asked. "Is the room soundproof?"

"Unfortunately, it is not, but I have come up with another idea that may help soften your screams during your nightmares."

Father reached into a pouch against the wall and pulled out a piece of black cloth. "You know, sometimes the simplest ideas work the best. Here, put this over your head and let the fabric cover your mouth."

Father handed me what looked like a ski mask. He helped me pull it over my head and down over my mouth. It did not hurt, and I was able to breathe without any problem.

"Now say something," said Father.

I started talking; I could easily move my mouth, but I could hardly hear myself talk at all.

Father smiled. "I can't hear a word you're saying. Now yell as loud as you can."

I yelled a couple of times as loudly as I could, yet I could barely hear myself.

"Do you think you can sleep with that on?"

I took the mask off and said, "Yes, Father. I could sleep with this on with no problem. It does not bind me at all. Did you come up with idea?"

"No, my dear. Let's just say some of your old friends back at the homeland came up with it."

I gave him a slow understanding nod.

"There are a couple more things we must discuss, Sophia. I have a trusted servant who lives in the same apartment building. I will inform him of the situation and have him strap you down each morning and then undo your bindings each night. I will also have him text me every morning and evening so that I know you are okay. If I do not receive a text, I will send someone over to the apartment."

Father smiled at me. "And if you're there for more than a week or two, I hope you won't mind if your old man stops by from time to time. I'm going to miss you, my dear."

I gave him a hug and said, "Thank you, Father. As you said, at least we are trying something. Now I have some hope."

"Don't thank me yet," said Father. "I still don't know if this will work. But if it doesn't, we'll try something else. You're going to get through this, Sophia." He rose from his chair, gave me a courtly bow, and said, "I am at your service, lady Manori."

I laughed but did not want to spoil the moment, so I stood up, curtsied back, and said in my most regal tone, "You honor me, my lord, with your kindness. I will be forever grateful." Then Father turned around like a servant, left the library, and went upstairs. I gave a long sigh of relieve after he left the library, thankful that I would not have to be put somewhere for insane vampires, if there was such a place.

28. THE WHITE SWAN

The next evening I started packing, getting ready for my move to the Big Apple. New York was always a fun place to visit, but I never would choose to live there. I loved the outdoors too much, and New York was so crowded, yet I knew I was going there for a reason and hoped that I wouldn't have to be there very long.

By the end of the week, I was all packed and ready for my big move. As I got ready to leave, no one except for Sara and Father came to wish me luck or even say good-bye. Only Sara was there by my side. She wanted to come with me and see the apartment.

"Tell everyone good-bye for me and that I will miss them," I said to Father.

Father just gave me a quick hug and said, "I will, my dear. Have a good trip. I will come by next week to see how you are doing."

As Sara and I got into the back of the limo, I sat close to her and rested my head on her shoulder. "Thanks for coming with me," I said.

"Of course, sis. Can you tell me the real reason you're going to New York? Father just said that it was for the safety of the family. There has to be more to it than that."

"Well," I said. "Father just thought it would do me some good to be on my own for a while. Since all my abilities were brought out at the mansion as I trained with each member of the family, he thought that a change in my environment might help."

"Well, that's a load of crap," said Sara boldly. "But don't worry, I won't ask any more questions. I know Father well enough to trust him." I didn't say anything. I knew that my silence would confirm exactly what Sara was thinking.

Once we arrived at the apartment, I could not believe how beautiful it was. I had the entire top floor of the apartment building. There were two bedrooms, a large living room, a kitchen, and even a formal dining room. The most amazing thing was the view. The balcony looked out over Central Park. Being up away from everyone with the smell of trees was going to make my stay much easier.

Sara looked out over the balcony. "I think I'm jealous."

"You know, sis, you can stay here if you want," I said.

"I just might take you up on that. I'm starting to get claustrophobic cooped up in the mansion every day."

Just then, there was a knock on the door. I opened it, and a human male stood next to Randolph.

"Miss Sophia," said Randolph. "This is Justin. He is the person your father spoke of who will help you during your stay. He understands the situation and is happy to help."

He reached out his hand and said, "It's a pleasure to meet you, Miss Sophia. This must be Miss Sara. Your father has told me so much about you both. I am happy to finally meet you."

"It is a pleasure to meet you, Justin. You can call me Sophia."

"Very well then, Sophia. I see Randolph has brought up your things. Is there anything I can do for you?"

"Not right now, Justin," I replied, "but thank you for asking. Just come back about an hour before sunset. I'd like to see the basement and make it as comfortable as possible before I go to bed."

Justin smiled. "Yes, I understand completely. Well, if you do not need me, I will go back to my apartment. I live in the apartment just one floor down from you. If you need me just use the intercom. It's over there by the kitchen door, and here is my cell phone number in case I am out."

As soon as Justin left the apartment, Sara said, "We need to get back on the road if we want to make it back home before sunrise."

"Of course, I understand. Thanks for coming with me, sis. You don't know how much you mean to me."

Sara gave me a hug, and Randolph gave a slight bow. As the door closed behind them, I suddenly felt completely alone.

I went into the kitchen, poured myself a glass of blood, and walked out onto the balcony. It was a chilly September night, and I cradled the warm glass of blood in my hand, listening to the city's ever-present traffic noise far below.

Before I knew it Justin came knocking on the door, and we both headed down to the basement. I was surprised to see that there was already a sturdy bed there with restraints.

"Your father wanted to make sure you were comfortable, Miss Sophia. I hope it is to your liking."

"Yes, Justin, it is perfect. Thank you. I think it's about time to strap me in."

"Yes, ma'am."

As I lay down on the bed, I put the mask over my mouth and nodded for Justin to strap me in. He asked me if that was tight enough, and I just gave him a nod. Then he said, "I will be here to release you directly at sundown. Sleep well, Miss Sophia." With that said, he closed the steel door as he left the room and locked it.

That night I had another one of my nightmares, but thanks to Father's mask over my mouth I'm sure no one heard me. The next morning, as promised, Justin came in and undid my restraints. I then went upstairs, poured a glass of blood, and waited. That was my routine each and every day.

Almost a month had passed since I sent my e-mail to the White Swan from a computer at the Boston library, and there had been no response. I was quite bored in that apartment all alone. Luckily, I found a nice little bar down the street where I went when I wanted to get out of the apartment. After all my adventures with Sara, not having any social life to speak of took some getting used to.

October arrived, and my nightmares continued. In a way, I was getting used to them; I was able to get some sleep. When I woke from a nightmare, I took a few deep breaths, reminded myself that they were not real, and tried to go back to sleep. Most of the time it worked; but there were times when my nightmares were so bad, all I could do was lay there until morning.

Finally, six weeks after moving to Manhattan, I woke up one evening to find an e-mail waiting for me on my phone. It was just two sentences long: "One night soon there will be a white limousine waiting outside your apartment. Tell no one."

I lurked around the apartment all that night waiting for the limousine to appear, but it didn't come. I waited again the next night and the next. After that, I decided I might as well go out; there was no point hanging around every night if nothing was going to happen. For all I knew, the White Swan thought *soon* meant any time in the next decade.

The week before Halloween, I was walking home from the bar around three in the morning when a large, muscular man stepped out of an alley right in front of me. The streetlights gleamed off his bald scalp, and he didn't seem to have much of a neck—just massive shoulders that jutted out to either side right below his ears. I sensed right away that he was a vampire.

"What you're doing is forbidden," he said gruffly. "Contact that witch again, and you'll regret it. Do I make myself clear?"

Before I could respond, there were a couple of thumps behind me, and I glanced back to see two more vampires about fifteen feet behind me on the sidewalk. They must have dropped from a nearby rooftop. I cursed myself inwardly for being so careless.

"I haven't the foggiest notion what you're talking about," I said aloud, opening my eyes wide in mock innocence. "But if you boys want to play, I'm sure that can be arranged." As I spoke, I heard the two vampires behind me edging closer.

The big one in front of me pulled a wooden stake from inside his jacket and held it under my nose. "Mock me again," he growled.

That was one foolish vampire. Before he knew it I had snatched the stake from his hands. I sidestepped and spun with my arm outstretched, burying the stake in the chest of one of the two vampires charging me from behind. He doubled over, spewing blood onto the sidewalk. I ducked as the big one with the shaved head tried to hit me. I jumped back far enough to keep my two remaining assailants in front of me.

I didn't really want to kill them, but they knew I was looking for the White Swan. I couldn't let them live. The big vampire who had first confronted me took another swing. I jerked my head out of the path of his fist and sank my fangs into his forearm. He howled in pain as my venom coursed into his veins. I leaped away, and he fell on his face.

The last vampire was a bit scrawny compared to the others. He was wearing a leather jacket and had black, slicked-back hair, no doubt trying to compensate for his small size with a tough-guy look. He took one look at his fallen companions, turned, and ran.

The vampire I had staked had already turned to dust, so I picked up the wooden stake from his ashes and threw it overhand like a knife. It struck just below the fleeing vampire's left shoulder blade with a dull thud, and he sprawled forward onto the concrete.

I grabbed the big vampire by the collar and dragged him into the alley, out of the sight of any passing cars. Then I sat on his back and waited for my venom to wear off. When his burbling noises started to sound almost like words, I rolled him over and pushed my knee against his chest. "All right, big guy," I said, "who sent you?"

His eyes rolled in their sockets, and a little saliva bubbled out of the corner of his mouth, but he didn't say anything.

I slapped him across the face, hoping it might sober him up a bit. "Come on. I haven't got all night."

"I can't say," he slurred. "He'll kill me."

"Yeah? Well, so will I. The only difference is I'll do it sooner. So start talking."

He shook his head violently and clenched his teeth. I could tell I wasn't going to get anything out of him. Unless ... all of a sudden various implements of torture from my nightmares paraded in front of my mind's eye. I turned my head to one side and spat as if I had a foul taste in my mouth. My nightmares must be influencing me even, while I was awake, if I was seriously considering torture. This White Swan woman had better show up soon.

I looked down at the vampire. My venom must have worn off almost completely by then, but he still wasn't struggling. He was soaked in sweat and trembling; he knew he was about to die.

"Guess what?" I said. "It's your lucky day." I bent down and bit him almost tenderly in the neck. When I had injected a massive dose of venom, I stood up and wiped my mouth with the back of my hand. "Well, that should keep you from following me home," I said. "I don't expect it'll matter, but if you could tell whoever

FAITH OF A VAMPIRE

sent you to back the hell off, I'd appreciate it." Then I turned and trotted off into the night.

When I got back to my apartment building, to my surprise there was a white limo waiting out front. As I approached, a uniformed driver got out and opened the door for me. "Good evening, ma'am. I believe you've been expecting us."

I paused and looked through the open door of the limousine. I could see only a silhouette of a woman. I looked back up at the driver, who wore an impatient look on his face.

This had to be the White Swan, the one person who could possibly help me. I slowly slid into the backseat, and I found myself sitting next to an attractive woman who looked like she was in her early forties. She had curly blonde hair, and her hazel eyes seemed to shine even in the darkness of the limo. "Hello, Sophia," she said. "I understand you need my help. My name is Clarice."

She held out her hand, and I shook it. As soon as I felt her hand in mind, I sensed a feeling of trust and compassion that almost overwhelmed me.

"So," said Clarice. "What's your story?" She flashed me a smile, and her white teeth gleamed in the dark.

It sounded like a casual question, but it must have flipped the right switch, because it all poured out. The driver took us on a meandering ride through the city while I told my story. I told Clarice everything, starting with the day Sara showed up on my doorstep and ending with the fight just before I discovered the limo in front of my apartment.

"I don't know what's happening to me," I concluded. "Tonight—tonight I thought for a minute about actually torturing someone for information. I feel like I'm turning into some kind of monster."

"You're a vampire," said Clarice. "Fighting, killing—these things are part of what you are. But there's also a part of you that's human. Your humanity is fighting against the instincts of a vampire, but because of your dhampir bloodline, you are also fighting against the will of this Vadim Preda."

I hung my head, ashamed of what I had become. "Is there anything you can do to help me?"

"That depends on you," she said. "What are you willing to do to purge yourself of these nightmares and quiet the beast within you?"

My head snapped up, and I looked Clarice in the eyes. "Anything," I said. "I would do anything short of selling my soul, anything you could ask of me."

"What I teach is called the path of kohinoor," said Clarice. "You may have heard of it."

A thrill of excitement shot through me. I nodded.

"The path of kohinoor isn't for the weak or faint-hearted," said Clarice. "If you agree to take this path, you will suffer more than you have ever suffered before. You may even wish you could die. However, I have been watching you. You have a good heart and a strong spirit, and I wouldn't offer to help you if I didn't think you could take it, but I need you to understand that it won't be easy."

I started to tell Clarice that I understood, but she wasn't finished.

"I want to make it completely clear what this will cost," she said. "If you accept my help and follow it to its end, you will no longer be a vampire. You will be human once again. You will lose all your special abilities; you will once again be mortal." She fixed her hazel eyes on me. "There is one more condition that you must agree to. You will have to leave everything behind—your vampire family, your vampire father, and your sire, Sara. If you choose to come with me, you must never see them again. Think carefully, Sophia. I will not give you a second chance. You must decide tonight before you leave this limousine. Do you have any questions?"

"Just one, Miss Clarice. If I leave with you, my family will be worried. They will no doubt come looking for me. May I send them a message simply that I am all right?"

"Sophia, if the vampire council finds out that you have gone with me, your entire family would be in danger. However, since Sara sired you and Lord Manori sired Sara, you three share a common blood bond. If you were to die tonight, they would both know it. If you simply disappear, you would actually be protecting your vampire family. I know that Lord Manori helped you to find me, so he will no doubt know that you are with me. Remember that if you agree to go with me you can never return to see your vampire family again. So Sophia, what is your answer?"

I swallowed hard and stared through the window of the limousine at the streets of New York. I knew I could endure whatever suffering was required, but to never see Sara again? Tears stung my eyes, and I felt like my heart was breaking. But then I remembered waking up to find that I had nearly killed her. If the dreams kept getting worse, and especially if they started to take over my waking mind as they had tonight, who knows what I might do? I gritted my teeth.

"I'll go with you, Miss Clarice," I said. "I have no other choice."

29. The Path of Kohinoor

Clarice smiled and told the driver to take them to the airport.

"We are leaving now?" I asked.

"Yes, Sophia, we must. You see, the vampire community watches me constantly. I have no doubt that if you were to return to your apartment, you would be in danger just because you have talked to me."

"I understand, Miss Clarice, but what about my nightmares? The sun will be up soon. If I am not restrained while I sleep I could hurt you."

"Do not be concerned for my safety, my dear. I have all that we need on the plane, even restraints if necessary."

"Yes, ma'am," I said.

The limousine pulled up on the tarmac next to a private jet, and just as the first light of the dawn bled into the eastern sky, we boarded the plane.

The windows inside were closed and curtained. Clarice led me to a compartment at the back of the cabin, where there was a metal-framed bed equipped with leather restraints. She produced a bag of blood from a refrigerator and tossed it to me. "Here," she said. "Drink all of it."

I was famished. I tore open the top of the bag with my teeth and took a huge gulp. It was cold, bitter, and tasted of tin. I gagged and made a face.

"It's pig's blood," said Clarice. "And some herbs mixed in to help you sleep. You had better get used to it, because it's all you're getting from now on. Drink up. I'll be back in a minute to tuck you in."

I choked down the rest of the foul liquid and lay down on the bed. A warm, drowsy feeling spread out through my body, and I closed my eyes.

The next thing I knew, Clarice was standing over me, unfastening my restraints. I stared up at her in confusion. I had no memory of being strapped in. "What's going on?" I asked.

"We're almost there. Time to wake up," said Clarice.

As she unbuckled the last leather strap from around my wrist, I realized I had slept through the whole day without any bad dreams. I almost laughed; it was my first restful sleep in months. I jumped from the steel bed and threw my arms around Clarice's neck without thinking.

She gently pushed me away. "As much as I appreciate your gratitude, I need you to remember that I'm your teacher, not your mother," she said sternly.

A little embarrassed, I nodded, but I couldn't keep the smile off my face.

The jet landed. As the cabin depressurized, warm air rushed onto the plane, carrying with it the lush scent of vegetation and the sharp salt smell of the sea. I followed Clarice out the door into the damp, tropical night.

The runway was surrounded by trees; I couldn't even see any roads leading to it. A little way away up a gentle slope was a house built of stone and wood. I neither saw nor smelled any other sign of civilization.

I followed Clarice down the runway and then along a path through mossy tree trunks to a flight of stone steps leading up to the house. She held the door open for me. The interior was sparsely furnished with a grass rug and a few wicker chairs, and the walls were simple undressed stone.

Clarice motioned for me to take a chair and then sat down across from me. "Before we begin," she said, "I want to tell you a little bit about how this is going to work. The path of kohinoor will push you to your limits—and past them—but if you do as I say, I feel certain you will succeed."

I listened solemnly as Clarice explained what I was about to endure. The first step, it seemed, was to learn to control my emotions. She would intentionally drain my blood in order to put me into a bloodlust, and I had to learn to maintain control of my mind and body despite the beast raging inside me.

"Now," she said, "I have some rules you must follow while you are under my care. Rule one: you can ask questions, but never question my motives or my competence. I have been doing this a long time, and I know what I'm doing.

"Rule two: you are never to enter my home without my permission. If you do, I will end your training and send you back to Boston, where the vampire council will probably question you, and perhaps kill you for what you know.

"Rule three: from this day on, you are never to drink human blood again.

"Rule four: if by some chance we make a mistake and you escape during a bloodlust, I expect you to come back here as soon as you regain control.

"Do you understand these rules?"

"Yes," I said.

"Good. Now let's get started." Clarice rose from her chair, and I followed her through the house and out the back door. She led me down a dirt path past a grove of bamboo to a clearing where tall poles supported a circular roof made of palm leaves woven closely together. Under this roof, six massive stones stood in a circle. Each was about six feet high and three feet wide, and a heavy steel chain stretched from each standing stone to the middle of the circular structure.

Clarice then stopped under the structure and said, "This here is called a *chikee*. Its primary use is to keep the sun off you. Now please stand in the center, Sophia. We must attach these chains to you. Tonight we will force you into a bloodlust. As I said, it is your job to try to control it. We will continue to do this every night until you can control yourself while in a bloodlust and overcome your vampire instincts. It may take you ten times or a thousand times. No matter what, we will not stop until you've achieved your goal."

Two of Clarice's servants appeared, and I allowed them to shackle me to the chains: one to each ankle, one to each wrist, one to my waist, and one around my neck. As long as I stayed in the center of the ring, the chains weren't too uncomfortable, but they prevented me from moving more than a couple of feet in any direction.

"Okay," said Clarice, "we're ready to begin. Hold out your wrist, Sophia."

I did as she asked, and one of the servants stepped forward, drawing a long knife from his belt. He cut my wrist across the vein, and a stream of blood began to flow. When the wound healed, he cut me again.

As the dark blood spilled from my veins and soaked into the earth, I felt panic begin to build in my chest. It wouldn't be long before I would go into a bloodlust, and I knew I had to allow it to happen. Each slice of the knife took longer to heal than the one before as my body became weaker, and a slow burn began to spread throughout my body. My instincts were beginning to take over. My eyes turned back and my fangs extended. Saliva began to form in my mouth, and I stared at the servant's protruding vein in his neck each time he cut me.

"All right," said Clarice. "That's enough."

The servant stepped away just in time. As my instincts took over, I lunged towards him. Fortunately for him I was brought up short by the ring of steel around my neck. My fangs snapped shut on empty air. I watched helplessly, trapped in the recesses of my own mind, as my body struggled and pulled against the restraints. The steel shackles dug into my skin so hard that they drew blood.

From just outside the circle of stones, Clarice watched. "I know you can hear me, Sophia," she cried out. "You must take control. Do not allow the beast to control you. As soon as you can quiet your body and mind, I'll give you more blood, but not before."

My eyes focused on Clarice's face, and I pushed with all my strength against the chains. The metal groaned, and one of the stones tilted a couple of inches in my direction.

Clarice's eyes widened, and she took half a step back, but the restraints held. "I know you're in there, Sophia," she said. "Fight back!"

I heard her, but I was powerless to quiet the beast. I raged long into the night like a wild animal, snapping at Clarice, hissing, and struggling against my shackles. Finally, a little before dawn, my blood-starved body gave out, and I collapsed onto the ground. I lay there, gasping for air, until everything went black.

When I woke up, it was day. I was still chained to the stones. The green roof overhead prevented the sun's rays from falling directly on my skin, but I winced and squinted against the light. My head throbbed and my body ached. I looked around and realized there was an IV in my left arm, and my gaze followed the tube up to a nearly empty bag of blood hanging from a metal stand. I groaned, closed my eyes, and fell back to sleep.

"Good evening," said Clarice's voice.

My eyes snapped open. It was dark; I had slept throughout the day. I staggered to my feet, feeling almost like my normal self again. "Good evening," I mumbled.

"Are you ready to try again?" Clarice said.

I took a deep breath to try to clear my head. I looked around and in a flash it all came back to me. The bloodletting, my bloodlust, and the reason I was there. I looked over at Clarice, took a deep breath, and gave her a nod.

"Good." The servant with the knife appeared, and I offered up my wrist as I had the night before.

Tonight was no better. Again I watched, helpless, trapped in my own mind, as my body raged for blood like a wild animal. All night long, Clarice stood just out of the reach of the chains, calmly urging me to take control, but again I failed.

The next night was the same, and so was the night after that. Blood and sweat stained my clothes, and my unwashed hair formed greasy clumps as the days went by, but my determination never faltered. It is a testament to how bad my nightmares had become. Even though I was living in chains, drinking nothing but animal blood, and being forced into a bloodlust every night, I never once doubted that I had made the right choice.

Finally, when I had been chained to the stones for almost a month, I had my first breakthrough. At first, I tried to break free from my chains like always, but soon instead of struggling to get free I remained in the center of the stone circle. I still kept a defensive posture, crouched down, ready to attack, eyes looking in every direction, but the important thing was my reaction was different.

"So the beast can learn after all," said Clarice, smiling grimly at me. "But is this simply animal cunning, or is Sophia really in control? Only time will tell." She tossed me a couple of bags of blood marked with a red *x*, a reward for my accomplishment. I wolfed them down and slowly came out of my bloodlust.

It was another month before I gained enough control to speak. I was raging at Clarice and pulling against the chains when suddenly I looked her straight in the eyes and croaked out, "I control—me." Then I turned, walked back to the center of the circle, and sat down.

We had both been waiting for this breakthrough. After that day, I was able to communicate with Clarice more and more. Of course, I had my setbacks, but in time, I was able to control myself within a bloodlust.

Then it was on to the next step. It was time for me to learn to control my urge to kill while in a bloodlust. Clarice had determined the exact distance from the chains that bound me to the stones to the point where I could go no further. She then had a servant stand at that point beyond my reach and cut his hand just enough to bleed. As the scent of fresh human blood filled the air, I lost control and lunged for the servant. Time and again I tried to get to my victim. But since Clarice was able to talk to me now during my bloodlust, she was able to help me to control my urge. Finally one day I said to her in a growl, "I am hungry. May I feed?"

My reward was enough blood to take me out of my bloodlust but this time, the *x* was blue. It tasted horrible—even worse than the pig's blood and herb mixture. I coughed and spluttered, spitting some of the foul stuff down the front of my shirt. "What the hell is this?" I shrieked.

"Pig's blood," she said primly, "mixed with pomegranate juice."

I threw the bag against one of the stone pillars, and it exploded like a water balloon, spraying its sticky contents in all directions. Clarice shrugged and walked back to the house, leaving me to my rage. After realizing that the new blood was the only food I was now going to get, I ask for another bag and forced it down.

Despite my setbacks, I made steady progress from that night on. Little by little, I learned to tolerate the pain of the bloodlust, though it affected every nerve in my body.

At last, a full three months after I was first chained to the stones, there came a night when after going into a bloodlust I sat cross-legged in the middle of the circle, completely still, with my gaze fixed on Clarice.

"Very good, Sophia," she said quietly. "You're doing very well. Now you must learn to control your body." In a commanding voice she said, "Retract your fangs."

For almost two weeks, I sat there each night, trying to retract my fangs without results. Then Clarice said to me, "Sophia, you are trying too hard. You need to relax and let your mind do all the work. As a vampire, you can extend and retract your fangs with a simple thought. You should be able to do the same while you are in a bloodlust."

After listening to Clarice's advice, I no longer tried to physically force my fangs to retract. I just imagined it happening. One evening as I sat there focusing, it happened. To my surprise, they simply retracted back into my mouth. I was astonished.

Clarice then picked up four bags of blood and stepped between the stones to where I sat. I tensed, afraid the beast would take over and I would attack her, but my body obeyed me and remained still. She kneeled down, smiled, and placed the bags on the ground in front of me. They were marked with the blue x again. As she stepped away, I grabbed the first bag in my greedy hands and drank until my body returned to normal.

When I had finished the last bag, two servants appeared from the house. Clarice nodded to them, and they stepped forward and began to unlock the chains that bound me. As the shackles fell from my wrists, tears rolled down my cheeks, and I sobbed. Clarice stepped forward and helped me to my feet, apparently oblivious to how filthy I was. I put my arm over her shoulders, and with her support, I limped back to the house, weeping all the way.

She led me to her bathroom and told me to shower and clean myself up. Bathed, well fed, the tangles combed out of my hair, I felt like a new woman. When I got out of the shower, there was a fresh white terrycloth bathrobe waiting for me; after my sweat-and blood-stained clothes, it felt like heaven against my skin.

Clarice was waiting for me in the living room. I settled into one of the wicker chairs across from her, savoring how good it felt to be clean and relaxed after being chained up for months.

"You're doing well," said Clarice. Her tone was crisp, businesslike. "Are you ready for the next step?"

I wanted to lounge in that chair for a week at least, but I forced my back straight and nodded that I was ready.

"Good," she said. She hesitated for a moment before continuing. "Tell me, Sophia, have you ever heard of a device called the iron maiden or the Virgin of Nuremberg?"

"I have heard of the iron maiden," I replied. "Wasn't that a torture device used back in the medieval days?"

"Well, that is what most humans believe, but actually that's a misconception. In fact, it's a crucial step along the path of kohinoor."

My heart jumped into my throat. "You're not going to put me inside one of those things, are you?"

"Clam down and listen to me." Clarice said firmly. "It's not as bad as it sounds, but I will not lie to you, Sophia. It can be dangerous. This device, when used correctly, has the ability to reveal to a vampire their past sins."

"Reveal a vampire's sins. How is that possible?" I questioned.

"When a vampire enters the iron maiden, or blood maiden, as the vampires call it, their skin is pierced by dozens of metal spikes," explained Clarice. "The blood from the wounds is collected, mixed with a hallucinogenic herb, and then fed back to the vampire through a small hole. Because the vampire is drinking their own blood, they will see their own past and be forced to relive all the sins they has committed against others. However, this time the vampire will experience each interaction as the victim rather than the attacker."

I swallowed hard, thinking back on all the things I had done since leaving the family farm. I became anxious and began to fidget in my chair, making the wicker crackle and echo throughout the room.

"Okay," I said. "You said that it can be dangerous—in what way?"

"The older a vampire gets, the more likely they are to embrace their dark side and their lust for blood. Vampires, who go down that path knowingly, usually commit horrific sins. As they relive these sins as the victim, some vampires can't handle it and don't survive the process. Others go mad.

"The process is simply meant to open the eyes of the vampire and show them what they have become. While in the blood maiden, if the vampire accepts what they have done is immoral, then they will pass the test. If not ... well, that is when things can go wrong."

"The best advice I can give you is to first take responsibility for the sins you have committed. Once you have done that, then you must forgive yourself. Remember this and you will do just fine."

I didn't quite understand the reason for this test, but I figured after months of bloodletting and going in and out of a bloodlust, I could handle being inside this Blood Maiden.

"I hope that helped answer your question," said Clarice. "Is there anything else you would like to ask?"

"No, Miss Clarice. I still don't understand everything that is expected of me in the blood maiden, but as I have told you before, I will see this process to its end, no matter the outcome."

"I'm glad to hear that, Sophia, especially after all the progress you have made so far. Tonight I want you to relax and rest. You will not be chained or forced into a bloodlust. In fact, I want you to drink as much blood as you can, because the last thing we want is for you to go into a bloodlust inside the blood maiden."

The rest of the evening, I sat on the beach looking out over the water, just thinking about my past. My biggest concern was when I killed Devin. Even though he tried to kill Sara, Nora, and Father, I know I killed him out of pure anger; I could not blame it on being in a bloodlust. I knew I could take responsibility for what I did, but the question was, could I forgive myself?"

30. Dagon

Marcus Manori was sitting on the sofa in the living room with a heavy leather book in his hand and a glass of Blood at his elbow when his telephone rang. He leaned over and fished the phone out of his jacket pocket.

"Yes?"

"Marcus, you had better be able to explain this."

"Lord Illyrius, what a pleasant surprise," said Marcus smoothly. He had been expecting this call for weeks. "But I'm afraid I don't follow you. What seems to be the problem?"

"Where is your daughter Sophia right now?" Even over the phone, the ancient vampire's voice rattled like dead seeds in a desiccated pod.

"In New York, my lord."

"You're sure of this, Marcus?"

"She was there when last we spoke, my lord," said Marcus, pinching the bridge of his nose.

"And when was that?"

"Well, let's see ... about a month ago. But it would be unlikely for her to leave the city without telling me."

"Then why," asked Lord Illyrius, his voice deepening into a menacing growl, "why, Marcus, did I just receive a report that your daughter is looking for the White Swan? Can you answer me that?"

"With all due respect, my lord, that's preposterous. I doubt Sophia has ever even heard of the White Swan, let alone—"

"Preposterous? You *dare* to tell me what's preposterous?" the old vampire sputtered. "She was seen entering a white limousine outside your apartment building two weeks ago. Since then, my sources have been unable to locate her. And you know nothing about this?"

Marcus rolled his eyes, but he was careful to keep his voice neutral as he replied. "My lord, are you certain your sources are reliable? Getting into a white limo is hardly—"

"Enough! I want her found, and I want her found now. You know I have plans for the girl."

"Of course, my lord. I'll call her as soon as we're done speaking, and if she doesn't answer, I can have one of my people in New York check up on her at once."

"That's not good enough," said Lord Illyrius. "One of *my* people has already checked your apartment. Her belonging are there, but she has not been seen for days. He's on his way to you now. You are to assist with his investigation in every way possible—short of revealing council secrets, of course. Do I make myself clear?"

"Perfectly, my lord," said Marcus stiffly. "May I ask when we can expect our guest?"

"Expect him when he arrives! This isn't a social call, and he isn't your guest. He's a vile piece of shit, but he gets results."

"I understand, my lord. I'll call as soon as I've found her. I'm certain this White Swan business is nothing more than a foul rumor."

"I hope so, Marcus—for your sake." The connection went dead.

Marcus cursed under his breath. He had expected Lord Illyrius to investigate Sophia's disappearance, but the intensity of the old vampire's interest in her was highly disturbing.

Marcus barely had time to gather his thoughts before Randolph stepped into the room with a discreet cough.

"A Mr. Dagon here to see you, sir."

Marcus let out a heavy sigh. "Thank you, Randolph. Show him in."

Randolph returned a moment later followed by a tall, thin vampire with broad shoulders wearing a black overcoat, black pants, and gloves. His jet-black hair was swept to one side with a neglectful casualness, and his smile was as fake as a three-dollar bill.

"Good evening, Mr. Dagon," said Marcus, rising from the sofa. "I understand you're here to help me find my daughter."

"It's just Dagon, if you don't mind, Lord Manori," said the newcomer, stepping forward with a deep bow. "And you are correct."

"Very well," said Marcus flatly. "How may I assist you with your inquiries?"

"Ah, straight to the point, I see," said Dagon. He began to remove his gloves and overcoat, making himself at home. "Well, then. I will need to taste just a little blood from everyone in the family—except you, of course, my lord—and then I will have some questions for you."

Randolph raised an eyebrow at Marcus from behind the intruder's shoulder; it was an outrageous request, but Lord Illyrius had commanded Marcus to cooperate with Dagon. Fury welled up inside Marcus's chest, but he showed no emotion.

Marcus stood up slowly, and in a commanding voice he said, "Dagon, let us be clear about this investigation of yours. Lord Illyrius may have given you the authority to interrogate my clan but in this house, you will follow my orders. That means you will treat each of my clan with respect, including Sophia. Also, understand that if you happen to find her, you will contact me before taking any action. Have I made myself clear, Dagon?"

Dagon stood there for a minute, thinking of the proper response. It was easy to see in his eyes that he did not like being told how to do his job, but he was fully aware of Marcus's authority as an elder; he had no choice but to agree.

"Of course, Lord Manori," said Dagon. "There is no evidence at this time that your daughter, Sophia, has done anything wrong. I promise I will treat this investigation with the respect it deserves."

"Very well," said Marcus. "Randolph, please inform my children that I would like to see them in the parlor."

When everyone was gathered, one by one each member of the family submitted to Dagon's fangs. Nora offered up her wrist meekly, while Nikolai complied with stiff shoulders and a hard stare. Dante, Vanessa, and Carmilla were expressionless as he lapped the blood from their veins. Sara made no attempt at all to disguise her rage, but even with her blatant protest, she did not disobey her father.

Marcus looked on as the interloper drank from his children. He knew none of them could betray Sophia, because none of them knew the real reason for her journey to New York. Marcus alone kept that secret. He also knew Dagon wouldn't dare ask for his blood. As an elder, he held many secrets that only the vampire council members were privileged to know.

When Dagon was finished, he turned his eyes to Marcus. "Most enlightening," he said, grinning. "However, it seems none of your clan knows anything about your daughter's disappearance." His mouth twisted into a meager yet mocking pout.

Marcus stood in stony silence, waiting for the intruder to tire of his own performance.

"Well," said Dagon at last, "if you don't mind, my lord, I'd like to ask you some questions."

"Certainly," said Marcus, grinding his teeth. "Why don't you join me in my library?"

The library was dark, and the grate in the fireplace was cold. Marcus turned on a lamp and settled into his usual chair. Dagon dropped into the other chair without being asked.

"Ask your questions," growled Marcus, staring directly into Dagon's dark eyes.

Dagon leaned back and threw one leg over the arm of his chair. "Do you know the story of Circe from Homer's *Odyssey*, my lord?" asked Dagon.

"We're sitting in a library," he replied slowly. "I would ask you to note that it is *my* library." His right hand rose up from the arm of his chair in a sharp gesture, almost a spasm, to indicate the rows upon rows of books that lined the room. As he continued, his voice rose until it was almost a roar. "How many times do you suppose I've read Homer—in how many languages—during the countless many centuries I have lived on this earth? Did you come here to insult my intelligence or to help me find my daughter?"

"My apologies, my lord," said Dagon blandly, apparently unfazed by the criticism, "but the question is relevant to my investigation. You see, the jet in which I believe your daughter left New York was chartered by someone using the name Smith. Clearly as an alias."

"The jet *you believe* Sophia left in?" questioned Marcus. "Care to explain how you came to this conclusion?"

"Before I came to see you I found out that a white limousine drove up to a private jet at New York's International Airport around the same time Sophia went missing. I also found out that the flight plan for the jet was from New York to Naples. My sources told me that the plane went from Naples to a place called Circe. After a careful search, I could not find anyplace call Circe with an airport.

"Don't you see, my lord? Circe was a goddess of magic who had extensive knowledge of herbs and potions; by all accounts, so does the White Swan. Circe turned men into animals, and I wouldn't be surprised if the White Swan thinks of herself as someone who is turning animals into men," explained Dagon. "It makes perfect sense. Circe is a code name for the White Swan."

Marcus rose from his chair with his fists clenched at his sides. "And this is the evidence you would use to try and condemn my daughter—speculation and myth? Leave my house at once before I do something I *might* regret later."

"My lord—"

"Now!" roared Marcus as his eyes turned black and his long fangs extended. He then let out a long, low hiss.

Dagon sprang lightly from his chair and grabbed his coat and gloves. "Very well, my lord," he said. "I will take my leave." With a mocking bow, he turned on his heel, strode out of the library, and left the mansion.

When Dagon's back had disappeared into the gloom of the hall outside the library, Marcus retracted his fangs and permitted himself a smile. If a suspicious alias was the best evidence Dagon could come up with, his family would be fine. He only wished he knew how to get a message to Sophia, though it was probably for the best that he didn't know where she was—even if Lord Illyrius drank some of his blood, Marcus wouldn't be able to betray her. Sophia was now completely on her own.

31. THE BLOOD MAIDEN

The next evening I followed Clarice down a dirt path for more than a mile through the trees, until we came to a narrow strip of beach. The sand was coarse and white, and I could feel the warmth of the sea as the waves gently lapped toward me unto the sand. A little way up the beach was a shallow cave. Moss and ferns grew around its dark mouth, which did not look very inviting at all.

Clarice led me inside, and to my surprise, I saw an upright iron sarcophagus. It was open, and rows of iron spikes lined the interior. At the top of the device, was the head and face of a woman, also made out of iron.

"You'll need to remove your clothes," said Clarice.

I peeled off my clothes, grateful that at least the air in the cave was warm. Clarice nodded toward the blood maiden, and I stepped toward it.

As I entered the blood maiden I began to get nervous, but I was able to stay relatively calm basically because of the trials Clarice had already put me through. As I turned around to face the open door, Clarice sent me a look of encouragement and then began to close the door. The spikes in the door pushed me backward until my back touched the spikes behind me. As the door continued to close, the spikes began to cut into my flesh in all directions. Once the door finally came to a stop, I had spikes in my head, arms, back, chest, stomach, and some in my legs. The spikes pierced my skin only about an inch, which made the pain bearable as long as

I didn't squirm. I had to force myself to remain motionless in the dark, confined space of the iron coffin.

Moments after the door closed, warm blood began to trickle over my skin; I could feel it running down my legs. The air inside the blood maiden was still except for my panting breaths. With each breath, I tasted iron, blood, sweat, and rust.

After what seemed like hours, a small opening appeared in front of my face, and a piece of surgical-like tubing was thrust against my lips. I closed my teeth around it and began to suck. Blood poured into my mouth.

Once the tube was empty, it was removed, and the small opening was closed tight. After what seemed like only a few minutes, I began to see mental visions of my life as a vampire. They seemed very real, but for some reason I was watching everything as a spectator.

I first saw the car accident where I almost died. Then my vision changed to when I fought Vaine. I saw the fear in his eyes as my shuriken scored cruel gashes along his face; a moment later, I watched my fist thrust into his chest and pull out his heart. Then appeared the face of the pizza boy, his eyes wide with shock, his mouth open in a gasp of terror as my fangs sank deep into his throat. I could actually smell the pepperoni on his clothes and taste his sweet blood as I watched myself take his life. A sob caught in my throat. "I'm sorry," I whispered. "I'm so sorry."

Although I was upset by what I had done, I realized that I was still a spectator. I did not experience the act of killing that boy as the victim. The only explanation I could think of was that because I had been in a bloodlust, I'd had no control over what I did then. Since my actions were purely instinctive as I searched for blood, I guessed that the act was not considered offensive enough for me to relive it as the victim.

One by one, incidents in my life as a vampire flashed before my mind's eye. I saw myself pin the vampire who had attacked Sara to the wall, the assassin's test where I was almost killed, and the look on Lord Vladimir's face as I took his life.

Suddenly, everything went black. I sniffed the air but smelled nothing at all. It was as if the world had ceased to exist. There was only me, trapped inside the blood maiden, and the darkness.

I'm not sure how long I waited there in the darkness, but it felt like a long time. I wondered what it could mean. I was no longer having visions, and I had not been given any more blood. Had something gone wrong? Maybe one of Clarice's servants hadn't prepared the hallucinogenic herbs correctly. *How long am I supposed to be in this thing, anyway?*

Many hours went by and I began to feel the need for blood. I remember Clarice saying that she did not want me to go into a bloodlust inside the blood maiden. I was beginning to worry, and I sensed something was wrong. I opened up my sense of smell and was surprised to catch the scent of fresh human blood. I knew right away that someone had recently been hurt or killed.

Many thoughts went through my mind. What if some vampires discovered where Clarice was and had killed her and all of her servants? How was I supposed to get out of the blood maiden? As I sniffed the air again, I detected a lot more human blood. Something was definitely wrong. I knew I had to find a way to get out of this stupid device. My only thought was to rock the blood maiden back and forth and try to tip it over.

I began to shift my weight back and forth: left, right, left, right, left. The spikes tore deeper into my flesh, but I had to endure the pain. Luckily the ground was soft and eventually the blood maiden began to rock. I gritted my teeth against the pain and pushed harder: right, left, right, left. Iron bit into the muscles of my thighs and calves, but I had to keep going: back and forth, right, left, right. When I felt that the iron maiden was almost at the tipping point, I threw myself left again with all my might.

I felt a moment of weightless vertigo as it toppled, and then it struck the floor of the cave with a rending crash. The door of the iron case spilled open, and the spikes sank deep into my left arm and side. I felt their hard points scrape against my ribs and hip; I cried out in excruciating pain.

Gasping, I gingerly freed my body from the iron spikes and rolled away from the blood maiden. Moss and sand clung to my torn flesh. I lay there panting for several minutes as my wounds slowly closed. I had lost a lot of blood and would need some more soon.

The scent of fresh human blood tingled in my nostrils. I had to find Clarice and make sure she was okay. I struggled to my feet, put on the robe that was lying on a nearby chair, and staggered out onto the beach.

The moon had set, but the stars burned brightly in the clear sky, sending me plenty of light to see clearly, even in my weakened state. A little outside the mouth of the cave, I discovered a body sprawled face-down on the sand. The sand under the corpse was stained dark red. I crouched beside the still form and rolled it over. It was one of Clarice's servants. His throat had been cut.

I sniffed and then scanned the beach for intruders. I smelled only blood and the salty sea air. Down the beach, the dark shape of a speedboat's prow stood out against the starry sky.

The sand was warm between my toes as I hurried along the beach. Nearing the boat, I saw that the stern was still afloat in the surf, while the prow rested on the sand. I smelled motor oil and something else—there was at least one vampire nearby. As I approached, I realized that the vampire I detected was on the boat. I crouched low beside the hull and peered over the edge.

In the stern beside the outboard motor lay a figure. Its hands and feet were bound tightly with rope, and a black hood was pulled over the head. I glanced quickly back at the line of palm trees along the beach, looking for any signs of activity, but everything was quiet. I jumped lightly into the boat, and it rocked gently under my weight.

"Who's there?" said a muffled voice. The hooded vampire squirmed and tried to sit up, straining against the cords around his wrists.

Before I got too close, I asked. "Who are you?"

"I am a prisoner," said the voice. "Help me, please."

I slowly walk up to the vampire and carefully grabbed the dark hood. When I pulled it off I got the shock of my life. It was Devin. I stepped back, staring at him in disbelief.

"Sophia? Is that really you?"

"You can't be Devin," I whispered. "I killed you."

"No. I mean yes, you did, but it didn't kill me," said Devin. "One of the Németh boys came back while you were tending to your friend and gave me some of his blood. That not only healed me, it turned me. I'm a vampire now—I'm just like you."

"No," I said. "No, I saw you die." I stumbled backward, tripped over a life jacket, and fell into the prow of the boat. I shook my head. "I must be hallucinating," I said aloud. "This can't be real."

"What?" said Devin. "Sophia, it's me. Can you please untie me? I don't know when the others are coming back."

If this was a hallucination, it sure didn't feel like it. And if Devin was a figment of my imagination, then I was supposed to ask for his forgiveness, wasn't I? I pulled myself together, made my way back across the boat, and began tugging at the ropes on his wrists.

"Who did this?" I asked. "How did you get here?"

"I don't know. The last thing I remember was something sharp hitting me in the back. When I woke, I was tied up with a hood over my head."

Reluctantly, I worked the ropes loose. Once Devin was free, I took a seat on one of the boat's padded chairs and said as calmly as I could, "Devin, we need to talk."

He looked at me like I was crazy. "Talk? Not now, Sophia. We need to get out of here. They could be back any minute."

"This is important," I said. "And anyway, if anyone was coming I could smell them in time for us to get away."

He scanned the shoreline nervously, but he didn't try to argue. "Okay," he said. "What's so important that it can't wait?"

"I need to tell you I'm sorry—for killing you. After you shot Sara I lost control, and—well, I'm sorry," I finished lamely.

"Oh, you don't need to apologize," said Devin, as if having his throat torn out wasn't anything to worry about. "I understand now why you left. Being a vampire is amazing. It's almost like being a god compared to being human. Now I understand why you chose that over me."

"No, you don't understand," I said, confused. "I'm not apologizing for leaving. That didn't have anything to do with you. I'm apologizing for killing you."

"Didn't have anything to do with me?" he repeated. Then he looked at me with his head cocked to one side, and the starlight cast a pale sheen over half of his face. "Tell me something, Sophia. Did you ever love me?"

Taken back by his the question, I said, "Oh, Devin, I thought I did when you asked me to marry you, but I was young and my life was just beginning. I had hoped that in time, after we were married, I would come to love you, but as you know, we never got that far. I guess in a way I deceived you, but I didn't do it on purpose. I just thought marriage was the next step for a farm girl like me."

Devin's voice became bitter. "Tell me, did you ever think about me after you moved in with those vampires?"

"Devin, you don't understand. It's complicated." I said quietly.

"I see, so it's complicated. Too complicated for someone like me to understand, I suppose." said Devin sarcastically.

As I tried to explain, I saw Devin slide his hand into his trouser pocket. When he pulled it out again he held a leather pouch that fit in the palm of his hand. He opened it up, and to my surprise, he pulled out one of my shuriken.

"Devin," I said cautiously. "Where did you get that?"

"I found it after the battle," he said.

"Please put that away," I said. "It's not a toy."

Devin held the shuriken up to his face, turning it from side to side as if he was admiring it in the pale light. Then Devin got a weird light in his eyes that started to frighten me.

"Oh, I know exactly what it is, Sophia," said Devin. "It's one of your weapons, isn't it? How clever of you to take my hollow arrowhead design and use it to make a weapon of your own. I particularly admire the reservoir in the center. It's for your venom, right?"

I didn't answer.

"Sophia, do you remember when I said I had developed a stronger poison?"

Before I could respond, Devin's expression twisted into a snarl, and he hurled the shuriken at my face. I threw my arms up instinctively, and the shuriken stuck me just above my right elbow. I quickly pulled it out of my arm and scrambled to get away from Devin, but the poison was already starting to take effect. The world around me began to spin, and I felt my strength leave me. I crashed onto the deck of the boat, unable to move. I stared up at the night sky, helpless and afraid. Then Devin loomed over me, blocking out the stars.

"Why are you doing this?" I asked.

"You don't know?" he exclaimed. "You lied to me, Sophia, when you said you loved me. Then you left without even saying good-bye." His voice rose to a crescendo, and I felt his spittle spray on my cheek as he look down on me. "So being the lying bitch that you are, I'm going to make you pay for your sin. You took my life; now I have taken yours."

He lifted me roughly from the deck and heaved me over the side. I landed face down in the sand. I tried to get up, but Devin's toxin had already turned my muscles to jelly. Darkness clouded the edges of my vision, and my breathing became quick and shallow. After a moment, I heard the outboard motor start. Devin was leaving me to die alone.

"Good-bye, Sophia," Devin said over the sound of the motor. "We could have been happy together. All you had to do was love me. But you had to run off, searching for that damn vampire. I'm going after her next so you can both rot in hell together. Your abilities can't stop me now, Sophia, because—you're dead."

Devin started laughing as he sped off into the darkness. Before long all I could hear was the sound of the waves as they gently washed upon the shore.

As I lay there in the sand, the warm water of the surf began to wash over my legs and lower back. It was almost pleasant, but I knew I was dying. *The tide must be coming in*, I thought. I drew one last ragged breath, and that was all. Everything went black.

* * *

The next thing I knew I was on the floor of the cave, in extreme pain. My body was caked with dried blood, and the open blood maiden lay on its side a few feet away. Clarice kneeled beside me, a look of concern on her face as she cleaned my wounds. "What happened, Sophia?" she asked. "Why did you break out of the blood maiden?"

My eyes darted around the cave. My head throbbed. "What—where's Devin?" I stammered. "Is he gone?"

"Devin is not here, Sophia. You are safe. It must have been a hallucination from the herbs. The first thing you need to do is drink some blood. You cut yourself up badly. You need blood so you can heal."

I was scared. I did not know what to believe. I grabbed Clarice by the arm and nervously asked, "Is this real? Are you real? Please tell me it is over. Don't let him hurt me, please!"

Clarice had to change her tone to get me to listen to her. "Sophia, it's over. You're safe, but you need to drink this blood now." Clarice literally began pouring blood in my mouth. As soon as I tasted it, I grabbed the bag and began to drink. I went through four bags before I started to calm down. My wounds began to heal as I got more blood into my system. Clarice helped me up off the ground and had me sit in a nearby chair. Then she opened up a small black leather pouch and took out a syringe and a small glass vial. She filled the syringe with the liquid from the vial and without asking stuck the needle into my arm and injected me with the liquid.

"Hey, what are you doing?" I questioned.

"Don't worry. This is just a mild antibiotic to protect you from getting sick. Your body has gone through a lot, Sophia, and even though you are a vampire, with all the blood you lost during your trails, your immune system is weak. The last thing we need is for you to get sick. From now on you'll be getting an injection once a day."

I was too tired to argue. My mind was still on the events I had experienced in the blood maiden.

Once my wounds had completely healed, I looked at Clarice and asked, "If you don't mind, I'd like to take a walk on the beach before we go back. I have a lot to think about."

Clarice fixed her eyes on me with an unblinking gaze, and I had to look away. "I think that would be all right," she said after a moment. "Just don't stay too long. You need to rest."

I looked up, and her smile flashed in the dark before she turned and walked away, leaving me alone in the cave. When she was gone, I removed the blood-soaked robe Clarice had covered me with, put my clothes on, and strode out onto the strip of white sand. My encounter with Devin still seemed horribly real, and I needed to make absolutely sure that it truly had been just a hallucination.

As I walked along the shore, I saw no corpse lying on the beach, no boat, and no sign of any recent activity. I turned my gazed out to the starlit sea and listened to the surf rolling in over the sand. I don't know how long I stood like that, breathing in time to the rhythm of the waves, but at last my shoulders relaxed. "I am sorry, Devin," I said quietly.

I was about to go when I heard footsteps on the sand behind me. I assumed it must be Clarice or one of her servants coming to fetch me, but when I turned, Devin was standing right in front of me. I stumbled backward in panic. He lunged forward, and his hand closed around my neck and lifted me off my feet. I grasped his arm with both hands and flailed at him with my legs, but he was too strong for me. A nasty, leering smile spread across his face.

"Die, you lying bitch," he said. His grip tightened, and his fingertips gouged painfully into my throat. I felt myself choking. My windpipe collapsed with a sickening crunch, and blood spewed from between my lips. There was a rasping, gurgling sound as I tried but failed to suck in a breath of air. Then Devin released his grip, and my legs buckled beneath me.

*   *   *

The door of the blood maiden swung open with a groan, and I fell forward. Clarice was there to catch me. She gently laid me on the ground. She wrapped a robe around me, which began to soak up all the blood on my skin. After a moment, I opened my eyes and saw Clarice standing over me.

"Hello," I said mindlessly. "I'd like to be done now." My tongue felt thick, and I slurred the words.

"Hello, Sophia," said Clarice.

As she helped me to my unsteady feet and offered me a bag of blood from her backpack, somehow I knew that the trial was really over. There had been no Devin, no boat, and no escape from the blood maiden. It had all been part of my blood maiden trial.

Clarice had me sit in a chair and gave me some more blood to drink. Then the strangest thing happened. Clarice pulled out a black leather pouch and opened it. Inside I saw a syringe and a small glass vial.

"You're going to give me a shot of a mild antibiotic, right?" I said. "My immune system is weak from the loss of so much blood, and you don't want me to get sick."

Clarice looked at me curiously and said, "That's right. How did you know that?"

"I saw it while in the blood maiden."

I nodded and silently offered up my arm. I almost laughed at the gentleness with which Clarice gave me the injection; a moment ago, a hundred iron spikes were buried in my flesh, and she was afraid of hurting me with a needle.

When she was done, she brushed a matted clump of hair out of my face. "You're doing wonderfully, Sophia," she said. "The worst of your trials are over. Not long now, and you'll be free."

32. The Illusion of Death

Although I was no longer chained, I slept outside under the shelter of woven palm leaves in the circle of stone columns. One of Clarice's servants brought out a cot for me to sleep on, and fortunately, the mosquitoes left me alone. I guessed they didn't like the taste of vampire blood, being like tiny vampires themselves.

The evening after my ordeal in the blood maiden, I woke up long after the sun had set. Apparently Clarice felt I had earned the right to sleep in for once.

I stretched my aching muscles and swung my bare feet to the ground. I wandered up the path toward Clarice's house. As I drew near, I saw her sitting on the stone steps out front with a glass of what looked like iced tea in her hand. She patted the step beside her. "Good evening," she said. "I was wondering if you were ever going to wake up. How do you feel?"

"Still a little groggy," I said, taking a seat.

She reached behind her and produced a second glass and a bag of blood. "Here. I thought you might like to drink out of a glass instead of a bag for a change."

I cradled the glass in my hand and looked up at the stars. After a moment, I said, "Clarice, can I ask you something?"

"Of course."

"Do you believe in fate?" I asked.

"Well, that's a bit complicated," said Clarice. "Why do you ask?"

"Sometimes I feel like I've had almost no control over my life. It's almost like I'm a passenger in a car. I don't know where the driver is taking me, but at every stop I'm the one who has to pay the toll. You know what I mean?"

Before Clarice could respond, one of her servants came running up the path. He stopped at the foot of the steps. His face was red, and his chest heaved as he tried to catch his breath.

"What is it?" said Clarice, rising to her feet.

"I think there is a vampire on the island," he said between gasps. "We heard a boat land on the beach, and Philippe went to see who it was. When he did not return, we went to the shore to look for him. When we got there, we found him dead in the sand with bite marks on his neck. I then ran here as fast as I could."

I immediately jumped to my feet. "I can take care of it," I said.

"No," said Clarice, thrusting out her arm to stop me. "Getting into a fight at this point could undo everything you've accomplished. And killing one spy won't do much good anyway; Lord Illyrius can always send another. The question is who is he after, you or me?"

"Then what should we do?" I asked.

"Go to the center of the stone circle right now and start digging. About twelve inches down, you will hit a large stone. Lift the stone, and you will find an old water well under it. Be sure to roll the stone far into the woods so it won't be seen. I'll meet you there in a few minutes."

I hesitated.

"Go!" shouted Clarice. "We don't have much time."

I ran down the path to the shelter and dropped to my knees at the midpoint between the standing stones and started digging. I didn't know what Clarice had in mind, but I knew I had to trust her. I pulled up the gray earth by the handful and threw it behind me, pausing every few seconds to sniff the air for the scent of the approaching vampire. About a foot down, my fingers scraped against something hard and smooth. A bit more digging revealed a round stone about three feet in diameter. I lifted the stone and discovered a deep, dark hole under it. I then rolled the stone into the woods to hide it.

I heard hurried footsteps behind me and whirled around. It was Clarice, along with some of her servants. They were each carrying armfuls of chopped firewood and dried tree limbs. Clarice had a large red gas can in her hand.

"Okay, Sophia, listen carefully. The ultimate goal here is to create the illusion that you die in a fire. To do that I need to make the vampire believe that I have captured you. You will stand in the center shackled like before but the locks won't be closed. We will then place all this wood around you, high enough to hide you from the waist down, and then pour gasoline on it.

"Once the vampire shows himself, I will threaten to kill you buy burning you if he does not go away. Your job is to pretend that you want his help. Also, make sure he sees the chains. It will help with the illusion."

Clarice continued. "I will be standing close to the edge of the firewood with a lit torch. As soon as he makes a move, I will drop the torch into the wood. The gas will ignite the wood, and soon a large burning fire will surround you."

I stood there awestruck at this ruse, listening intensely to ever word.

"As soon as you see the fire, start screaming for all you're worth. When the flames are high enough, remove the shackles, lock them up tight, and then jump down into the well. At the bottom you will find a lever. Push the lever up and down to close off the top of the hole and prevent the fire from getting to you. After the fire has burned itself out, the vampire should believe that you have died and leave."

"What about you, Clarice?" I asked, sliding the steel ring around my neck. "Will you be okay up here?"

Clarice smiled. "I'll be fine," she said. "If one vampire was all it took to kill the White Swan, I would have died a long time ago."

As she finished speaking, a whiff of hair gel and vampire sweat reached my nose. I snapped my fingers and jerked my head in the direction of the smell.

The servants had just finished surrounding me with wood and branches dowsed in gasoline, and Clarice motioned for them to run in the opposite direction.

Clarice then picked up a makeshift torch in her hand. With the other, she fished a lighter out of her pocket. Then, loudly enough for the intruder to hear, she yelled, "It's time for you to die, demon!" She lit the torch and swept it dramatically into the air.

There came a violent rustling from the vegetation to my right, and the vampire crashed between the trees and into the clearing that surrounded the hut. Clarice and I turned to look at him. He was tall and broad-shouldered, and as soon as he saw that he had our attention, he paused and swept a hand through his jet-black hair, trying to regain his composure.

"I'm sorry," he said. "Am I interrupting something?"

"Help!" I wailed. "She's going to kill me!"

"Well," he said, tilting his head to one side and scratching his chin, "can't have that, can we?" He turned to Clarice. "I'm here for the girl. Put down the torch, and I promise no harm will come to you."

"I know what you are, demon," spat Clarice. "Your promises mean nothing to me. Come any closer, or she dies." She waved the torch menacingly toward the nearest bundle of wood.

"Come now," said the vampire, taking a step toward us, his palms held up in front of him in a placating gesture. "Surely we can come to some kind of arrangement? I've already said I only want the girl. What is it that you want? I can offer you money. If money does not suit you, I can get you gold. Perhaps diamonds are more to your liking."

"I want you and all of your kind to burn," hissed Clarice.

"What an ugly thing to say," said the vampire. He shook his head in mocking disappointment. "And here I've worked so *hard* to find you. I expected a warmer welcome."

"Warmer? How's this for warmer?" Without hesitation, Clarice thrust the torch into the gas-soaked pile of wood. She spun around as the first flames leaped up and sprinted into the woods.

The wood ignited instantly. Flames danced and flickered in a circle around me and licked along the roof of the shelter. Even though Clarice had been careful to leave some space between the wood and me, the heat was still intense. Beads of sweat formed on my forehead.

"Help me!" I shrieked over and over. Then I started screaming as loud as I could, as if I were being burned. I finally let my voice trail off into one blood-curdling wail.

The vampire dashed forward and tried to find a way through the flames, but Clarice had done her work well: a solid wall of fire encircled me. Swearing, the vampire jumped back, beating smoldering cinders from the front of his shirt.

Black smoke billowed into the humid night, filling the chikee hut so that not even a vampire could see me. I curled up into a ball on the ground and began to tear off my shackles. The flames crackled around me, and sweat soaked my clothes. Ash and smoldering pieces of palm tumbled down on me from above.

As I snapped the last shackle shut, I noticed the assassin's ring on my finger. The diamonds flashed red in the light of the fire, and I remembered the day Lord Illyrius had given it to me. Suddenly, the ring filled me with a sense of revulsion. Acting on instinct, I slipped it off my finger, tossed it into the flames, and jumped down into the old well. Once I hit the bottom, I found myself in a puddle of dirty stale water, roots jutting out from the walls in every direction. I quickly found the lever and pushed it up and down until all the light above me was gone.

A moment later, I heard a long, creaking groan and then a violent crash: the hut had collapsed above me. I stood there listening to the crackling fire for a long time. The air in the old well was damp and stifling but all I could do was to wait.

I worried about Clarice. What if the vampire went after her? Could she really protect herself? I never saw any evidence that she could fight.

As I stood there in the dark, I closed my eyes and prayed for the safety of Clarice and her servants. The last thing I wanted on my conscious was for them to get killed because of me. I also prayed that this illusion would work. I knew that the only way I would truly be free, was if Lord Illyrius thought I was dead.

After what seemed like hours, I heard footsteps above me, and then the hatch opened. Clarice stood looking down at me with a smile on her face. Behind her, a hint of pink light filled the sky. "Come on," she said. "It's almost dawn."

She threw down a rope, and I quickly pulled myself up out of the dark well into the fresh air. I looked down at myself. I was caked with mud and sweat, and the smell of rank, stale water rose from my clothes. "Did it work?" I asked. "Is he gone?"

"Let's hope so," said Clarice. "Your screams were certainly convincing. But I'm not taking any chances. We're getting out of here as soon as the sun sets."

She glanced down at my hand. "What happened to your ring?"

"I threw it away," I said.

She nodded. "So that's what it was."

"What do you mean?" I asked.

"After the fire died down, the vampire kicked through the ashes and inspected the shackles," said Clarice. "I saw him pick something up, and then he left. It must have been your ring. He'll no doubt take it back to whoever sent him as proof that you're dead."

I held my naked fingers up to the predawn light. "That's not why I threw it away," I said quietly.

"And yet it will work to your advantage. It's funny how fate works, isn't it?" said Clarice, putting her arm around me. I smiled at her, and together we walked back to the house.

33. A ΠEW LIFE

C larice loaned me a change of clothes, and I spent the day on her couch with the blinds and curtains drawn over the windows. As dusk fell, I woke to her gentle grip on my shoulder. I sat up, and she handed me a glass of blood.

"Thanks," I said.

She settled into a chair across from the couch and watched as I sipped the lukewarm beverage. I almost didn't notice the bitter taste anymore.

"The plane is waiting for us," said Clarice. "We can leave as soon as you're ready."

"Where are we going?" I asked.

"To a hospital. It's time for your last step on the path of kohinoor," said Clarice.

"My last step? You mean I'm almost done?"

"Yes," said Clarice, smiling at the eagerness in my voice. "After the procedure, you'll be human again."

"Procedure? Exactly what kind of procedure are you talking about?" I asked, suddenly filled with apprehension. In my mind's eye, I saw myself strapped down on a table while a figure in a bloodstained lab coat went after my fangs with a pair of pliers.

"It's nothing to be too worried about," said Clarice. "Essentially, it's a blood transfusion. The antibiotics I've been giving you should have weakened the virus enough by now that your body will accept human blood again. You see, vampirism is really nothing more than a virus"

"It's just a virus?" I asked, with skepticism and a little anger. "Like the flu or something? Then what was all this other stuff you put me through? Why not have the procedure right away and get it over with?"

Clarice sighed and said, "I suppose it's time you know the complete truth. As the White Swan, I do not work alone. There is an entire community out there working to find a cure for vampirism."

"What do you mean, a cure?" I asked.

"Vampirism is really nothing more than a virus, but it works in ways we do not yet understand. Some sciences believe it is a mutated virus strain from back when we were primitive creatures. They think the virus unlocks some of the dormant genetic traits in our DNA from back when we were primal. Otherwise the infected host would not change physically, like growing fangs, or going into a bloodlust.

"You see, Sophia, once humans get enough vampire blood in their systems, the virus changes the very cell structure of their organs. No longer does the host have to process food. It's organs can get nourishment directly from the blood. High amounts of adrenaline have also been found in vampire blood. We believe this is how a vampire acquires their heighted abilities. Other benefits from the virus are a slowdown in the ageing process and fast healing. The trade-off, as you know, is that the infected host can only get nourishment by drinking blood, and skin exposed to the sun will burn. We think the virus considers the skin to be a secondary organ. Only when injured will the skin get the blood it needs to heal—hence the pale complexion."

"So if vampirism is nothing more than a virus," I asked, "then why all the bloodletting and putting me in that damn blood maiden?"

"Well, Sophia, the vampire virus is a very resistant strain. None of our antibiotics work on a healthy vampire. We have found that the only way to get rid of this virus is to weaken the immune system by continuous bloodletting, while at the same time teaching you to take back control of your body with your mind."

"Those shots I have been giving you each day are an antibiotic, but it is a specific antibiotic that fights to destroy the virus. It only works when your system is weak. In short, we had to weaken your body and strengthen your mind before we could get to a point where we could start killing off the virus with antibiotics."

"Okay, that makes sense, but what about the blood maiden?" I asked.

Clarice leaned forward and took my hand. "Treating only the physical part of the disease doesn't work. You have killed people, Sophia. If we had made you human again before you had a chance to come to terms with that, the psychological trauma might have destroyed you."

"You see the virus actually does change the way you think, by changing your brain chemistry. We have found that vampires have an unusually high amount of dopamine in their brain, which can suppress the feelings of fear and remorse. We have also found very low amounts of serotonin, which we believe is the reason from much of a vampire's violent behavior."

"The blood maiden by having you experiencing your violence as the victim, showed you how malicious and brutal you can be. Once you accepted responsibility for what you were shown, your thoughts literally changed your brain chemistry to a more normal level, making the final phase of your transformation possible."

Clarice folded her hands back in her lap and looked at me with her piercing hazel eyes. "There are still some risks involved," she said. "The final procedure involves draining most of your vampire blood. We've never tried this with a dhampir before, and it's possible that could complicate things."

I gulped, but I certainly wasn't turning back now. "Okay," I said. "It won't exactly be the first time my life's been in danger."

"Well, that's one way to look at it," said Clarice. "Sophia, you have a good heart and, more importantly, you believe in God. We don't know why, but that seems to make a difference. I feel sure you'll be all right."

"Thank you, Clarice," I said, and I meant it. I drained the last of the blood from my glass. "Would it be all right if I went for a short walk on the beach before we leave?" I asked. "I could use a little time to myself."

Clarice told me not to take too long, and I jogged down the path to the beach. The sharp smell of the salt tickled my nose, and I kicked off my shoes and buried my toes in the sand. The moon was rising, and its reflection stretched out like a silver shimmering path over the waves to the horizon.

I tried to remember what it was like to be human. My sense of smell would be dull again. It was funny, considering how much trouble my sensitive nose had caused me at first, but I knew I would miss being able to pick out every scent on the air. And of course my heightened strength and speed would go away. On the other hand, I'd be able to eat chocolate again. That had to count for something, right?

I laughed to myself in the darkness. Then, on a sudden impulse, I sprinted down the beach at full speed. My hair streamed out behind me, and the wind rushed against my face. This was something else I knew I would miss. Maybe I could take up skydiving, or something. I knew it wouldn't be the same, but it couldn't hurt.

Before I made my way back to the house, I picked up a sharp rock and carved *SM* deep into the trunk of a tree beside the path. Above my initials, I carved a cross—a marker for the final resting place of Sophia Manori, who had died slowly in this place over the course of several months. I pressed my hand against the trunk of the tree for a moment and then hurried up the path to the house.

Clarice was waiting for me on the runway next to the plane. We boarded, and as the landing gear left the runway, I strained forward in my seat and peered through the window: lush foliage, a strip of white beach, and then the moonlit sea. I didn't know the name of the island or even what ocean it was in, but I knew my old life was buried there.

All those months I had been focused on freeing myself from the beast inside me. Now that my journey was almost at an end, I wondered what I would do when I was human again. If word got out that the daughter of an elder had taken the path of kohinoor, there would always be those in the vampire community who wanted me dead. It would cause chaos. I would have to assume a new identity. With a shock, I realized I would need a day job. I wondered if maybe Clarice would help me find a job. As soon as the thought popped into my head, I knew what I wanted to do once I was human. I would help Clarice help others like me—vampires who didn't like what the virus caused them to become. Somehow, I would find a way to spread the word that the path of kohinoor was real. There was no need to use assassination to control the vampire population when there was a cure! My jaw clenched. Right there on the plane, I decided to make it my mission in life to see that the vampire community learned the truth, even if it meant my death.

"A penny for your thoughts."

I turned away from the window and saw Clarice standing beside me with a syringe in her hand. "Oh, just thinking about what I'll do once I'm human again."

"And?" said Clarice.

"If I live to be human, maybe I'll tell you," I said. I rolled up the sleeve of my shirt and held out my arm to receive my shot.

"Have it your way." She focused on the syringe, gave it a flick with her finger, and then proceeded to give me the injection. "This isn't your usual dose of antibiotics," she said. "We have to keep the location of the hospital a secret, so I'm giving you a tranquilizer. It'll put you under for several hours, and when you wake up, you'll be in the hospital."

I nodded, knowing that if Lord Illyrius ever found out that a facility for curing vampirism existed, there was no doubt he would have everyone there killed. All it would take to reveal the secret was a vampire snacking on the wrong person's blood, so the fewer people who knew where it was the better.

"Sweet dreams," she said and walked toward the back of the plane.

I leaned back in my seat as the sedative started to kick in. My last thought before I succumbed fully to the drug was a line from the manuscript I had discovered in Father's library: "Beware, for the path is hard, and the way is set about with sharp thorns. Yet it is hope for those who wander in darkness." A slight smile spread across my face as I fell fast asleep, knowing that my journey was just about over.

*　　　*　　　*

Marcus, alone in his library, clutched the phone to his ear with his right hand as he paced back and forth in front of the fireplace.

"And you're quite sure of this, my lord?" he said, his voice choked with emotion.

"I'm sorry, Marcus, but I'm afraid there can be no doubt," said Lord Illyrius through the phone. "Dagon says he saw her burn with his own eyes. He brought her ring to me as proof. I'm holding it in my hand as we speak."

"Do you mean to tell me, my lord, that Dagon was there—that he watched my daughter die and failed to stop it?" Marcus made no effort to suppress the growl in his voice.

"According to his report, that would seem to be the case," said Lord Illyrius. "If it's any consolation, I've already taken a … personal interest in his failure. He will be feeling the consequences for a very, very long time."

"That is some comfort, my lord, but it doesn't bring my daughter back," said Marcus. "If you will permit it, I would very much like to pay him a personal visit."

"That is your right, of course. His fate is in your hands. Marcus, I want you to know that I am deeply saddened by this news. As you know, I thought very highly of Sophia. I will miss her."

"As will I, my lord," said Marcus. "As will I."

Marcus ended the call and stared into the fire. There was a choked off sob behind him, and he spun around to see Sara standing in the doorway. Her face was pale. Before he could say anything, she turned and ran crying down the hall.

Cursing, Marcus hurried after her. She dashed up the stairs to her room and slammed the door behind her. Marcus stood in the hall and listened until her sobs began to subside. Then he tapped gently on the door. "Sara, may I come in?"

"Yes, Father," she responded in an unsteady voice.

She was seated on the edge of her bed hugging a pillow to her chest. Tears streaked her cheeks. Marcus sat down beside her and put an arm around her shoulders. "How much did you hear?" he asked quietly.

"Enough," she said, sniffling. "But this just doesn't make sense. Sophia and I have a blood bond. If she's really dead, then how come I didn't feel it?"

"I don't know," said Marcus. "I don't feel that she has died either, Sara. Our family bond is very strong. Then there is the fact that Dagon found Sophia's ring. Doesn't it seem a little convenient that among the ashes he should happen to find exactly the thing that would most easily prove to Lord Illyrius that Sophia was dead?"

"Are you saying Sophia is alive?" asked Sara. She stared up at Marcus, and he could see the hope in her eyes.

"I can't be sure," he said. "But yes, I do think that's possible." He offered Sara his handkerchief, and she took it and blew her nose.

"But why?" she asked. "What reason could Dagon possibly have for lying?"

"Oh, I'm quite certain Dagon believes what he says," Marcus replied, "but I think Sophia may have faked her own death."

"Why would she do that?" said Sara.

"I can't tell you the details, I'm afraid, but Lord Illyrius had plans for Sophia—plans she didn't want any part of. Her refusal would have made him extremely angry. And she was also seeking help for her nightmares from someone the council wouldn't approve of, to put it mildly. Faking her death solves both problems, and it also protects the family from any repercussions for her actions. I think that sounds like the sort of thing Sophia might do, don't you?" Sara nodded and leaned against Marcus's shoulder. He stroked her hair with his hand and let out a heavy sigh.

"We have to keep this a secret," he said. "You can't tell anyone of your suspicions, not even your siblings. They have to believe that Sophia is dead."

"I understand, Father," said Sara.

"I know you do, but that's not enough," said Marcus. "We need to be sure that if anyone ever tastes your blood, they won't be able to see what you suspect."

Sara sat up looking curiously at Marcus. "Is that even possible?"

Marcus reached into his jacket pocket and produced a small, unmarked bottle made of dark glass. He unscrewed the top and handed it to Sara. "We have your sister Carmilla to thank for this lovely little concoction," he said. "Just one sip, and none of your memories from the past few hours will imprint onto your blood—you will still remember them, but no one will be able see them by drinking your blood."

Sara took a sip, made a face, and passed the bottle back to Marcus.

"Good," he said, as he returned the glass bottle into his jacket pocket. "Now let's go give your brothers and sisters the bad news. It will hurt them, but it's for the best."

34. The Ultimate Choice

When I woke, I was strapped to a bed. For a moment, I thought I was back home at the mansion and had just woken up after one of my nightmares. Then the smell of antiseptic filled my nostrils, and I opened my eyes.

As I looked around, it looked like I was in a typical operating room. Leather restraints held my wrists, ankles, and neck to the metal frame of the bed. This did not bother me, but when I saw that I had IVs in my arms and legs, I stared to get nervous.

"Good morning," said Clarice as her hazel eyes swam into focus above me. She was wearing a surgical mask and gown.

"Morning," I mumbled. My tongue thick in my mouth.

"The sedatives will wear off in a minute," Clarice assured me.

I did my best to nod.

A man appeared next to Clarice. He looked to be in his midfifties and wore a white lab coat. A thick shock of brilliantly white hair stood out from his head.

"Sophia, this is Dr. Allen," said Clarice.

"Hello, Sophia," said Dr. Allen. His voice was deep and rasping. "I'm sure you are wondering why you have so many IVs in you."

I nodded.

He checked each of the IVs while he explained how the procedure would work.

"Well, first we're going to remove as much vampire blood as we can without putting you at any undue risk," he said. "Your body will at some point try to put you into bloodlust, but the longer you can resist, the more likely it is that the procedure will be successful. Once we see signs of you going into a bloodlust, we will then start you on a heavy round of antibiotics to kill the virus in the remaining vampire blood in your body for good. When we're sure the antibiotics have done their job, we will slowly start reintroducing healthy human blood into your system."

He adjusted a knob on the heart monitor. "Are you ready?"

"Would it make a difference if I said no?"

Clarice sent me a disapproving glare from behind her mast.

"I'm just kidding—yes, doctor, I'm ready." The truth was I was scared. I didn't want anyone to know, but the heart rate monitor gave away my secret.

Clarice took my hand in hers, which gave me some comfort.

"All right," said Dr. Allen. "Let's begin." He flipped a couple of switches, and a low hum emanated from a piece of medical equipment. I watched as my blood started to flow through the IV tubes toward the humming machine.

Clarice looked at me, still holding my hand, and said, "This is what your training was for, Sophia. Stay calm for as long as you can. When the virus is about to die, it usually … fights back, for lack of a better term. It'll be rough, but you can beat it. Just remember what you've learned."

After about five minutes, I started to feel that all-too-familiar burning in the pit of my stomach; I knew a bloodlust was coming on. I gripped Clarice's hand tightly and stared into her eyes, trying to force myself to relax. Panic surged into my throat, but I took deep breaths and forced it back. The time between the beeps on the heart monitor grew longer and longer, until it seemed as if several minutes passed between each one. My muscles throbbed with a slow, burning ache.

My fangs shot out of my mouth, and my eyes turned black. Clarice jumped back, pulling her hand away as if it had been burned. The beast quickly took control, and I could only watch passively as my body struggled against the restraints. Then, to my horror, the beast spoke. My eyes darted wildly around the room as the words rasped up through my throat: "No, stop! I've changed my mind! I don't want to be a human."

No one listened. My back arched away from the table. A scream started deep in my guts and wailed up through my chest with so much force I thought it would tear me apart. The straps that held me down cut into my flesh, but the beast pulled harder and harder, putting every last ounce of my strength into the effort to escape.

A ripping sound came from my right wrist as the leather restraint gave way. The needle pulled free of my arm, and a jet of blood spurted across the room as I struggled with the other straps with my free arm.

"She's coming loose!" Dr. Allen yelled.

Within seconds I had freed myself and was off the off the table. I stood in a defensive stance. Dr. Allen grabbed a syringe off a tray and approached me. My hand quickly found his throat, and I snatched his bodily off the ground and slammed his back against the wall.

Behind my rage, I saw what was happening and tried my best to stop it, but it was no use. My mouth was opened wide, fangs fully extended, ready to feed. Just before I could bury my fangs into the doctor's neck, a sharp pain in my back brought me up short. I released my grip on my prey and whirled around. Clarice stood before me, clutching an empty syringe in her hand. I snarled at her, but the room was already beginning to spin. I quickly fell to my knees, and as I tried to right myself, I crashed face-first onto the linoleum floor.

There was a rush of footsteps all around me. I heard someone shout as if from a great distance away, and I heard the buzz of the heart monitor flat-lining. Was I dying? For some reason, I didn't seem to care one way or the other. The sound faded, and I found myself alone in the dark.

*   *   *

When I woke up I was lying on soft grass with the sun warming my limbs. The air smelled of summer. As I sat up, I looked around. "I know this place," I said out loud.

A little ways off, I saw the worn path that twisted its way into a grove of trees. I rose and followed it. A short way down the path I heard the sound of laughter drifting through the trees. A sense of joy welled up inside me, and my steps quickened.

"Sophia!" The voice came from behind me. I turned and saw Clarice running toward me along the path. "Sophia, wait!" she called again.

I stopped, and she quickly caught up with me.

"What happened?" I asked. "Is the procedure over?"

"Yes, the procedure is over, but it didn't go quite as we planned. When you broke free, I had to sedate you. In your weakened state, it was just too much for your body to take."

"What do you mean?" I asked.

"Your body died, Sophia. Your soul is here, between life and death."

"So that's what this place is," I said remembering it from after the car accident.

"Sophia, I followed you here because I want to ask you something."

"Okay," I said calmly.

"A long time ago, I was a vampire. With the help of the White Swan from that time, I went through the path of kohinoor and became human again. Many years later, when I was about to die, a visitor came to me and offered me a choice: I could go to heaven and be with my loved ones, or I could return to earth to become the next White Swan. Well, you already know what I chose.

"Sophia, you have a good and kind heart and a strong will. I have been given permission by my 'visitor' to offer you the position as the next White Swan. If you agree, you will be endowed with unique gifts, some very similar to those of a vampire. But these gifts will come from God, not from some virus. That is how I am able to speak with you now."

"Are you an angel?" I asked.

"No, not exactly," explained Clarice. "I am more of a teacher and a guardian, but I can tell you this much. If you choose to be the White Swan, you and I will be able to sense each other's thoughts no matter where you are, and I promise that you will never be alone again. You will also gain all the knowledge I have attained to help vampires on the path of kohinoor.

"So now you must make a choice, Sophia. Continue your path and be reunited with your loved ones, or return to your body and take over as the next White Swan."

"So you will leave and I will take your place?" I asked.

"That is correct, Sophia, but as I said, you will never be alone. This I promise you. I am sorry, Sophia, but we don't have much time. I must have your answer."

I glanced over my shoulder toward the clearing, remembering where I met my grandfather after the car accident. He'd told me I still had many things to do yet before I could go with him.

I then took both of Clarice's hands in mine and met her gaze. "Last night I thought long and hard about what I wanted to do when I was human, and all I could think was that I wanted to help other vampires like me. Well, at least now I know for sure that vampires do have souls. That's good to know," I said smiling. "You said the gifts you talk about are from God?"

Clarice nodded.

"Well, if someone up here has enough faith in me for me to be the next White Swan, who am I to say no? I would be honored, Clarice."

A child's laugh drifted through the trees from the clearing, and I thought of the people waiting there by the pool. *Well, they will have to wait a little while longer*, I thought to myself. *As my grandfather said, I still have some work to do.*

*   *   *

The next moment, my eyes snapped open. I was lying in the hospital bed, and a florescent light shone brightly above me. Every muscle in my body ached. Scorch marks from defibrillation paddles covered my chest.

As my eyes adjusted to the light, Clarice's face came into view. "Welcome back, Sophia," she said.

I sat up, groaning, and looked around the room. The restraints on the bed were completely destroyed, and blood was spattered in all directions. The heart monitor continued its steady beat.

Dr. Allen appeared in the doorway. His white hair was a mess, and bright purple bruises ringed his neck. He looked from Clarice to me and back again. "I … I can't believe it," he stammered. "I could have sworn you were dead!"

"Don't look at me," said Clarice. "You're the doctor. I was just standing here, and she woke up."

Dr. Allen hurried forward, and as he bent to check my pulse, Clarice winked at me over his shoulder. He straightened and looked at me sternly. "You're lucky to be alive, young lady."

"No," I answered. "I'm pretty sure luck had nothing to do with it."

35. Saying Good-bye

The doctors confirmed that I was human again, despite the interruption in the procedure. I could have told them that—my craving for blood was gone, and the burns on my chest were slow to heal.

That first morning after the procedure, I sat in a chair by the window and waited for the sun to rise. I watched as the eastern sky faded from blue to purple to pink, and then the golden rim of the sun appeared, and a ray of light fell on my face. I didn't laugh or cry; I just sat there and felt the warmth on my skin. It was a wonderful feeling.

They didn't release me from the hospital for several days, but I had Clarice to keep me company. She sat by my bed late into the night, talking about what it meant to be the White Swan. It turned out she was only one part of an organization that had been around for thousands of years, and she had dozens of spies who brought her regular reports on vampire activity throughout the world. The house on the island where I had spent the past several months was one of many that the organization maintained around the globe.

When they finally released me, Clarice took me straight to the airport, and we boarded a plane for Rome. I didn't even bother to ask why we were going there; by this time I trusted Clarice completely and would have followed her anywhere.

It was the middle of the night when we landed. We collected our luggage, and I was yawning by the time we climbed into the waiting limousine.

"You can't go to sleep yet," said Clarice. "I have something to show you before we go back to my flat." Turning to the driver, she said, "Take us to St. Peter's Basilica."

Even though I was tired, my eyes popped open when I heard that. "Wait a minute," I said. "We're going to the Vatican? Are you telling me the Catholic Church knows about vampires?"

"Of course," said Clarice. "Why do you think the Vatican archives are kept such a secret? Within the estimated fifty-two miles of archives is a lot of information about vampires, but the Church will never admit it. If the Church even hinted that they knew vampires are real, there would surely be panic. Fortunately, the vampire council also realizes the need for secrecy and desires that their race remains a secret among the human population."

"Are you allowed in the Vatican archives?"

"Oh, no. In fact, they have no idea who I am. Fortunately some priests and bishops that are part of our organization are allowed inside the Vatican. They simply help us with specific ceremonies and certain rites of succession. Do not worry, Sophia. I assure you that you will soon know everything you need to know about being the White Swan."

After about an hour's drive, the limo pulled up outside the Basilica. "We'll have to walk from here," said Clarice.

As Clarice and I got out of the limo, it was already way past sundown. Saint Peter's Basilica had already closed. I could only assume that whatever Clarice had planned, she didn't want any spectators.

We walked past the front entrance to one of the side doors of the church, where a priest in a black robe was waiting for us. He gestured for us to enter, and I followed Clarice inside. He gave us a slight bow and said, "Welcome. The bishop is waiting inside."

As we entered the church, I could not believe how beautiful it was. I craned my neck to look up at some of the statues above me and the paintings on the ceiling. They were magnificent. Even in the dim light, the church was beautiful, but I could tell from the way Clarice strode purposefully across the floor that we were here for business, not as tourists.

The priest led us to a chapel with a stone altar draped in white cloth. On the altar I saw a Bible, a chalice, a tall jeweled flask, and a knife with a golden hilt. To each side of the altar were two beautiful bronze angels, their wings outstretched as if they were guiding you toward the crucifix that stood in the center. Behind the crucifix was a large dome. Not being Catholic, I had no idea what many of those objects represented, but the sight was awe-inspiring just the same.

Clarice told me to wait by the gate as she went to go talk to the bishop. After a few minutes, the bishop looked at me and motioned for me to come up to the altar. I walked up to the altar as quietly as possible. Without saying a word, the bishop motioned for Clarice and me to kneel.

The bishop placed one hand on Clarice's head and made the sign of the cross with the other, saying something in Latin. Then he did the same to me. I didn't understand what was going on, but as the bishop's ancient words filled the chapel, a sense of reverence and awe came over me.

The bishop walked back to the altar, picked up the knife with his right hand and the chalice with his left. He then looked to his right, where the priest who'd welcomed us stood. The priest walked up to the altar next to the bishop. He bowed and then picked up the jeweled flask and a piece of white cloth. They both walked over to where Clarice and I were kneeling.

Clarice held out her right arm, exposing her wrist, and the priest poured a thin stream of what I assumed was holy water from the flask over her wrist, catching the excess water with the cloth below. The bishop, holding the chalice under Clarice outstretched wrist, drew the blade across her skin, allowing her blood to flow freely from the wound into the cup.

When it was almost full, the bishop gave a nod to the priest, who then poured more water over the wound. It stopped bleeding. The priest then took the cloth and carefully wrapped Clarice's wrist with expert precision. Clarice then folder her arms over her chest, bowed her head, and prayed in silence.

The bishop placed the blood-filled chalice on the altar next to the Bible. After making the sign of the cross over the chalice and praying again in Latin, he took the chalice in both hands. He walked over to me and said, "Blood is the life of the flesh, and it is through the atoning of the blood of Christ that the believer receives redemption, forgiveness, justification, spiritual peace, and sanctification. For the life of every creature is the blood of it."

He paused and looked down at me. "Sophia, the duties of the White Swan are not to be taken lightly. Do you willingly take up this office as a sacred covenant with God, agreeing to accept the hazards you will surely face, and agreeing also to keep this covenant a secret from all save those whom you have chosen to lead along the path of kohinoor?"

"I do," I said.

"Drink then this cup," said the bishop. "For the blood of all creatures is the life thereof. Therefore, by drinking this blood shall the knowledge and wisdom of those who have held this office before you be passed onto you."

I took the chalice from the priest's hands and brought it to my lips. I hadn't tasted human blood since I first met Clarice. I expected it to be sweet, but it tasted of salt and iron. When the cup was empty, I handed it back to the priest. He took it, and with the thumb of his right hand, he made the sign of the cross on my forehead.

He took a step back toward the altar, and I bowed my head and silently asked God to give me the strength and wisdom to do his will as the White Swan. I also thanked him for bringing Clarice into my life and asked him to bless her.

As I prayed, I started to become dizzy. I opened my eyes and tried to stand up, but the world spun around me. I toppled backward into the priest's waiting arms, and everything went black.

After a moment, I saw a white light in the darkness. At first it was small, like a tiny hole in a dark curtain with the sun directly behind it. It then grew and became brighter. Pulsing rays of light stretched out from it toward me, and I felt them as physical sensations on my skin. The pulses came faster and faster, and the light became so bright it almost blinded me, even though my physical eyes were closed. There was one final flash, brighter than all the others, and the light winked out.

When I woke up, I was lying on a couch in a room I'd never seen before. I had a splitting headache. I closed my eyes, and splotches of color swam across the insides of my eyelids.

"That light's pretty intense, isn't it?" said Clarice's voice.

"What happened?" I asked. "Did I die again?"

Clarice laughed. "No," she said. "You're in my home—one of my homes, I should say."

I opened my eyes just enough to peer at Clarice through my eyelashes. "What was that light?" I asked.

"I'm not really sure," said Clarice, "but it's part of the ritual."

"Over the next few days, you'll start to understand what you've been given—memories from all the White Swans, along with many other gifts."

I sat up and opened my eyes all the way. It was a bad decision, and I winced. "You're not leaving right now, are you?" I said.

"Not right this instant," said Clarice, "but soon. Don't worry, Sophia. I promise you'll have all the help you need to get you started." She rose from her chair and pressed two aspirin into my hand. "For now, I think you should take these and try to get some sleep. There are still a few hours left before dawn."

"You're probably right." I said. I took the two aspirin, thanked Clarice, and went straight to bed.

The next morning I woke up feeling much better. I saw Clarice sitting out on the balcony, so I went to join her.

"Good morning," I said

"Good morning, Sophia. There is fresh coffee in the kitchen if you want some."

At the sound of the words *fresh coffee*, my eyes lit up, and I ran to the kitchen to get a cup. When I returned to the balcony, I said, "Do you have any idea how long it's been since I last had a cup of coffee?"

"No," said Clarice with a smile

"Well, I don't either, but it's been a very long time."

"It sounds like you're feeling better."

"Yes, I'm feeling much better. Those aspirin did the trick."

The sun shined brightly in the sky; it felt so good on my face and shoulders. It had been too long since I felt the sun on my skin without burning. I closed my eyes and allowed my body to soak up the sun's rays.

"I have a gift for you," said Clarice, holding out a battered notebook. "These are all the notes I took when I was first learning to be the White Swan."

I took the notebook from Clarice and looked at it as if it were some kind of treasure filled with secrets.

"Thank you," I said, thumbing through the first few pages. "This is great."

"Before I became the White Swan, I was one of those people who took meticulous notes about everything. Once I became the White Swan, I became almost obsessed with taking notes. I didn't want to forget a thing. However, after a few days, all the knowledge I needed was just there in my mind, and I stopped taking notes. I thought these would help you get started. Eventually you won't need the notebook anymore, but do me a favor and hold on to it. Maybe the White Swan after you can use it too."

"Of course," I said. "Thank you. I promise I'll take good care of it."

"Sophia, I cannot stay here much longer. You see, they want you to do things your own way. You are so different than I am, and they are anxious to see what you can accomplish after the experiences you have been through.

"Remember when you asked me if I believed in fate?"

I nodded

"Well, I believe you were chosen to be the White Swan even before you were born. Just look at how unique you are. You were born a human dhampir who Sara turned into a vampire out of love, because of an accident. During your life as a vampire, you experienced so much. You even learned what vampires were like centuries ago, thanks to your nightmares, which then led you to me. In a sense, you even died—twice. Sophia, you have experienced things no one in the world has ever experienced, and I believe God will use you to help others in ways I could never do.

"Everything that you have experienced, every choice you have made, has led you to this day, and I believe it was not by accident. I am so proud of you, Sophia. I feel blessed just to have known you."

Clarice finished her coffee and went into the kitchen.

I followed her inside and asked, "They? Who are *they*?"

"You have not felt their presence yet? I guess I have forgotten what it was like to go from a vampire to a human. Let me just tell you that from this moment on you will never be alone again. I envy you Sophia. There is a new and wonderful world ahead of you to discover. I wish I could stay, but there can only be one White Swan."

"When do you have to leave?"

"Very soon, Sophia, so if there is anything else you want to ask me before I go, ask now."

I walked over to Clarice and gave her a hug. "Thank you so much, Clarice, for everything. You have truly been my angel."

"So you have no more questions?"

I shook my head and tried to hold the tears back.

Clarice then looked at me with angelic eyes and said, "It's time now, Sophia." She stroked my head and said, "You are going to make a wonderful White Swan. Remember that I love you and will always be with you."

I tried to be strong, but my heart felt like it was breaking. Through sobs and tears, I manage to say, "I love you too."

She took both my hands in hers and closed her eyes. As I looked at Clarice, I began to see a bright white aura surrounding her. The light grew so bright that I had to close my eyes. Then from Clarice's hands I felt energy flow into mine and pass through my entire body. It was amazing. I can only describe it as the feeling of unconditional love. I became so overwhelmed that I actually started laughing.

As my heart and mind focused on the incredible feeling, I suddenly realized that I could no longer feel Clarice's hands. I quickly opened my eyes, but she was gone.

Within that moment, I felt like someone was stroking my hair, and I heard a voice inside my head that said, *Remember, you will never be alone.* I smiled, wiped away what was left of my tears, and into the silence of the room said a quiet good-bye.

That evening as I was reading Clarice's notebook, I realized I was hungry. Being human meant I had to eat food again. There was very little food in the kitchen, so I went out and found a store within walking distance of the flat and picked up a few things. On the way home, I came across a young boy sitting in a doorway folding little animal shapes out of paper on his knee. As I watched, he took out a new sheet of paper and skillfully folded it into a little origami swan. When it was finished, he jumped to his feet and held it out to me. I took it, somewhat taken by surprise—surely he couldn't know who I was. "Grazie," I said. That exhausted my Italian, so I added in English, "Thank you. You're very talented." He smiled, nodded at me, and ran away down the street.

I stood there for a moment with the paper bird in my hand. I couldn't keep it, of course; it would be foolish to have anything in my possession that so obviously singled me out as the White Swan. I held it up to the evening light, admiring its simplicity and crisp lines. I couldn't keep it, but maybe I could put it to good use.

* * *

After paying a visit to Lord Illyrius and dealing with Dagon personally, Marcus arrived home just before dawn. He knew he had to make the trip to give the impression that he believed Sophia was dead. After his long trip, he was tired and thirsty. So he picked up a bottle of blood out of the parlor, went straight to his room, threw his jacket on the bed, and poured himself a glass of blood.

The image of Dagon's sweating, tormented body stretched to the breaking point on the rack was still fresh in his mind. The master of pain did his work well. It wasn't the sort of thing Marcus approved of as a general rule, but in this case ... he permitted himself a grim smile.

As he put his glass down on the dresser to remove his cufflinks, an unfamiliar object caught his eye. It was a little origami swan. Puzzled, he picked it up and held it up to the light. Written along the side of the paper swan in Sophia's looping handwriting he saw the words *Tell only Sara*.

A grin spread across the old vampire's face. "Sara!" he called out. "Come here at once, my dear! I have something you'll want to see!"

Epilogue

As I start my new life as the White Swan, a peace has come over me that I have never felt before. No longer do I feel compelled or obligated to do anything except help those who seek the path of kohinoor.

Clarice told me that I would never be alone. As the days have passed, I have begun to feel a presence around me. I'm not sure what to make of it yet, but in many ways I find it comforting. Maybe I have more help than I realize.

Not a day goes by when I do not think about Sara. Even though I'm human now, we're still connected, and sometimes I see her face in my dreams. I know in my heart that one day I will see her again—Father too.

My sources tell me that the vampire population is growing fast, and I have no illusions about what Lord Illyrius is willing to do to maintain the balance between humans and vampires. This can only mean the deaths of countless vampires. However, if balance isn't maintained, the council could lose control of the vampire population. If that ever happens, God help us all.

My only appointed task as the White Swan is to aid those who seek the path of kohinoor. But if there comes a time when the lives of hundreds, perhaps thousands, of vampires are threatened, should I interfere? All I know is that dark days will be coming soon. But now, more than ever, I have the faith to believe that whatever difficulties are ahead of me, I will not face them alone.